Granjon's gun leaped in his hand. The flashing thunder of the black powder pulsed against the walls. The ball went through the doorway and whined off an adobe brick. Grif kept moving, sprawling to his knees, getting up and plowing straight forward at Sam Granjon as he fired again. This time Grif felt the ball whip his coat-tails, like Death plucking at a man's sleeve to say, *About time, pardner—about time!*

Charter Westerns by Frank Bonham

BLOOD ON THE LAND
CAST A LONG SHADOW
DEFIANCE MOUNTAIN
THE FEUD AT SPANISH FORD
HARDROCK
LAST STAGE WEST
LOST STAGE VALLEY
SOUND OF GUNFIRE
TOUGH COUNTRY
TRAGO
NIGHT RAID (coming in August '84)
FORT HOGAN (coming in September '84)
BREAK FOR THE BORDER (coming in October '84)
BOLD PASSAGE (coming in November '84)
LOGAN'S CHOICE (coming in December '84)
SNAKETRACK (coming in January '85)
RAWHIDE GUNS (coming in February '85)

FRANK BONHAM

LOST STAGE VALLEY

CHARTER BOOKS, NEW YORK

LOST STAGE VALLEY

A Charter Book / published by arrangement with
the author

PRINTING HISTORY
Berkley edition / May 1978
Second printing / February 1981
Charter edition / July 1984

ISBN: 0-441-49513-3

Charter Books are published by The Berkley Publishing Group,
200 Madison Avenue, New York, New York 10016.
PRINTED IN THE UNITED STATES OF AMERICA

For Gloria

Foreword

THE TRAIL OF the Great Southern Overland Mail, the nation's single attempt to forge a transcontinental stage line, has long since been obliterated. Where a stage station once stood, in Eighteen Fifty-nine, a small historical marker may be found. Towns have grown at the sites of lonely relay stations. Freeways may parallel the course of a trail engineered to the strength of horses bred especially for the headlong rush from one "stage" to another.

But here and there, especially along the infamous "Fourth Division" between El Paso and Tucson, one can still find, not far from the highways, a suggestion of wandering weed-grown ruts—a low mound of adobe bricks where a building once stood—a cut in a mountain pass, which silently commemorate the shining Abbot and Downing stagecoaches that passed in that single year of the stage line's existence.

Lost Stage Valley is a story of the watershed year of Eighteen Fifty-nine, the year before the Civil War. It records and celebrates the courage and determination of the men who drove the stages, and the passengers who rode them.

The Great Southern Overland Mail was years in the making—the dream of one man, a stage man named John Butterfield. Yet it lasted but a single year, for by the time the war had ended, another dream had been born—that of a transcontinental railroad.

That was a dream of steel and steam, and primarily it was a triumph of engineering. The Overland Mail was a victory of horseflesh, skilled handling of coaches by courageous drivers, and the guts of shotgun guards and horse handlers at lonely relay stations.

Along that trail from St. Joseph, Missouri, to San Francisco, California, horses and drivers were killed by Indians whose ancestral lands were violated by the road; passengers fell ill and died, to be buried by the road; and other passengers literally went mad from sleeplessness and illness.

In this book, I have attempted to tell the story of some of the men and women whose lives were touched and altered by that crucial year of Eighteen Fifty-nine.

Frank Bonham

San Diego, California
November, 1977

1

THE HOTEL ROOM was poor even for the Mexican border. The ceiling was hardly higher than a tall man's head, and displayed a herringbone pattern of cottonwood poles supporting a layer of mud plaster. Occasionally a trickle of earth would patter onto the dirt floor. Each morning, when she came to remove the chamber pot, a Mexican girl threw a bucket of water on the floor to settle the dust.

There was a window which opened onto a corral and gave entry to flies and the hot animal odors of the stable. By the window stood a reeling table bearing a tin pitcher and basin, and one rawhide-slung chair. Grif Holbrook sat there, smoking and brooding over the spectacle of the wind-swept corral and plaza beyond, sere and yellow in the cold winter sunlight. Dust eddied along the street. The manes and tails of horses streamed in the wind.

He drew on his cigar, and thought: Blow, damn you, blow! In a week I'll be in California. A man can ride in his shirtsleeves all winter out there.

He laid the cigar on the mud sill and walked to a battered chest of drawers to resume packing. He was a solid, roughly made man with no pretensions to elegance. At the moment he needed a shave, a bath, and a shine, but these deficiencies were the fault of the San Antonio and San Diego Mail, which had brought him to El Paso in one of the line's thundering mud-wagons. Over a pleated shirt he wore a plaid vest. His wrinkled trousers were tucked into the tops of black knee-length boots. The shirt needed washing, but it was his best shirt and he knew that if he let a Mexican

1

washwoman take it, it would wind up on the back of some knife-throwing dandy across the river. Yet, clean or dirty, there was nothing even a pleat-front shirt could do to make him look other than unpolished and direct.

His packing consisted of dumping the contents of the drawers into the maw of a black india-rubber bag. A rain of coins, matches, and loose cigars vanished into it and he turned to drag soiled linen from under the bed. He stuffed shirts and underwear into the bag and tramped it down to make space.

He kept listening for the blare of a stage horn. The westbound, as usual, was overdue. Holbrook had worn out a week in El Paso, waiting for Butterfield.

John Butterfield was a fine man, a great figure in staging, but after twenty years with him Holbrook was ready to quit. He had, in fact, already quit. The meeting in El Paso was in the nature of a last handshake before they parted; Butterfield to his gray hairs and transportation headaches, Holbrook to retirement and a California ranch.

He concluded his packing and looked at his watch. It was one o'clock. A healthy man's hunger took possession of him. He shrugged into a square-skirted black frock coat and went out onto the plaza. He considered the stage restaurant. The cuisine—beef, shortcake, and raw onions—had begun to depress him. He decided instead on a Mexican café around the corner. It was a cramped, murky, low-ceilinged hole in the wall with tottering iron-legged tables and chairs. Smoke from a table of American diners balanced in rocking layers on the air. At one table a Mexican youth was belaboring a stringed instrument with small felt hammers.

Holbrook washed his hands in the basin in one corner, shook them dry and took a table. The proprietor appeared, a mustachioed Mexican with uncombed black hair. *"Mande?"*

Old suspicions of restaurant-keepers rose. You'd think they could get together on a simple thing like an enchilada. Yet he had unrolled tortillas to turn up everything from grapes to spoiled beef. "How do you make your enchiladas?" he asked the man.

"Cheese, onions and chili, *patrón*."

"What kind of chili?"

"Chili verde." Green as grass. *Sabroso!"*

Holbrook grunted. "If a thing's hot, it ought to look hot.

The only chili for enchiladas is red chili. What do you put in your tacos?"

"*Como quiera, caballero.* Beef? Cheese? Frijoles?"

"Bring me six with cheese. *Prontito.* I've got a stage to catch."

His attention was drawn by the Americans, loudly discussing politics. He had a mental retching. More and more he hated the rant and bluster of politics. It had come to the point where you could not buy a beer without telling the saloon-keeper whether you were a Buchanan or a Lincoln man.

"Fight!" one of the men exclaimed. "They don't dare fight! Who's going to give them the weapons to fight with?"

"England," said another man. "The minute the tariff's off, England's going to dump more manufactured goods in N'Yorlins than you could shake a singletree at."

If anybody around my place in L.A. mentions politics, Holbrook brooded, I'll hang him by the thumbs for a week.

"You watch," said the first man. "They'll come dragging back asking to be taken into the Union again. The North will starve 'em to death. England's not going to land any cargo in New Orleans if the Navy won't let their ships through."

Let them wrangle. Let them fight duels in Washington. Let the wives of New Hampshire senators snub the wives of North Carolina senators. But just let him have fifty thousand acres, some cattle to run, and a porch to sit on. He was sick of politics and he was sick of working for John Butterfield.

He thought back over all those years of staging and allied griefs. The freight line in Panama. The Great Lakes steamer line. The telegraph line and system of stage routes in the East. For twenty years transportation had been his wife . . . no, not his wife, his mistress, for she had made few demands on him, leaving him free to roam almost as he liked. But now, as sooner or later a man must, he had tired of the jade. He was forty-nine. He could not go on shoveling out Butterfield's Augean stables forever. The last forty years of his life would be for himself.

The tacos were not bad. He ate four, had the other two wrapped in corn husks and tucked them in his pocket to eat on the stage. Suddenly, down the street, a copper bugle cried like a cock. He left the café in time to see a Concord stage, yellow wheels flashing, varnished panels shining under a layer of dust, come lunging onto the plaza behind a six-horse team. He hurried to meet it.

In a year's time, John Butterfield had changed little. He was a large and corpulent man of about sixty, his black beard streaked like the head of a badger. His flushed and dusty countenance was no tribute to his own stages, which had brought him down from St. Louis.

They drank whiskey from thick china cups, talking of old times and of times to come. Holbrook could not escape the feeling that behind Butterfield's grave yet cheerful manner lay a small, cocked gun of craft. He had tried to retire before and always been outmaneuvered. Finally he rose and began to buckle the frogs of his capacious india-rubber bag.

"This won't be the last time we have a drink together, Admiral. But if I don't catch that stage, I'm going to have another four days in this burg."

"Lots of time," the stage man said. But he stirred and brought a small box from his pocket. "I thought you might find this useful."

Holbrook opened it to find a gold watch as big as a turnip. It was decorated with chip diamonds and rubies on the cover, outlining an engraved representation of a stage-coach. On the reverse was the inscription:

To Grif, for he knows what. From John Butterfield.

Thanks were hard for Holbrook; he was touched, and hardly knew how to start. Butterfield waved a hand. He had acquired the patina of casualness that greatness bestows on a man. "You've earned it, Grif," he said. "Some day, after you've retired, it will remind you of the old days."

Holbrook's eyes began to cool. "I've already retired."

"Of course. Only—you see, there was something I wanted you to do for me, a sort of errand, on the way out."

"What was that?"

"Why—" Butterfield struck a match and got a cigar going. "You've heard about the trouble I've been having on the Fourth Division?"

"Apache Pass? Yep."

"I've lost eleven stages between El Paso and Tucson last six months. Most of them near the Pass."

"You're a damned fool if you haven't replaced them."

"At twenty-five hundred apiece? I'm not making that

kind of money. I can't stand such losses, Grif. And, anyway—Abbot and Downing aren't taking orders for coaches just now."

"Thought that was all they did make."

"Used to be. Their yard is knee-deep in shavings, but they aren't turning out a thing but ambulances and caissons. Army stuff."

Holbrook put the watch back in the box. "If I've got to get my behind shot off to earn this thing—"

Butterfield looked injured. "Now, look here! Don't try to connect the gift and the favor. But I thought, as long as you were going through there anyway, you might kind of look things over and find out who's raising all the fuss."

"No," Grif said.

Butterfield frowned at the tip of his cigar, turning something in his mind. "I had a talk with Abe Lincoln the other day. He's worried. While Lincoln waits to take office, Buchanan's throwing Army contracts around like confetti, with a Southern delivery point on everything. Lincoln told me that if war comes, an operating stage line will be worth two divisions of foot-soldiers. California gold is going to pay for a lot of guns. But they can't send gold by carrier pigeon. Hockaday's Central Overland is staggering. It will be my line that fights the war." He paused. "That is, if there's a line left."

Holbrook began to feel the tightening noose of a trap. "Call in the Army," he said sharply. "Get escorts."

"I asked for escorts six months ago. Buchanan talked out that frozen face of his for an hour, and never said a word a buck private couldn't have. It adds up to this: They'll be damned if they'll make an effort to save the biggest gun the North may turn on them!"

Holbrook set his bag by the door. There came an outbreak of yells and thudding hoofs in the corral. In a milling fog of dust, hostlers were hazing a team through the gate. He scratched his neck.

"Admiral, I'm sorry. I wish I could help. But what could I do that you couldn't? I've got the urge to build me some houses and barns, like the Good Book says. If I can find a red-headed widder with the right bust dimensions, I may even get married."

"And maybe you'll find that all those houses and barns bring you is vanity and vexation of spirit," Butterfield snapped. "Also from the Book. What do you know about ranching?"

"Nothing. But I know plenty about setting on a veranda, drinking beer and ruminating. You can't do that on a stagecoach, not with somebody trying to decide whether to knock over you or the driver with his first shot."

Butterfield began to tour up and down, swinging his arms vigorously, working out the stiffness of a thousand miles on the trail. "It's damned queer. They've taken all those coaches and the horses, but they've never touched the mail nor hurt any of the passengers. Does that sound odd to you?"

"It sounds like somebody was starting a stage line somewhere."

"Exactly! If it were Southern saboteurs, why wouldn't they simply burn the coaches right on the road? Grif," he said, "I'm down to the last of my reserves. That Fourth—damn it, I hate to travel over it myself! Hay's short and horses are beginning to show it. At Apache Pass, a driver's life isn't worth an iron washer. When I think of the fight we had to build that road," he grumbled, "it makes me want to get somebody's neck in my hands."

Then he seemed to soften, saying musingly, "Remember the year we built it? The papers saying it couldn't be done? Everybody saying we were crazy? And a couple of times I thought we were, too."

Lights warmed the depths of Holbrook's pottery-brown eyes. He remembered, all right. When the first Great Southern Overland stage rolled west from St. Louis two years ago, he and Butterfield had felt like the God-anointed prophets of transportation. In all those years of staging, nothing had ever stirred him the way the working of this Western miracle had. One year after signing of contracts to link by stagecoach a hundred places the East had never heard of—Soldier's Farewell, Alamo Mocho, Colbert's Ferry, Indian Wells! It had been like a poker game, the biggest one ever played on the dusty gaming-table of the frontier. Butterfield and his men against the house—Apaches and dust storms, thirst and heat and flash floods.

The game had taken a lot out of every man in it. But now he, Grif Holbrook, was ready to quit while he was still ahead. And it took only one shot or arrowhead to empty a chair in this game. He reached for a gun that leaned against the wall.

It was a Dragoon model Colt with a detachable shoulder stock, which was in turn eccentric by virtue of a canteen concealed in its walnut bosom. He slipped his arm through a leather thong and slid the gun up under his right armpit, barrel down.

Butterfield stood looking out the window. "Remember Sam Granjon, Grif?" His voice was almost gentle.

Holbrook paused in the act of donning his coat, his eyes lighting with old reminiscence. "As good a whip as I ever saw, for all he wasn't over twenty. Wonder how young Sam's making out?" On the backdrop of his mind walked the picture of a lean blond boy with a man's frame and a youth's eyes and grin, and the lanky hands of a born driver. Butterfield did not reply. Suddenly suspicious, Holbrook demanded: "What about Sam?"

Butterfied stirred from his reverie. "Sam's dead, Grif. I moved him to the Fourth a year ago. They shot him off the box last month. He's buried near Dragoon Springs. They named a wash after him."

"Well, I'll be dogged!" Sentiment came into Grif's head like smoke, obscuring his clear thinking. Sam Granjon had been a fine driver, and forty years too young to die. Somebody'd ought to swing for that. Head down, over a slow fire.

Outside, the stage horn blared. The mail was aboard. Butterfield stood quickly and began to button his gray frock coat.

"Well, Sam won't be the last. But if that doesn't bother you—if it doesn't turn you inside out to think of young fellows having their eyes blown out by homemade muskets because the gold to buy new ones is bottled up in California; and men freezing to death in summer uniforms while bales of wool rot in warehouses— Well, that's your problem, Grif, not mine. *I'm* not the one God will be looking at when He says, 'Who is this who comes before Me with bloody hands?'"

His voice rolled like thunder in the room, and then he seemed to choke up and turned away. He set his gray beaver on his head, gave it a tap with his palm and extended his hand to the other man. Tears stood in his eyes.

"Good luck to you anyway, old friend," he said. "Think of us once in a while, dying for our principles while you sit on a veranda—drinking beer."

Holbrook said bitterly, "I'll be danged if you couldn't talk a sand rattler into climbing a tree! Why didn't you wave the flag in the first place, and save all this jawing?"

Butterfield reached for his hand and gripped it. But Holbrook turned away gloomily and snapped the frogs of his suitcase. A dream had gone shimmering. Los Angeles and his red-headed widow were a million miles away.

2

HE PAID HIS hotel bill and they walked down the street in the sallow winter sunlight. Before the stage station, on a street that formed one side of the sere, frost-nipped plaza, the westbound stage was receiving its last passengers, the final piece of baggage was being thrown in the rear boot. The team minced in the traces, while on the box the driver sat teetering his foot on the brake. The express messenger lurched from the office with the strong-box.

A small crowd was on hand to watch the pageant of departure. Butterfield stopped short of it and stood with his back against a sun-warmed adobe wall. Grif set the bag down and pulled the greasy lanyard of his Stetson up under his chin, turning his face from the gritty wind.

"The details are up to you," Butterfield said crisply. "All I can do is give you some suggestions. First thing you do when you reach Tucson, look up Blaise Montgomery, editor of the *Tucsonian*. 'The Senator,' they call him. I met him last month when I went through. Seems he served two terms in the Georgia senate, until he got too outspoken against secession. He left for his health. He's got to be careful though, because according to him there's an organized secessionist crowd right in Tucson. But he'll help all he can."

Grif gazed off across the Rio Grande. Yesterday it had seemed to him he could almost discern the trees of Los Angeles beyond the distant haze. Now they were no more that gauzy dust clouds.

"Another thing," Butterfield said. "The acting station agent at Apache Pass is a woman named Kate Crocker. Her husband held the contract before his death. She's got the idea a man's contracts go down to his widow just like his clothes. Besides, she doesn't know any more about how to operate a stage station than I know about having babies. Man named Chantry is waiting yonder by the stage to go up as her replacement."

"Number one," Grif said, "evict one widow. Any orphans you want murdered, while I'm at it?"

Butterfield laughed. "There's an orphan named Heydenfeldt in Tucson—Fourth Division section boss. At least his parents ought to've been hung for not drowning him. You'd think his office was in Cambridge, for all the help he's been in stopping the raids. You'll go in ostensibly to take over his job. Pay him off and boot him out.

"The rest—well, your guess will be better than mine. Stop the raids and find the coaches and stock. Maybe there's an underground market in them, operating through Mexico down to Texas and on south. I've given up guessing. In other words, I'm licked. I'm handing it to you."

"Who do I hand it to when I'm licked?"

"Nobody's going to lick you, Grif. That's why I picked you. I can't tell you how much better I feel about this already."

"I wish I could tell you how much worse I feel." Holbrook put out his hand. "Well, so long. If they knock me over, write me a nice epitaph. 'Here lies Grif Holbrook. You could talk him into anything.'"

He heard Butterfield laughing as he walked up the street.

About the coach milled the usual crowd: relatives of departing passengers, old men who read dead dreams of adventure in the dust of varnished panels, Mexican children waiting to run alongside the big yellow wheels as the stage rolled up the road.

Grif tossed his bag into the boot, the big valise-like pocket, flap-covered, at the rear of the coach. As he approached the door of the coach, a man stepped quickly from the wall of the station. "Mr. Holbrook?"

Grif nodded. "You're Chantry, I guess."

Chantry shook hands with him, a farmerish man in his late thirties who wore a black coat, too tight across the shoulders, and odd trousers. He carried his belongings in a sack over his shoulder. He did not have the appearance of a man who would be brilliant or heroic, but perhaps lack of imagination was the most important thing in a station-keeper in Apache country.

They entered the coach and took places between the front and rear seats, facing forward. The interior of the Concord could accommodate nine passengers; there was one empty seat. Two new passengers, a man and his wife, had taken seats on the deck.

A final time the driver sounded his copper bugle, and now, as the horses went into the collars, the coach rocked on its bullhide thoroughbraces and the wheels spun forward. Dogs barked and children ran screaming alongside. Soon they dropped behind, and the stage shook the town and ran smoothly up the river road, in and out of mottes of willow and withered salt cedar. At their left the Rio Grande was a shallow brown trickle ribbed with sandbars. Mexican farmers had their corn and chili patches in the bottomlands, but the slopes that mounted to the abrupt base of Franklin Mountains were a barren world of ocotillo and greasewood.

Under the floor, gravel spattered and sandboxes chuckled. It was an old, old story to Holbrook. Looking at the tired faces of the other passengers, he thought it had become familiar to them too. The Oxbow was fast, but it was brutal. After a thousand miles, tossed about like pullets in a sack, men and women either sank into a coma or went mad. At Phantom Hill, he had helped truss up one man who lost his mind after five days without sleep. Of course, this was unusual. But it was a wearing business at best, slamming endlessly over a raw, half-graded trail where the floor-boards crashed interminably down on the reach-and-bolster. Two meals a day, perhaps sour beans and fat port, perhaps flinty shortcake and coffee. Forty minutes to get it down. Then crawl in again, body sobbing for rest, eyes inflamed with the corrosive kiss of alkali dust. Hit the back of the packed horsehair seat as the horses ran, and pray that you would either sleep that night or die.

Chantry was talkative. "Been with Butterfield long, Mr. Holbrook?"

"Too long." Grif added philosophically, "But I reckon there's been good mixed with bad. One time, down in Panama—"

"I've been with him since 'fifty-eight," Chantry interrupted. "Colbert's Ferry station. Gets tiresome sometimes, don't it? I read a lot, though. *Book of Facts*. Best reading in the world."

Grif waited. "This thing I was going to tell you about—" He started the story, aware of a vacancy in Chantry's eyes.

"Did you know," Chantry interjected, "that a boat forty-five feet high can be seen eight an' one-tent' miles at sea?"

Grif cleared his throat. ". . . No. I didn't know it."

"Fact! And here's a funny one: A woman's got one chance in eighty-nine of birthin' twins, but she's only got one in five hundred ninety-nine thousand, nine hundred and twenty-one of havin' quadruplets! . . . This is interesting, too," he said. "If you deposited a hundred dollars in a bank at nine percent interest and left it there, it would double itself in eleven and eleven-hundredths years!"

"You know," Grif said, "I think you're going to make out all right at Apache Pass. Just don't let yourself think. Reckon you can do that?"

Chantry blinked and said he thought he could. Holbrook leaned his head back against the seat, convinced of it.

The afternoon wore away in a series of river settlements passed, of breathless swing stops where they changed teams, and then again the steady, lurching roll toward the sun. Fatigue and monotony came to roost in the darkening coach. At one station there was a ten-minute stop while a new driver inspected the axles; a cut spindle, the result of failure to lubricate, was the fault of the man at the reins when it happened. A passenger disembarked here. The man and woman on the deck came down to take seats inside, wind-blown and red-nosed. Night was rushing on, and evening wind cascading across Black Mesa, on the west, the Rio Grande silent between its eroded banks.

The station-keeper, hurrying from his adobe shack with a pair of lighted lamps, set them in their sockets. There was a shout, a jingle of trace chains, and iron tires ground across the yard.

Grif looked at the new couple, who had taken seats across from him and Chantry. The husband was a small man with a sallow, rutted face. It seemed as though, in thumbing the pages of his life, time had left them slightly dog-eared. Yet about him there was a certin backhouse gaiety, a ruttish good humor. He would catch Grif's eye, wink, and grin for no particular reason.

His wife, years younger, was nicely stacked-up, Grif decided. She had a waist you could have spanned with your two hands, and a bust you could hardly get your arms around. In addition, she was possessed of extremely personal eyes, pointed up by the ridges of high cheekbones. Yet they had glitter rather than glow, and there were lines to be seen about her mouth, strident lines a heavy paving of powder did not soften. She was pretty, but her kind of beauty could be duplicated in many a bagnio.

The light died. Cold wind lashed the leather curtains, pale flashes from the lamps fitfully invading the coach. Ten miles to Mesilla, capital of New Mexico Territory, now the seat of Doña Ana County, which included all of Arizona. There was a dark mood over this whole country, it seemed to Grif, which touched him with melancholy. The West was like a man just out of the operating room, threshing in torment, his wounds still raw. The wounds were a hundred Indian treaties made and broken; the Gadsden Purchase, sale at gunpoint; the Mexican War. Each act signed in blood.

In a purgatory of half-finished thoughts, his mind drugged by fatigue, Holbrook drowsed.

... The night, dark and dangerous. Yet safest for travel, the Indians hating it too. But white men liked it, when they were on the prowl. After we pass Mesilla, I'd better sit up on top with the boys. Cold enough to freeze the balls off a brass andiron. He turned up his collar.

A man was snoring, the stout one who looked like a successful cattle buyer. *Why should a man like that go to California? Why should anybody, for that matter? California was a cruel metate, impartial about whom it ground, so the meal was fine. Grinding lives out in the mines; crushing them in in the saloons. But also forming giants in her mold. And who in this tiny coach on the limitless plains would believe that anything but fortune awaited him? Yet some were hurrying to their deaths, and only a few would work out the kind of lives they wanted. But they were the raw materials of which the West was being built.*

With a ripple of gooseflesh Holbrook dimly perceived that he was sharing a seat with history.

A hand touched his knee. The roguish little man was peering at him in the gritty, clattering darkness. "How much farther to Mesilla, friend?"

"Three miles, four miles. Meal stop."

The man sank back. "Travel over this section often?"

"Too often."

His wife whispered something and he said, extending his hand, "My name's Prentiss, friend. This is my wife, Aimee."

Grif shook hands with them. Aimee smiled. "I'll bet Mr. Holbrook could use one of those samples, Ira."

Prentiss, it developed, was a whiskey drummer. A leather case of samples rested between his feet. He bent to open it; struck his palms together and rubbed them. "What's it going to be—J. H. Cutter, Mountain Brook—?"

Grif let a small flask of Mountain Brook be forced on him. It contained about a large mouthful. He drained it. "Good whiskey," he said. He could feel its warmth scorch clean to his toes.

"Have another. On the company." Prentiss produced another miniature, then chuckled. "Hell, take half a dozen! The only way to travel by stage is drunk anyway!"

It was unexpected, but Grif stowed all the liquor in his coat pockets except one bottle, which he drank. In his belly the whiskey was as pleasant as a hot brick on a cold night. Whiskey warmed him without tampering with his inhibitions or tongue. He supposed he must have a capacity, but he had never quite plumbed it.

The stagecoach whipped through a grove of cottonwoods. A mile ahead, he saw the lights of Mesilla at the foot of the mesa. "Here she comes!" he said.

The horn bleated. The soft thunder of hoofs livened. Aimee Prentiss turned to look for the town, placing a warm little palm on Grif's knee as she did this. She flashed him a sudden glance, at once provocative and roguish. "Oh, excuse me!"

She was red-headed and wore earrings. She was pretty, though with the brassy beauty of a fire engine, and Grif had a not-quite-proper tingle. Prentiss gave him another of those ruttish winks.

"Just can't keep her hands off a good-looking man!"

"Ira!" said Aimee. And she giggled.

Grif was left feeling left-handed. Before he had recovered,

the stage was rushing through the outskirts of the town, shaking dead leaves from the chinaberry trees, stirring clouds of dust as it passed between gap-toothed rows of houses. Lamps burned softly in the windows. The business section was poor, indeterminate, entirely Mexican. This was a mean and unswept village which a few years before, after the Gadsden Purchase, had received hordes of angry Mexicans who had moved in under the belief that they were leaving the United States.

They approached a long corner building afire with lighted windows. The horses turned the corner and entered the yard of the La Posta, stage station, restaurant and hotel. Hostlers took the team in hand. The driver climbed down, pulling off fringed gauntlets. The express messenger opened one of the doors.

"Forty minutes, folks. Grab a bite."

Chantry, slumped beside Grif, awoke with a grunt. His obtuse features stared about. "Where we at?"

"Mesilla. For a buck and a half, you can ruin your digestion."

Drunk with sleep, Chantry lurched from the coach, looked about him and headed for a backhouse. Aimee brushed past with a rustle of petticoats and a scent of lilac. Grif waited for Prentiss to follow the girl, but the drummer merely hitched forward, planted an elbow on a knee, and winked.

"One for a man's sweet tooth, ain't she?"

Grif hesitated, feeling that the remark was not quite in good taste. Prentiss made a furtive clearing of his throat. "Tell you a secret, brother. She ain't my wife! Just a friend. Met her in Missouri. We kind of throwed in together, being we're both for California."

A cooling process began in Grif. He was not unfamiliar with the games professional passengers played. But Ira Prentiss laid a hand on his arm.

"I don't know if you're like me, but travel gets mighty irksome. You're livin' in a bottle: life goes on, you get hungry, you get thirsty—you, ah, feel certain other needs, eh? but you can't get out to satisfy 'em."

The hand on Holbrook's coat wheedled like a beggar's claw. He stood under it, staring out the door while the drummer brought his mouth closer to Grif's ear.

"Well, there's no use carrying those certain other needs any farther, friend. We've got forty minutes. If you'll just drop five dollars in my pocket, I'll say a word to Aimee and..."

Grif stared at him until Prentiss' hand fell away and he said petulantly, "Forget it, then! I just thought, with all the liquor you'd drunk—"

"You just thought," Grif said, "that I was a lamb for shearing. If I went behind the bushes with your friend, all of me that would go on with the stage tonight would be my wallet—in your pocket. It happens I'm with the line. I'm going to recommend to the station agent that you get off here. We're freighting enough riffraff to California without carrying pimps."

Prentiss bristled. On an angry impulse, Grif seized his wrist and yanked him across the floor. Stumbling and swearing, the drummer lurched out the door and sprawled on the ground. Grif threw his sample case after him. He stepped down. He stood over Prentiss a moment. Then, making a settling motion with his shoulders, he walked past him.

He had almost reached the rear door of the La Posta when he turned his head to glance back. His heart gave a wild bound and he made a run for the door. It was too late. A small-caliber gun cracked sharply in the darkness. Grif heard the bullet splinter a panel. There was a sound of shattered china within the restaurant. He lunged against the wall and turned to face the man by the stage. He was not aware of swearing, nor of turning sidewise to make a narrower target, but he was shouting profane warnings at Prentiss as his hand tore back the skirt of his coat to get at the gun slung against his right side. Inside the station, a woman screamed. The team just entering the corral began to rear. A thought jammed in Grif's head: *It's too late! too late! too late...*

Prentiss took his second shot. The bullet exploded against a brick beside Grif. Then the drummer ducked, running around the back of the stage with a hand on a wheel as a pivot. Grif's gun locked solidly against his shoulder with the blazing rush of gases. The short barrel lifted, but when the glare cleared from his eyes Prentiss was gone. Somewhere he ran down an alley between the outbuildings.

The dark stage yard awoke with quizzical shouts and rearing horses. A man ran from the feed barn with a lantern.

"What the hell's going on?"

Grif jumped the long tongue of the Concord to follow the drummer. He halted before a huddle of sheds. He had his choice of three alleys. Prentiss was no longer moving. Or, if he was, the racket overrode his footfalls. Grif waited for the man with the lantern before he proceeded.

"Feller shot at me," he said. "A damned pimp. He went on the peck when I threw him out of the stage."

Stablehands were collecting. Another man arrived with a storm lantern. They broke up into two search parties and began to screen the buildings and weed jungles behind the yard. They searched for fifteen minutes, but Prentiss had vanished. They found no more of him than a smear of blood where he had cut himself on a plow, against a wall.

3

IN A WARM murk of smoke and fragrance of food, Aimee Prentiss was being comforted by three women inside La Posta. Grif sat on the end of a bench at a long table and watched them. The room was low and unfloored, with whitewashed walls. A corner fireplace crackled cheerfully with a rosy pyre of mesquite roots. It was here, on a bench, that the women sat. Chantry and the other men were inspecting a shattered gravy boat in a cabinet set in the thick mud wall, where Prentiss' first shot had gone home. The station agent, Collis, a big frowing man with a pocked face, came in from the yard. "Now, what *is* all this?" he demanded of the room.

Aimee raised a tearful face, a white dish of tear-gullied powder and mascara, stared at Grif and sobbed again as she buried her face in her hands. Collis went over and stooped before her.

"What's the matter, lady? Was that your husband out there?"

Aimee nodded, sobbing: "That man at the table—he—he propositioned—! And Ira—hit him, and—"

"I—see." Collis straightened. The ladies rose, presenting a solid front of alpaca and set lips, like three judges of the Holy Office about to recommend the Iron Maiden. Collis walked to the table. He propped his heavy upper body above Grif with his hands gripping the edge of the table and frowned upon the unshaven, wrinkled man who sat on the bench. Grif stirred, never having felt more like a sexual delinquent. He wiped his nose with a thick forefinger.

"Been drinking, brother?" Collis asked.

Grif shrugged. "A snort. That is," he amended, "it was an hour ago. Fact is—"

"But it ain't wore off yet, has it?"

Grif's jaw went out. "If you'll ask the ladies to leave, I'll tell you what really happened."

"Nobody's going to leave," Collis informed him, "but you're going to tell us anyway."

Grif's glance speculated upon Aimee. "All right. I threw her husband out of the stage for—" he paused; wasn't there a respectable word for it? "—for pandering. He said he was a whiskey drummer. After he poured a couple of samples down me he figured I was ready for the kill. It's an old story. They'd have knocked me on the head and taken my money, if I'd fallen."

Aimee swept across the room with claws out, her face wild. Grif caught her wrists while she struggled to scratch his face, screeching: "You God-damned dirty . . . !"

There was that in the expressions of the other ladies which said Aimee's case had been weakened. One of them drew her elbows against whaleboned sides and hurried from the room.

The door from the hotel side opened. A very bulky, white-haired, florid man stood in the entrance. "Blue blazing hell, Collis!" he shouted. "Has a man got to listen to gunfights and domestic wrangles every night in your confounded tavern?"

Collis said deprecatingly, "'Twarn't nothin', Senator. Couple of boys got exercised over a woman, best way I can figure. Now, you run along to the bar and I'll have things straightened out and dinner on the table in ten minutes."

Aimee had torn away from Grif. She looked at him, at Collis, in focusless fury; then, with a low and prolonged ripple of contumely, she flounced from the dining room.

Collis looked at Grif, tugging at the lobe of his ear. Then he smiled ruefully, and Grif chuckled. "Brother," said the agent, " 'pears to me I owe you an apology." He peered more closely. "Say, do I know you?"

"Might. I spent a night here three years ago, before you got the stage contract. I remember you served the best enchiladas I'd ever eaten. In fact, that's why I recommended your place to the Admiral."

"Holbrook!" Collis slapped him on the shoulder.

Half of Grif's attention had been on the elderly, pompous-bellied man whom Collis had called the Senator. Almost at the door to the bar, this man now turned and put a questioning glance on him. Collis was declaring his good intentions, but the Senator said loudly, "I'll let the bartender crush the mint in my julep if you ain't Grif Holbrook!"

They took places at the bar, Grif, Senator Montgomery, and Chantry. Presently Chantry was in conversation with a man who had not previously known that the first adding machine was invented by a Frenchman named Pascal, in 1642; and that a thing called a torpedo submarine, invented in 1776, might destroy all life on this planet, if misused.

Grif and the Senator engaged in conversational sparring. The Georgian had the good sense not to come bursting out with anything better left unheard by the general public. He took his mescal like a man: a pinch of salt thumbed from a saucer, a half-lime sucked between drafts. He had shiny cheeks, red as pippins, and his upper lip hid under ragged ramshorn mustaches. His eyes were blue under thorny brows, but the lower lids were red and loose, like a St. Bernard's.

"Heard all about you from John Butterfield, Holbrook," he said loudly. "Fine man, Butterfield, fine man! Sorry I couldn't help him in his business plans. But what I don't know about raising onions, suh, would comprise a volume." A slow wink went with the remark.

Grif held his glass to the light. "Yep. John was disappointed. By the way—you were in Tucson last time I heard of you."

Montgomery stabbed at him a look of dark portent. "Had to come down the other day on—ah—business. But nothing doing, nothing doing."

In the dining room, someone pounded on a tumbler to signify that dinner was served. The room was fragrant with enchiladas, fried pinto beans, a thin chili sauce capable of taking the bluing off a Colt, onions and jerked beef. With his taste for Mexican food, Grif ran a thumb about the rim of his plate to corral the last of the melted goat's cheese and chili. His eyes raised to find the Senator scrutinizing him. Montgomery made a slight nod toward the door. Grif finished his coffee, smacked his lips, wiped his mouth on his sleeve, and, with Montgomery, left the room.

In the yard, a fresh team was being backed into the traces. By lantern light, the driver was doping the axles of the Concord. Freight was being loaded into the boot.

Grif and the Senator walked in the night.

The Senator paced along with his hands clasped under the claw-hammer tails of his shiny broadcloth coat. Once they had crossed to the dusty plaza, he spoke warmly.

"Most propitious, our meetin' here! I'd planned to return tomorrow, but since you've come along I'd be mighty proud to go back with you. Once satisfaction in an otherwise disappointing journey."

"Butterfield," Grif began, "said you could sort of draw me a map—"

Montgomery interjected, "Correct. We haven't but a few minutes; if you don't mind, Holbrook, I'll do the talking. I said I'd come down on business. It was this: I had information that someone would try to bring contraband guns up from Mexico, near here. But as usual, either the hounds gave a false point, or the bird had flown."

Grif grunted. "Guns! What kind of a crowd is this we're up against?"

"I wonder . . . I might mention that this man Prentiss, with whom you had the run-in, was probably no whiskey drummer at all. No doubt he was an agent of the Territorials, with orders to keep you from reaching Tucson."

Grif's mind faltered. "The Territorials? That's a new one, isn't it?"

"The Territorials are a supposedly social lodge with headquarters in Tucson. They hold rifle shoots, parades, dances, and all the rest of the la-de-da of the usual secret society. A sort of desert Masonic lodge. It may mean nothing—but the local grand master is a man named Benteen; a political mad dog if I ever saw one. Secessionist! He's sent in a petition every month for the last two years demanding that New Mexico Territory secede from the Union and declare all Northerners slaves! Crazy! But smart along with it. I'd watch him. I don't know why," he grumbled, "someone doesn't start a counterlodge. A lot of us are tired of being hind titmen at the chewed dugs of the ship of state."

There appeared to be something wrong with the

metaphor, but it was colorful. "Eleven coaches. Any theory what happened to them?"

"What would your guess be? The torch!"

"But why take them into the desert to burn them? They could have done that right on the road. I'm playing with an idea that those coaches are being held somewhere, in a hidden valley, let's say. That one of these days they'll roll again—south. There ain't any Concord, New Hampshire, in Dixie where they can be bought. There's only three things they produce down there that are worth a damn—women, whiskey, and horses. They might be able to fight a war with whiskey and horses, but those women are just going to have to be fed."

Montgomery smiled. "The legend of Lost Stage Valley! It sounds romantic, Holbrook. I'm afraid, though, that it will turn out to be just a legend. Let me ask you—have you any dependents?"

He was completely in earnest, his pouched pink face grave. Grif had a premonition that the Senator was one of those perennial Paul Reveres who hear tocsins in fragments of conversation, who read sinister codes in a scrap of torn letter. He was a little surprised that Butterfield had been taken in by him, if that were true, and he could not help chuckling.

"What are you going to do, Senator—sell me some insurance?"

"The best insurance I could give you would be this advice: Keep on that stage till it reaches California. But that's not the kind of man you are. The next best is—trust no one. If you're in doubt about anyone, ask me."

"I'll have it tattooed on my chest," Grif promised.

Sharply through the dark the stage horn cried. Grif jumped. "That's it!"

Five minutes later, with Montgomery jammed in between Grif and Chantry, the stage whirled into the night.

In the morning they breakfasted at a wind-harassed little station at the base of a hill. They ran on, skirting the mountains, while dust swirled and eddied inside the coach. They lunched at a dismal relay called Soldier's Farewell. In the middle of the afternoon they broke through a rampart of flinty hills into the broad San Simon Valley. The wide trough in the plains was golden with winter grasses. Beyond rose the blue Chiricahuas, steep and ragged. Apache Pass was a notch near the north end of the range, where it abutted against the brief bulwark of the Dos Cabezas.

Passengers began to sit up a little straighter, remembering stories they had heard about the pass, knowing that slaughter, at this spot, was as old as civilization. Grif thought of the Widow Crocker, operating a stage relay at the very mouth of the pass, and shivered.

With some old-fashioned ideas about the frailty of women, he detested altercations with them. As they crossed the valley and worked up through a desolation of grease-wood, stone and Spanish bayonet, he found himself rehearsing the scene with the widow.

No, ma'am. I'm sorry. Not a thing I can do. I don't make the rules, I just enforce them. And, if she became mean: *I'm sorry, ma'am, but it's out of the question! Absolutely! You can take it to court if you like, but Mr. Chantry, here, is duly appointed in your place.*

So that as they clattered higher through the foot-hills, his jaw bulged forward and he thought he might almost enjoy a brush with this hatchet-faced female.

The sun fell in a spray of peach-and-gold behind the mountains. In the evening breeze, Grif caught an odor of cedar smoke. A moment later the stagecoach swerved, causing the passengers to grab at the straps, and stopped with a squealing of shoes before Apache Pass station.

The station was a long, flat, mud structure fronted by a roofed gallery. A ragged woodpile sagged against the west end of the building. A tattered banner of smoke fluttered from the chimney. Horses stood attentive in a rangy corral made of spiny ocotillo wands placed on end in a bristling, five-foot barrier. Back of the station, a rough, reddish slope mounted to high, snow-crusted peaks.

By the time Grif swung down from the coach the rest of the passengers had dismounted and were hurrying for the warmth of the station. A woman, slight in build, hurried from the house with a red shawl over her head. Nettled by a sense of something being wrong, Grif glanced about. He discovered it. The relay team was not ready. In a blue-gray dusk, the horses pulled at heaps of hay in the corral. Mexican hostlers sat on the porch, smoking.

Bannock, the driver, began to shout. "Ma'am, *this* is the

last—! So help me, you had the breast straps and traces snarled last week; but tonight you ain't even started to hitch 'em up! How in the name of—"

The Widow Crocker said in a calm voice: "But you aren't going on tonight, Mr. Bannock. There was some trouble up the line. You're staying here tonight."

The face of Bannock was stringy and weathered as an old fingerpost. It now began a purpling process that was delayed by Grif's inquiring: "What kind of trouble, ma'am?"

Mrs. Crocker gave him a pleasant, unruffled glance. "Really, it's nothing to be alarmed over. Some trouble with the road. A flash flood. You folks could do with some sleep anyway, couldn't you?"

Grif discerned the professional I'll-take-care-of-everything manner of a physician, and said brusquely, "I'm with the line, Mrs. Crocker. What is it?"

She gave him a quick, studying look. "Why, it—it was another raid. It happened last night. There was some shooting this time. The driver is inside now. I don't think he'll live the night."

Bannock received the news with dull shock. "Last night, you say?"

The widow nodded. Studying her, Grif saw that she was a young widow indeed, but there was the sort of maturity in her eyes that even years did not bring to some folks. In the dusk he discovered little more about her than that her face was rather thin and that she stood with a kind of defiant erectness against the censure of Bannock's gaze.

She was saying, "It would be the third time someone was killed, you know. It's Tom Gilson this time. His passengers carried him down here from the pass . . . We might as well go in, gentlemen."

It was not a small room, but it was jammed. On the eastbound stage from Tucson last night there had been three women and four men. Added to the nine from the westbound, it made a capacity crowd for the station. Their talk buzzed in the room, the women gravitating to the corner fireplace, the men standing in a group near the door.

The widow placed bars across the door. One of the women at the fireplace was stirring with a long wooden spoon a stew bubbling on a crane. Mrs. Crocker said quietly, "Please don't stir it. It stuck, and I don't want the burned part stirred up."

The woman started and dropped the spoon. She gave the

others a glance. Then she gave a barely audible sniff. For
some reason Grif could not discover, the remark seemed to
have been judged in bad taste. There was an instant of
awkwardness, and finally the lady passenger turned her back.
The talk picked up again. Grif sat by the window on a three-
legged stool, gazing into the thickening dusk and letting the
conversation wash over him without disturbing his own
thoughts.

"... Think the company would do something to protect
us!"

"Did they take the express box, too? I had a watch in it."

"Your hard luck, friend. They warn you to carry your own
valuables."

"I won't vouch for it, but what *I* heard was that Butterfield
is bankrupt and he's simply *letting* the line go to pieces to
spite the creditors!"

Under this mattress of sound Grif heard a man cry out
somewhere, as if in sleep. He glanced across the room toward
a closed door. His eye was caught by the Widow Crocker's.
He had a pleasant shock. She had discarded the shawl and
stood under a hanging lamp, its soft light in her hair, gently
brushing the planes of her face. She could not have been over
twenty-five. Her hair was brown, with tiny sequins of copper
in the highlights, brushed and parted and worn in a chignon
on her neck. She had a young, firm figure, her bosom deeply
divided. Her skirt reminded Grif of the kind some Mexican
women wore, full and pleated but falling only a few inches
below the knee. It failed to conceal slim brown calves and
bare ankles. Grif couldn't recall having seen a white woman
without stockings before. He was surprised but pleased.

He saw her tilt her head slightly toward the door and turn
and go through it. He threaded the crowded floor to follow
her. They faced each other in the bedroom beyond. There
was a nervous intensity about her. Her arms were crossed and
she rubbed one upper arm as though trying to drive a chill
from her flesh.

"Will you try to do something for that poor man in there?"
she said.

There was a door leading to a third room. Grif glanced at it
without enthusiasm. "I'm no doctor," he said. "I might be
able to cut a bullet out of him, but I'm not saying he'd be any
better off when I got through."

Kate Crocker clenched her fists, but could not keep all the

emotion out of her voice. "A man is dying in there and they wrangle over whether or not they'll be paid back for torn clothes and lost watches!"

She went to open the door but did not go in, standing there staring inside as Grif entered. On a dresser, a small flame burned clearly in a polished glass chimney. Covered to his chin with a rough gray blanket, Tom Gilson lay on a cot. He was not a young man. He wore a clipped gray beard and his nose was lean.

Grif sat on the edge of the bed. Gilson made a low sound in his throat. "Sam! Is it you? Sam, if it is—I haven't got much room, I can't hold them—!"

He wrenched wildly on the rawhide springs, and now Grif saw that he was tied down. "All right, Tom! It's all right!" he whispered.

Gilson sobbed with the petulant hurt of a child. He had a coughing fit. Grif wiped blood from his lips. He stood above him with a frown between his eyes. "Sam—Sam Granjon!" He turned the matter over and found nothing in it but the maundering incoherence of delirium. He left the room, and met the widow's unvoiced question with a shake of his head. "I wouldn't touch him. Too late."

"Poor, poor fellow! He tried so hard to save his stage." With sudden weariness she sat on a chair and pressed her hand over her eyes. "I'm about done in myself, Mr. Holbrook. It's been hard, caring for him these last eighteen hours and trying to keep the passengers from becoming hysterical."

Grif's heart, always ready to leap up like a dog with dirty feet, softened. His hand touched her shoulder in quick sympathy, and the amazing part, when he reflected on it later, was that she let it rest there, and even sighed a little and leaned toward him, as if he were the support she had needed. Something recurred to him.

"Did he happen to mention somebody named Sam before?"

Kate Crocker glanced up at him. "That's the thing I can't understand. He thinks Sam Granjon was driving the stagecoach that forced them off the road. He wasn't delirious the first time he said it. And yet Granjon was killed a month ago."

Grif recalled Butterfield's statement that they had shot the blond Texan from the box in one of the last raids. When the rescue party came out later he was in pretty grim shape.

It wasn't hard to understand that a man in delirium might dream of an old friend. But the implication that another stage had crowded Gilson from the road was odd. Grif asked Mrs. Crocker about it.

"Why, the passengers tell me that a black mud-wagon swung out of the brush at a turn and crowded them off the road. All the outlaws were masked except the driver. They threw the baggage out of the boot and one of them mounted the box after they'd righted the coach."

She gave him a direct look. "Mr. Holbrook, why doesn't Butterfield do something about it?"

It was the ideal time to explain that Butterfield was going to do something about it. But there was that in Grif which refused to throw a new grievance at an already almost-tearful woman, and he said merely: "Why, I daresay he will, ma'am, when he's able to."

Bannock opened the door. "Excuse me, Mrs. Crocker. Folks are getting hungry. Reckon we could sling some hash 'fore long?"

Kate Crocker's brown eyes flashed. "I'm *so* sorry they're suffering! You tell them they'll get their dinner right away— just as soon as we bury a man."

4

Soon the crowd in the station realized they must fend for themselves. They ladled their own jackrabbit stew from the pot and found bread to eat with it. The women were slightly outraged by the widow. Their eyes disapproved of her slim waist and bare legs. Their ears burned at her explanation of why there was no butter: "The damned Apaches drove off my cow last month!"

But Holbrook sat in a corner with the Senator and Chantry, eating off the wide mud sill of a window, and chuckling over her handling of them. He received the impression that she had little tolerance for the complaining, short-tempered breed known as the overland passenger, particularly for the female of the species.

Chantry sopped bread in pot-liquor and stared at Grif. "This kind of corruption happen very often?"

"Depends on what you call often. Say once a month."

Chantry chewed on a stringy bit of jackrabbit meat. "When are you going to tell her I'm taking over?"

"In the morning."

Senator Montgomery set his coffee cup with a thump on the windowsill. "Have you heard this wild yarn about Sam Granjon?"

"Mrs. Crocker told me. Think there's anything in it?"

Montgomery frowned. "I—I don't know. I delivered his eulogy myself. Sam was dead all right! Dead enough for two men."

A doubt had come to perch in Grif's consciousness.

"*Somebody* that knows how to drive a six-horse team ain't dead," he speculated.

Montgomery raised one eyebrow.

"Ever handle a stage team, Senator? You've got six ribbons to manipulate. You can't do it by geein' and hawin', neither. You hand in the wrong horse, mister, and you've got him down in the traces. Hold those left ribbons too tight and your nigh string will fight the off animals until they're both wore out. It's a job only a few horsemen ever learn to do right.

"And think of the way this one was handled! Bring it out of a side road and nudge another wagon off the road without snapping spokes or letting your team get away from you! That's driving, mister! Whoever drove that Concord didn't learn it overnight. There aren't many drivers of that kind that I don't call by their first names, either."

He finished his fourth and last cup of coffee and hauled from his pocket the gold watch as big as a turnip, gift of John Butterfield, with the ruby-and-chip-diamond representation of a stagecoach on the cover. It gave him a secret satisfaction to feel its body-warmed weight in his hand, less that it was a jewel of watch-making than that it was an oblique boast of deeds accomplished. It corresponded to the notches on a gunfighter's Colt.

He snapped the cover open. Ten minutes to nine. The women were finishing up the dishes. Mrs. Crocker was trying to discover how to hang a tarpaulin across the room as a curtain between the men's and women's dormitories. A stubborn crease was between her eyes, those candid brown eyes that were at once so young and so wise. He went over.

"If you've got some nails, we could hang it from the vigas."

"Yes, we could do that. Do you mind helping?"

Grif helped hang the canvas and by that time the dishes were finished. Kate Crocker made a little speech to the crowd.

"The Mexicans will bring in straw for shakedowns. I've got extra blankets and comforters. The ladies will sleep in the section next to the fireplace. The extra gentlemen will sleep in the barn."

It would be necessary for three men to sleep outside, and a man who had a pair of dice suggested rolling for places.

Grif, having no desire to share his bed with packrats, hoped for boxcars as he rattled the dice. But Kate Crocker spoke to him from the door to her room.

"Mr. Holbrook—"

He relinquished the dice. She gave him a faint smile as she stood with one hand turning a gold locket she wore. "I seem to be putting upon you continually, but would you do me one more favor? I can't bear the thought of being alone next to— So if you'd sleep in the room with him, I'd be most grateful."

She had a way of asking favors which made a man want to jump to the task. On Grif, her request had the additional effect of expanding his chest an inch. Of the roomful of men, she had picked him to be her watchdog. He found himself patting her arm.

"You get your sleep and don't worry about a thing."

He went through to the chamber where Gilson lay wrestling with death. With his back to the driver and his grisly breathing, he removed his coat and hung it on a nail. He unslung the half-breed Colt and took a short and therapeutic pull at the whiskey in the gun-stock-canteen. In the middle of it he recalled that he was in this station for the express purpose of firing Mrs. Crocker. It seemed to him that he should have had the matter out before morning. This came in the category of stealing silverware from a host's board.

Gloomy, restless, and yet with a small spark of emotion burning in him, he lay on the cot across the room from Gilson.

He did not know when Tom Gilson died, but in the morning he found him rigid as whalebone. Grif had rubbed shoulders too long with violence to be upset by the fact that he had slept with a dead man. He covered Gilson's face with the blanket and rapped at Kate's door. She did not reply, but from beyond her room he heard the bustle of morning stir.

He went through, noting that her bed was neatly spread and the earth floor already sprinkled down. In curiosity, he paused to glance at the scarred mahogany commode against one wall. The marble top was chaste in lack of ornament, nunnish almost. A brush, a high tortoise-shell comb, a copper candlestick, a bottle of toilet water. Two ambrotypes in deep mahogany frames, half facing each other, dominated the dresser. One was of Kate, looking somewhat younger and certainly less mature. She wore a gown which exposed her shoulders and throat. Her hair was done in dark little ringlets like sausages, which spoke of hours with a curling-iron. She was smiling, with a sparkle in her eyes, as though she were flirting with the photographer.

He looked at the picture of the man, who stood in jaunty stance with one hand on his hip and one on the back of a chair, a cigar in his mouth. He was a young, hard-eyed fellow with sardonic eyes. So this was Crocker! This was Willy Crocker, who had brought his bride to live at the back door of hell, and who had ridden out one day to shoot an antelope and been killed by the Apaches. Well, he looked capable of bringing a young girl to New Mexico Territory, Grif thought indignantly.

The door opened. Kate stood in the entrance, glancing curiously at Grif as he stood with the picture in his hand. Color invaded his face. He made a pointless gesture with the picture, set it down so that it fell over, righted it, and smiled foolishly.

"Excuse me!" he said. "Just curious about how your— your late husband looked. A good-looking man, ma'am."

"Poor Willy!..." The widow let a pause gather. "The other one," she said, "is me. Not my daughter, as you might have thought. Me, four years ago."

Grif found himself bounding to her defense. "Your daughter! Why, any daughter of yours wouldn't be walking yet!"

Kate laughed. "Mr. Holbrook, you're gall*ahnt*!" Yet in her response there was almost a hunger for the kind of flattery a good-looking woman didn't encounter in a lonely stage station.

Grif was inspired to enlarge. "I mean—well, you're not the same woman you were in that picture. You've grown up. You can't stay in this country long without doing that. But out here, most men's taste doesn't run to schoolgirls anyhow. We like 'em pretty, but they ought to look like they could cook a meal too. And you're both those things."

The girl smiled, with a tinge of color in her face and an expression more of gratitude than of coquetry.

"You're too kind," she laughed. Then she walked to the door of Gilson's room. "How is— Oh!" She had seen the blanketed form on the cot, and stood a moment with her shoulders tightening, and then turned quickly and closed the door and stared at Holbrook.

"He's better off," Grif said. "We'll take care of him after breakfast."

Before the meal was over, a stage horn was heard down in the brush and rocks at the entrance to the pass, and in ten minutes a coach entered the yard. It appeared that Mrs. Crocker had sent a rider to Mesilla for a replacement coach as soon as she had word of the trouble. The eastbound passengers were noisy and excited as they entered the Concord. There was no expression of gratitude to Mrs. Crocker for favors rendered, only muttered comments on the stage situation. Holbrook saw Kate turn from watching the coach roll back down the road toward El Paso. Her lips were pressed tightly together.

"Your stage will be ready in a few minutes," she told the other passengers.

Time was plucking at Grif's sleeve. He inhaled deeply, held the breath, and said: "Mrs. Crocker."

She turned back. "Yes?"

"I'd like to talk to you."

Her glance was steady and curious. "Why, surely."

Near the corral was a well with a round adobe ring; a weelsweep dangled a limp rope in it, like a boy fishing for nonexistent fish in a tub. Kate Crocker, smoothing her skirt under her as she sat on the ring, with the gesture nearly as old as femininity, watched Grif plug tough shreds of tobacco into a pipe. The sun was full on her face, yet it was kind to her. Her eyes, her mouth, betrayed only the faintest of time's trial sketchings. The light sprinkled small catch-lights in her hair, a richer auburn than it had seemed last night. In fact, it was almost red, and Grif recalled what he had said to Butterfield: *I may even marry a red-headed widow, if I can find one.* Now, wouldn't old John have a double-barreled fit if I did, he thought, and the idea titillated him.

He lighted the pipe. He chased the proper words all over his mind and finally started, bluntly enough. "Mrs. Crocker, Butterfield sent me out here to tie some knots in this broken stage line of ours," he told her. "One of the breaks is right here. Chantry—the *Book of Facts* character—is the knot I brought along. I'm sorry, can't say how sorry, but Chantry is replacing you. We'll furnish transportation to any place you name."

Kate stood up with a quick frown and gasp. "Oh, now—see here! I *do* hold a contract, you know. Butterfield can't simply fire me, the way he would a—a hostler. I'm a contractor, not an employee."

Slowly, Grif shook his head. "If you were a contractor, it would be different. But the contract was with your husband. And contracts can't be passed down to the heirs, like a man's assets."

The widow's lips firmed again and the eye she put upon him was cool and steady. "I'm willing to go to court to find out about *that*," she said crisply.

"No use. Not a bit of use. You'd be fighting a million-dollar corporation. And besides—Kate," he said, "you're a level-headed woman. Do you know how long you're apt to last here, without a man's help? Do you know what Apache squaws do to white women their men bring home? If I've got to carry you out of here, kicking and screaming, why, I reckon, you're going. That's just the way it's got to be."

He had tapped a well of temper in the widow. She stamped one foot and clenched her fists and bridled right up to him. "Kicking and screaming is just exactly the way I'll leave here, too! My husband took this place over when it was nothing but a corral and a mud hut. He fought off Indians and rustled his own provisions when the company let him down. And then he died in the service of the line. And what do I get for all he did? A sympathetic letter from the great Mr. Butterfield! And you come along and tell me I'm not competent to run the station, so I can just run along and beg on street corners or something. Oh, I never heard anything so . . . !"

Inspiration struck from the clouds like a shaft into Holbrook's brain. "You mean, it's *salary* that keeps you risking your life in this Indian warren?" To a man who had never given money more than its bare due, the idea was incredible.

Kate gave him a look arch with contempt. "Is there anything but money that would make a person live in a stage station? I hope you don't think I'd be dedicating myself to ungrateful passengers and hungry horses for the love of them!"

In her fury, Grif was able to feel the desperation of her. It gave him the power to see himself as she must see him—as a single-minded representative of the line, cold-bloodedly separating her from the little measure of security she had clung to. And with this came a thought, bright and fresh as a new-molded bullet. "Kate, can you keep books?"

On the threshold of another tirade, Kate hesitated. "That's an odd thing to ask. Why?"

"I'm going to need a bookkeeper. I'll be taking over the Tucson office, and if there's anything I hate worse than bookwork, it don't come to mind. The pay might not come up to what you've made here, but if you'd like—"

Something was happening to her face. The stiffness was dissolving and her lip was trembling; joy was asking permission to enter and being asked to wait. "Can you do that?" she asked him.

Grif laughed, feeling a sort of exultation. "Can I do it!" He was moved to exhibit his watch in an excess of pride, drawing it from his vest pocket, snapping the lid open and shut, letting her see the jeweled stagecoach on the cover, flashing the inscription at her:

To Grif, for he knows what. From John Butterfield.

"I think it could be arranged," he said.

There were tears in her eyes, but they were regarding him with the glistening clarity of sunlight through rain. "Mr. Holbrook," she said softly, "I think you're the sweetest man I've ever known. I'm going to kiss you."

She put her hands on either side of his face and held him while she kissed him. Then she stepped back and laughed at his expression. "I didn't mean to frighten you," she told him. "Do you want me to go with you this morning?"

"Be best," Grif agreed. He wondered if his face looked as hot as it felt. There was a tingling in him as though his body had been numbed by cold and was just thawing.

Kate leaned on his arm as they went back to the station, beginning to sober as she looked about her. "If you knew how I've hated this station from the first day I saw it!" she said tensely. "How I hated it when Will was alive and dreaded it after he died." She sighed. "I saw Tucson once. It's a quaint little town, isn't it? I do believe I'll like it."

5

UNDER A GRAY blanket of tattered clouds, they buried Tom Gilson in the cemetery on the hillside. Here lay Willy Crocker; a Mexican hostler dead of smallpox; and three immigrants who had been murdered in the pass. Almost as many residents as some Western towns could boast.

A cold wind nettled with fine rain flapped the brush as the last spadeful of pebbly earth fell. The Senator delivered a brief eulogy. "... *Ashes to ashes, dust to dust ... In sure and certain hope of the Resurrection unto eternal life....*"

It was over. Tom Gilson was on his way, and Holbrook's heart was touched anew by the ancient mystery.

While Kate Crocker packed, Grif sat at the long table loading an extra cylinder he carried for his forty-four. He measured powder, inserted a ball, rammed the charge home with the priming lever. He did this six times and gave the cylinder a spin for luck.

Outside, Bannock blew his copper bugle. It sounded like a cry of fright. Kate came from her room with a canvas telescope bag. She wore a brown traveling cape and a bonnet. Something had happened to her during the half hour she had spent alone in her room. She was radiant, as though she had wrapped all her fears in a bundle and disposed of them. "Ready!" she said.

One of the men, rubbing his hands with cold as they stood watching the baggage being loaded and the women enter the coach, said: "Maybe some of us fellers better ride up on top. Get a shot at anybody that takes out after us before they can catch up."

The Senator grunted. "That's all right for anybody who likes dust and rain, but I'll be blessed if *Ah'll* sit up there!" He touched his forehead. "Get a most frightful pain when I ride outside. The dust and cold. Frightful! But the rest of you do as you like."

Grif told them: "I'll ride the deck. It isn't the healthiest spot, even if you can get a clear shot. I'll watch the back trail. You boys stand by in the coach." He swung up, taking the place beside the driver at the left side of the seat.

The stage rocked away. In an instant the station was out of sight. Another bend rounded and they were as lost to civilization as a cork on an ocean, an ant on a prairie. They were a self-contained cosmos whirling through a void. The road bent and doubled up the bottom of the canyon. Bannock drove with frowning concentration, his lean gloved fists backs up, the taut ribbons bridging the clattering void between footboard and the horses' rumps.

Nature had not been prodigal with vegetation in Apache Pass. She had flung boulder and mesquite, Spanish bayonet and creosote brush to fall where they might. Close to the ground clung tough black bushes that gave an impression of having been planted roots up. It was not large growth, but neither was an Apache large. The road was narrow, easily blocked. It had long been Apache heaven. But at the same time, the rough terrain made it hard to understand how a second coach could have overtaken Gilson's.

The climb grew steeper. The wind avalanched down the mountainsides, laden with the abundant odors of wet sage. Grif was acutely conscious of the canyon walls pressing in upon them, of being boxed up like an ox in a slaughter stall. Ten miles. The bloodiest ten miles in Arizona.

In an hour and a half, they had shaken the deeper cuts and mounted to a chain of shallow *rincóns* staked about with low peaks. There were many small oaks here, standing ruggedly against the slope. But Grif did not relax as they topped out on the summit. His eyes rummaged through the brush at both sides of the road. Thus it struck him like a thunderclap to realize suddenly that a team of horses was drawing in beside them, that almost abreast of them rocked another stagecoach.

He shouted a warning and reared up to throw his gun to his shoulder. The coach was a black celerity wagon, low and heavy, a Concord mud-wagon. The leather curtains were drawn. Only one man was on the box, a long and spare individual with his Stetson hanging down his back by the lanyard and his blond hair streaming. Grif got the face of his man in his sights. And then he slowly lowered the gun.

Granjon! Is it you, Sam? I wouldn't do this to you, Sam...

A dead man was crying in Grif's head. Tom Gilson was writhing on his death-cot and accusing Sam Granjon of forcing him off the road. But Granjon, the yellow-haired Texan, was dead. He was dead and buried, and they had named a dry wash after him at the spot where he died in the Sulphur Springs Valley.

And yet it was the Texan who sat on the box of the black mud-wagon, nodding pleasantly at Holbrook and smiling, while he urged his team ahead of Bannock's with gentle taps of the whip on the wheelers' backs.

Grif Holbrook was shaking; he was cold and soaked with perspiration. It was all a nightmare—the black hearse-like coach, the horses tossing their heads like wild things, and a ghost holding the ribbons.

He shook the spell loose. He brought the gun up again, hearing a gun crash beneath him. There was a ringing sound like an anvil stroke as the ball struck through the leather curtain. It was backed with armor. Kate Crocker's scream came through the clatter, rousing Grif to action. He fired at Sam Granjon, but Granjon only turned his head to urge the horses along, throwing them heavily against Bannock's team.

Shots flashed up at Grif from the blind belly of the mud-wagon. The iron rail at his side leaped and a silver streak creased it. He was firing steadily now, but the right wheels of the coach were crashing along through brush and rocks with a monstrous racket and jolting. The passengers thumped about, shouting, screaming, occasionally firing an ineffectual shot at the black stage.

Sam Granjon sent his long, silver-ferruled whip out and hauled on his off-reins, so that Bannock had to swerve to avoid a tangle. The wheels smashed down into the barpit; the Concord heaved up on two wheels and began to capsize.

Grif was not consciously frightened. He was looking for a soft spot, and he was tasting bitterness and regret. This was what the Admiral had picked him for. This was the only talent he had; and he had failed. He landed asprawl, rolling dizzily. He took two lunging strides, but a root snagged his foot and he went down flat and hard on his belly across a boulder. He had the sensation of having been projected into the interior of a soap bubble. The world shimmered and smiled; there were rainbow edges along the toothed blades of the Spanish bayonet. The bubble glistened, and suddenly it burst, and beyond the opalescence there was darkness.

He seemed to be riding a wave of discomfort which broke and dumped him miserably on the cold beach of consciousness. He lay on a bank pitching up from the road. The other passengers were sitting about on boulders. The stage had been righted and the driver and another man were working the team back onto the pole. A tall man with a flour-sack mask over his head watched them work. Two other men guarded the huddle of passengers near Grif, while at the rear wheel of the mud-wagon Sam Granjon stood with a horse-pistol held casually upon the scene.

Somewhere the Senator was loudly declaiming about Constitutional rights. Grif found him at the rear of the celerity wagon, rumpled and shaken. But he had stayed in character. He had come up making a speech.

Someone said, "Save it for the Senate, Pop!"

The voice plucked a humming wire in Grif's consciousness. He came onto his side, on one elbow, and sought the speaker. He was one of the pair guarding the passengers. In frame, he was about right to fit the picture his voice had conjured in Grif's mind. There was another clue: his gray trousers were torn above the right knee. Grif remembered a tuft of threads and a smear of blood on a plow behind the La Posta in Mesilla.

He saw Kate Crocker standing with her cape pulled closely about her. She glanced up at him. Relief lighted her face briefly, but she allowed only her lips to move, saying nothing. No one had seen Grif stir. Some dim idea of dropping one of the guards with a rock, the one standing nearest him, and acquiring his gun, was shaping up in his head. She seemed to sense this. But the Senator himself aborted the plan.

"Holbrook!" he called. "Are you all right, man?"

Grif sat up and held his head in his hands, muttering. Sam Granjon climbed the slope to him. Granjon had Grif's Dragoon pistol slung over his left arm. He stood meeting Grif's stare with a grin, a cocky, broad-shouldered blond young fellow.

"Sorry, pardner. One of the hazards of a hard trade."

There was a tinge of awe in Grif's bloodshot glance. "Are you dead, Sam? Or only about to be?"

Granjon, brownskinned and hard-jawed, chuckled. "Don't reckon I'm neither, Grif. But I don't aim to talk about it."

Grif let this remark lie between them a while. "Do you reckon you could see your way clear to giving me a drink? For auld lang syne? There's a canteen in the stock of that gun."

Granjon inspected the Colt. "Well, damn me! Ain't that clever?" He pulled the stopper and took a pull at the liquor. "But I don't know as it would be smart to put a gun in your hands, old timer. I remember you used to be *mucho hombre* with a smoke pole. Though I can't say I'm feeling much pain from the slugs you were throwing a while ago."

"I was rattled," Grif confessed. "You know what I think? I think that's why you're the only one of this pack that doesn't wear a mask. You like to scare a man out of his wits so's you've got the bulge on him."

Granjon's wide mouth smiled. Grif nodded at the gun once more. "The cylinder slips out," he explained. "I couldn't do much harm with a gelded Colt, could I? And you've got my powder-and-shot flasks."

Granjon dubiously slipped the cylinder from the Colt and tossed it on his palm with a frown. Then his arm pulled back and he hurled it deep into the brush. When he tossed the gun at Grif he was smiling again. "She's gelded! Don't try to ride that Colt, because you ain't going to get far on her."

The team reharnessed, the guard at the front of the coach brought Bannock back to the others. Granjon said curtly to Grif: "Get in the mud-wagon."

Grif finished drinking. "God's sake, boys! If you're going to hold me for ransom, you won't get more'n a stringhalted stud horse for exchange."

The other man turned. It began to be apparent to Grif that he was the bandmaster at this concert. As he approached, he had a glimpse of cool gray eyes behind the flour-sack mask.

"We're not going to hold you for ransom," he said. "In fact, I'm hoping we won't have to hold you at all." He had a pleasant voice, a deep-South voice, but the eyes behind the mask were chilly: eyes the color of old lead.

The fear Grif had kept at bay flapped up now as he realized that whatever chance he had had to amend things was gone.

"Are you going to harm the women?"

"I'm afraid our reputation has gotten out of hand," the other said. "No, we're not going to touch the women."

He turned back. When he spoke, it was to the men and women clustered on the road below. "You're all to get back in the stagecoach. No one will be hurt unless he makes us hurt him."

Bannock climbed to the box. The passengers were herded into the scuffed stage, some of them limping with injuries. Last to enter was Kate. She stood in the cold gray sunlight with her face turned up to Grif, an intense expression in her eyes. "It will be all right!" she said. "I just know it will. They won't hurt you. They won't dare."

Then she was gone, the door slamming behind her, but she had left something for him to carry like a medallion. He descended the hill stiffly, slipping the gun under his arm as he went. On the box, Bannock turned from watching him, shrugged helplessly, and accepted the reins from one of the outlaws. The pink-and-white head of the Senator thrust through the leather curtains for a last word.

"Young fellow," he shouted at the Southerner, "I'll see you hung from the highest tree in Tucson for this!"

The gray-eyed man laughed. "I daresay I'd still have my feet on the ground, old timer."

Bannock turned, kicked off the brake, and let the leaders have the buckskin popper. The stagecoach ran up the wet road and fell away behind the summit. With his rifle, the leader gestured at the black coach. As Grif turned to enter, the other swore and grabbed at his gun. "How'd he get *that* thing back?" he demanded.

Granjon shrugged. "I've taken the cylinder out. He's not going to make us no trouble."

"Oh—" the Southerner frowned. "Just the same, I'll keep it."

Despair settled damply upon Grif. He shouldered through the door into a gloomy interior smelling of sperm oil. Bolted to the side of the coach, a carriage lamp burned dimly. As the five men crowded into it and the door was closed, there remained only the weak flame behind a blackened bull's-eye for illumination.

There was a sensation of turning, of backing and switching. The stage started off. It was impossible to see anything through the slot-like gun loops without pressing to them. A thunderous crashing of bolsters told that they had left the road. It became a rough ride then, with each man hanging to the straps. Gray-Eyes had stood Grif's gun against the door, but his leg kept it from falling.

For some time there was only the dull booming of a half-graded trail under them, the sway and jounce of leather springs tossing the coach like a snuffbox. Then, abruptly, it ended. The coach sat level. The man beside Grif, and the three across from him, stirred in relief. But no one opened the door.

Grif looked at the small man on his left. He said, "You look better with a sack over your head, Prentiss. Lots better. You ought to wear it all the time."

The little pimp from the El Paso coach almost jumped from the seat. He said, "All right! I'm still going to settle for Mesilla, Holbrook." He hitched about, and Grif saw the dark ring of his gun muzzle tilt.

The Southerner snapped: "Cut that! Suppose he does know you? He's not going back unless it's as our man."

Ira Prentiss silently soaked in resentment and anger.

Grif smiled benevolently on him. "I see now the Senator was right. You and Aimee were out to put the big britches on me before I ever reached Tucson."

No one spoke, and Grif, realizing the advantage in having the deal for a while, said thoughtfully: "Tell me something..."

He began to grope in his pockets while he phrased the question, bringing his hands out empty in a moment and saying parenthetically: "I could use a smoke, fellers." Someone tossed him a pouch of pipe tobacco. He extracted his pipe from a vest pocket and began to fill it. "What I'd like to know is, how can Sam Granjon be up there on the box and be buried beside Granjon Creek all at once?"

The man across from him chuckled. "We could arrange the same kind of burial for you, Holbrook," he said. "Even a eulogy by the poor old Senator. I didn't go to all this trouble just to take you away from John Butterfield. I could have done that with a bullet."

"In fact," Grif chuckled, "you even had a fling at that gambit, didn't you?"

The gray-eyed man hesitated. "As a matter of fact, it was the way you handled Prentiss that persuaded me you could be of more use alive than dead. You're rough and homely as a mud privy, but you know your way about a tight corner. You're in one right now, but you're still talking, and that means you're thinking. Would you like to do some thinking for me?"

"Depends." Grif snapped open the bull's-eye of the lamp and held the pipe inverted over the flame.

"I'm what you might call a connoisseur of rolling stock," the other man said. "I collect rare old stagecoaches. I'd like to have you help me. You seem to be a man who gets things done, from what I hear."

"Now you're talking like a damned fool," Holbrook grunted. "If I get things done it's because people know me and they know I mean what I say. That puts a big zero in front of my name as far as you're concerned, doesn't it?"

"Not necessarily. They don't know you in California, do they?"

"Some of the agents do."

"Butterfield's agents. But there are a lot of other stage lines in California. Those independents are the ones I'm interested in. I'm skimming the cream off the Oxbow right here. Sooner or later, every coach on the line rolls through this pass. But they keep the short-lines at home. I'd like you to see about bringing some of them to me."

Grif continued to regard the pipe. "What if I could? What do you want with them?"

There was a pause which told him he had overstepped. The Southerner said coldly, "It seems to me you're doing a lot of asking and not much talking."

"Can't help bein' curious, friend." But suddenly he knew

he had damaged his position. "Let it lay, then," he said. "What's to keep me from deserting, once I hit a town?"

"Nothing. But I don't think you'd be very easy in your mind if you did. You'd get in the habit of never sitting with your back to a door. You'd keep the shades drawn at night."

"What's in it for me if I do it?"

The gray-eyed man shook his head. "You're still asking questions."

Grif sank back and chewed on the pipe stem. "Now I'm just smoking my pipe."

Prentiss shifted on the seat. "Christ's sake, are you going to blabber with him much longer?"

The leader continued silently to study Grif.

Grif managed a chuckle. "Son, I didn't mean to misput you. Come to a choice between working for you or shoveling coal in hell, I reckon you'd make an A-1 employer."

The gray-eyed man sounded like someone who was speaking of one thing and thinking of another. "You asked what was in it for you. Your life, to begin with." He stopped talking. His fingers gently rubbed the heavy cylinder of his rifle. They were long, small-jointed fingers; drawing-room fingers.

"This percentage, now—" Grif prompted him. The pipe had gone out. He leaned forward to relight it in the lamp flame.

"Oh, hell!" the outlaw snapped. "We could have got this over sooner and saved a lot of trouble. Ira—"

Grif protested. "Sho, now! This ain't giving a man half a chance!"

He looked in mild alarm at the outlaw leader. Then he let the pipe descend gently upon the frayed wick. The light perished.

6

IN THE DARKNESS men were shouting, but no one dared fire. Grif heard Prentiss' hand spidering along the leather cushion, trying to find out whether he were still there. He was not. He was standing in a crouch with his rump against the door. He held the Colt of which they had dispossessed him, and he was cramming the spare cylinder into it.

The gray-eyed man, holding his voice to a note of brittle coolness, tried to stem the panic. "Sit still!" he said. "If you feel anyone moving, put your gun against him and shoot. It won't be one of us."

But the impact of this statement was lost, inasmuch as Grif had just gone plowing across the floor, trampling toes and arches, to crash against the door. The catch gave, and as he sprawled out over the roadside, sunlight entered his eyeballs like a knife. He had a dazzled impression of a hillside sweeping up to a low ridge, of reddish ground spiny with starved vegetation.

He heard the flat bark of a gun. Then he piled headlong into a *cholla*, tore through it and crashed against the earth. His left arm, wrenched by the fall, ached until his whole body seemed involved in the pain. But he kept rolling and scrambling, gaining a blunt, blackish mass of boulders, and here he squirmed through an embrasure until he was sheltered from the stagecoach.

He found his left arm too weak to steady the gun. Resting the short eight-inch barrel on the rock which sheltered him, he craned forward to scan the coach. They hadn't found him yet, for only one masked head showed at the door, and it was turning about in frantic search. But up on the box, Sam Granjon had turned to stand with one smooth cheek against the stock of a shotgun. It must have been loaded with nuts and bolts, for when it went off Grif could hear shrapnel lashing the brush and rocks about him. Granjon went back with the recoil, his blond hair shaken.

Grif bent carefully to the sights. He took up the trigger slack with a single slow squeeze of his entire hand. The driver was a clear figure on his front sight, but Grif was panting so that the barrel of the Colt rose and fell. The coach was in three-quarter view against the brush; the blocky figure of Sam Granjon, feet placed wide, one elbow against his side and the other extended straight out for steadiness, was patterned against a gray, boiling void of clouds.

When the gun stopped weaving for a second, Grif let the shot go. Granjon dropped his gun and clutched his thigh. He slipped from Grif's sight behind the front boot.

Someone sprang through the open door and crouched by a boulder. Swinging the Colt to cover him, Grif saw the man throw his gun to his shoulder. He got off a shot too quick to be good. It split the air above Grif's head with a sound like the crack of a cap. This man then yanked the loading lever of his carbine and jammed a new shell into the smoking breech. Coolly Grif squeezed off his shot. He could almost see it rip into the middle of his target. The gunman got up, looking startled. He turned slowly as if on a pivot, and fell against the side of the coach.

Another man started through. With the taste of black-powder on his tongue, Grif felt a wine-like headiness rising through him. Fear had no part in his emotions; he could savor the situation. The old cannon bellowing and a long clean shot. In a way, it was art; he felt like a master painter depicting justice with lead and smoke.

Then he heard that deep-South voice of the gray-eyed man: "*Sam!* Get this thing rolling!"

He saw Granjon haul himself up on the seat, and as he kicked off the brake awkwardly with his left leg instead of his right, Grif set the man's head on the tip of his front sight. Then he knew he couldn't shoot. Not in the back, not with a shot already in the man. Killing ceased to be art, at that point.

The stage rolled, the door banging shut. Grif got a shot

through the leather curtain sagging over the rear baggage compartment. The stage went careening through a tangle of brush down a sandy *barranca*. On the trail behind it lay the body of the man Grif had shot. Among the rocks, Holbrook slowly stood up and rubbed his wrenched shoulder.

There was the matter of whether the shoulder was broken. He settled that by forcing his elbow about in a painful circle. Nothing broken, he reckoned. But nothing right, either.

It was beginning to snow—tiny crystalline flakes spinning in the cold air like salt. He was under-dressed, he did not know where he was; it was quite possible the coach would be back. But not with Sam Granjon at the ribbons: Grif's shot, in the right thigh, he believed, had taken him off the action list. Two out of five. You fixed 'em, old hoss! he thought. But against that he placed a counter-fact: It's not that you're so damned good, but that men do such damned fool things. In action, nine men out of ten were chickens flapping about with their heads off. The one who kept his head ruled the yard.

It seemed best to remain where he was. At last, his feet chilled, he tramped down the slope to where the wounded man lay. The gritty fall of snow was melting as fast as it touched the ground, but the wind had teeth. He went down on one knee, removed the man's pistol, and turned him over on his back. He pulled off the white hood he wore. His eyes were open, but filming. There was blood in his mouth. It was open grotesquely, with two upper teeth showing, like the mouth of a dead gopher. He was a stranger to Grif.

Being dead, the man would not need his purse nor his jacket. The first seemed by law of battle to belong to Grif; the second might be useful in the night that was ahead, if he failed to reach habitation. But when he started to remove the jacket, he found the back of it sodden with blood. He let the man keep it. The purse was a long chamois sack with a clasp top. It contained about fifty dollars in various coins, chiefly Mexican. There was a metal tag which was stamped *Good for One Beer. Congress Bar*. He appropriated this and his powder-and-ball flasks.

In another pocket, Grif found a letter. "Mr. William Fitzroy, Tucson, N. M. Territory." It was from the man's father, apparently, and complained of poor growing-weather in most of Illinois; it spoke wistfully of the small, everyday affairs of farm life. Then it complained, with an old man's snuffle: "Ma and me miss you, Billy, sure could use you on the place, don't want you to tie yourself down though if you still got this traveling bug. Ma not too well again. Asks why you don't write. A letter would help, feel sure."

The date was July, 1860. A dull anger invaded Grif's blood. Slowly he tucked the letter in his pocket, staring down at the dead man. *You son of a bitch! Not enough to desert them. You got to get yourself killed, on top of it!*

Somebody would have to write them, and he supposed it would be he, posing as a friend of their son's and setting down painfully the kind of lies parents liked to hear about even such a son as William Fitzroy.

Later he hiked to the top of a brushy ridge. It would be northwest, as he made it. He looked out on a succession of similar ridges stepping down into wet gray mist. Out there might be, he reckoned, the Sulphur Springs Valley. Or beyond the mist might be another bulwark of mountains.

He thought of descending to the stage road and trudging back to Apache Pass station. Yet he had little idea of which way to start, and he was afraid to follow the trail the black celerity wagon had taken. It occurred to him that the semi-weekly eastbound stage would be along sometime the next day. Best to work down to Sulphur Springs Valley and wait on the road.

He began to walk. A cold wind hissed through the spined wands of the ocotillo clusters and flipped brown, dime-sized leaves from the runted oaks. The toothed blades of a yucca rattled like sabers. His watch indicated two o'clock. Yet it was as dark as five, and the cold was pressing down more bitterly. He hated cold. He was entirely a warm-weather man, dreading frost, despising rain. He turned up the greasy velvet collar of his box coat. The wind lashed at the square tails of it.

At dusk he found a spot under a flinty ledge and prepared to spend the night.

He had feared to start a fire, this being Apache country. But the mist was lower, a screen for the flames, and there was not a remote chance of their seeing his smoke. An oak grew close to the rocky bank and he gathered dry kindling beneath it. All the larger deadfall was in the open, and damp. He spread leaves, arranged twigs artfully, sprinkled black-powder from the powder flask he had taken from Fitzroy. He struck a friction match and let the powder flare.

He was hungry. His shoulder ached. The cold tightened about him as the snow began to whirl in heavier fall. No sleep tonight. Just a night-long campaign against freezing, in this six-thousand-foot air that nipped like foxes' teeth at exposed skin.

Night came on. He took sips of whiskey and thought of fried onions and beefsteak. And as he hunched half frozen above the sick flame, he found his thoughts polarizing to the little auburn-haired girl from Apache Pass. He liked to think of her as warm and secure in the station at Dragoon Springs. Funny how a man in danger and misery liked to think of women surrounded by comfort. But there was a special tingle to his thoughts of Kate Crocker. A frank, sweet, and yet sad girl. And all alone. He was glad he had thought of that bookkeeper angle. He hated bookkeeping and letter-writing. She could do those things for him. And she'd seemed so grateful, taking his arm and leaning on it as though a long fight had ended.

He slept. When he awoke his fire was out and in a gray light he looked about him at rocks and shrubs mantled thinly with snow. He tried to stand up. God *damn!* His back was broken; no, bent and frozen into an L. He could hardly straighten his knees. He stood propped against the tree, feeling the wiry stubble on his face, looking down the slope and wondering whether he dared start now or must wait until the snow melted in a few hours. What more could an Apache ask than a trail of fresh boot-prints in the snow?

The hell with them. He grubbed in his cold fire until he found a still-warm branch; he held this in his two hands and let the stinging heat drive the chill from his fingers. He started to walk. Presently the clouds melted. The sun was a pale lemon color, almost heatless.

7

ABOUT TEN HE realized he must be on a road of some sort. He had drifted along more or less aimlessly, but now he perceived that where the slope was steeper, just ahead, it had been cut away to furnish a level roadbed. He had gone on about a mile when he heard a faint tinkle of mulebells. He scrambled through the cactus to the base of a steeple-like rock. Sprawled in rubble at its base, he had a view through his gunsights of the nearest bend when the first pair of small gray mules came into sight. There were seven more pairs in the team; then came a high-sided freight wagon with seven-foot wheels. Two wagons, hitched to the first, trailed behind it. Four such teams and wagons rumbled through the turn.

The skinner driving the first wagon was singing. He was a chunky individual, well bundled in heavy clothing. He had one leg cocked over the side of the wagon and the cotton jerk-line was snug about his ankle.

> My sweetheart's a mule in the mines;
> I drive her without any lines;
> As on the wagon I sit...

The song died. He stood up and reached for a rifle on the seat beside him in a jerky series of motions. A large black-clad man, with a strange sort of snub-nosed rifle in the crook of his arm, stood at the side of the road just ahead of him. This man was unshaven and glowering. His face was square and rough under the brim of his hat—heavy of nose, broad of jaw, the eyes deep-pocketed beneath brows like a blacksmith's thumb-smudges. Something about him kept the mule-skinner from trying to get his gun into action.

"Air you human," he demanded, "or air you some kind of rare shrub?"

The man said, "I was human the last time I ate. I wouldn't care to guess, right now."

"What do you want?"

"Grub. And a ride."

There was a moment of scrutiny by the skinner. Behind him a muffled grunt came from a pile of blankets atop the heap of freight. The sleepy face of a swamper emerged. The freighter moved his head.

"Climb up, then. Don't know what you're doin' out here afoot, but you'll find this easier'n shanks mares."

The men on the wagon in the rear were standing up to shout questions, most of them unable to see the head of the train. The first man bawled back at them:

"Got a passenger! What'll I charge him—seventy-five dollars a ton, like he was a piano?"

He glanced down at Grif, grinning, a man of ponderous build and knuckle-scarred features. A black felt hat obscured one eye and a quid of tobacco bulged under his cheek. From the neck of his blue Army shirt sprouted a thicket of blond hairs. But above his grin his eyes were still prudent.

Grif set a foot against a spoke. "I reckon we won't quibble over the price. If you can set me down on the stage road or in Tucson, whichever you hit first, you won't lose any money, I'll guarantee that."

He swung up. The mule-skinner moved his gun from the seat and Grif sat down, letting himself slump on the cold padded canvas, and sighed from the bottom of his soul. "Ah, Lord! If I never walk again, I'm telling you I've done my share since yesterday."

The skinner looked curious, but did not question him. His gaze speculated on Holbrook's features, haggard and tinged with the cold. He turned on the seat to confront the Mexican swamper who now sat on a crate staring at Grif. "Cruz," he said, "What's left of the coffee?"

Cruz dug a beer bottle from the blankets. It was corked, half full of an opaque liquid. He tossed it up to the mule-skinner. The warm ease of it descended through Grif.

"Now," he said, "if there would be a whang of jerky at hand—"

The mule-skinner slung a sack onto the seat and extracted hard biscuits, jerked venison, and dried onions. Grif chewed them and washed them down with coffee laced with whiskey. The driver watched him eat as they rumbled along. When he had finished he put out his hand.

"Name of Sig Johnson," he said. "Up from El Paso by way of Skeleton Canyon. You're lucky I ran acrost you. Not many bull-whackers on the Tucson run these days. What there are tend to get rich or dead real sudden."

Grif shook hands with him and presently, warming to the man's rough friendliness, told him an abridged version of the attack on the stage.

Johnson thought about it. "You're a little off your bearing, at that. We'll hit the stage road about ten miles northeast, where she sashays out into the valley. California stage won't be along till Friday. Better ride her on in with me."

"When'll you make Tucson?"

"'Bout the same time as the stage. We make thirty miles a day. Stage knocks off close to a hundred. We may not be fast," he added, "but we're shore purty."

They lumbered down shallow canyons where small streams ran, the snow melting in the sun. They came through a gap and gazed out on the wide reach of Sulphur Springs Valley, smiling in the golden day, a small stream glinting through unhurried turns. It appeared flat as a desert, but when they reached it they found it plowed by arroyos. Wild hay riffled in a breeze, hub-high to the wagons.

At noon they camped on the bank of a sandy arroyo beside the stage road. Johnson made coffee. Grif closed his eyes and leaned his head against the felloe of a wheel, letting the sun burn against his whiskered, fatigue-pinched features; and sitting like this he heard Cruz, the Mexican, say softly:

"Señor Seeg? *Por allá—Caballeros!*"

Horsemen...

Grif sat up with a grunt and found himself staring into Sig Johnson's eyes. Johnson's gaze had a pinch of wonder between the brows. On the stage road the clop of trotting horses rose briskly. Grif's mind rushed from its ease. He could get the drop on Johnson and Cruz; maybe on the whole parcel of them. But the men on the road, if they were accompanied by a gray-eyed man, would see what was happening and pick him off.

His desperation must have shown in his face, for Johnson winked and said gently, "Had a rough time of it, pardner? Well, if you don't feel like talking to strangers, just climb into the wagon and make like a sack of spuds. Don't forget to pull the tarp over you."

Grif regarded him steadily. Then he rose quickly and gripped the freighter's shoulder. "If you ever run for president, Sig, let me know so's I can cast my vote. You know you may get your feet wet in this ruckus, don't you?"

"I know they're going to see you crawling under that tarp if you don't shake a leg."

Grif climbed up and wriggled under the heavy canvas, burrowing beneath earthy-smelling sacks of potatoes. The cold lingered in here. As he crouched under the tarpaulin he heard hoofbeats swell and then abruptly stop. A man spoke.

"Howdy, freighter."

"Howdy. Light down. Hot coffee in the pot."

"Wish we had the time. Seen anything of a big, hard-looking gent in a black suit?"

"Ain't seen nothin' but the behinds of them sixteen oat-engines of mine."

"He's have been afoot, most likely."

"Was he wearing a black hat?"

The voice struck up. "That's it!"

"What was the feller's name?"

"Holbrook—Grif Holbrook."

"No, I ain't seen him," Johnson said casually. "But if I do, I'll tell him you're looking for him."

There was a charged pause, then a tart: "Don't bother. You don't mind," the voice of the gray-eyed man asked, "if we glance under the tarps? There's an off chance he might have crawled in during the night."

"Why, shore," Johnson said. "Just throw off the lashin's and pitch all my freight on the ground. Bust into the crates and scatter everything from hell to breakfast. You damn well bet I mind! Touch them wagons, brother, and I'll take time to dig three graves before I pull up stakes."

A new voice said: "You don't have to be so damned...Come on. He ain't got the sense to know Holbrook from a mountain canary anyhow."

Johnson inquired drily: "You like to step down off that horse a minute, mister?"

Again the Southerner spoke: "Never mind." He added: "For your trouble." Grif heard a coin clink on the ground.

There was a stir of horses wheeling, of hoofs striking the road and breaking into a high trot. After a while there was no sound but the murmur of the teamsters as they ate.

Grif emerged. He took his place at the fire once more without speaking and with no comment from the teamsters. Presently he said, "Give a purty to know what that fellow was with the Alabama accent. Think I've met him before."

Sig Johnson chewed on a strip of jerky. "Wisht I could tell you, brother. See him around Tucson often enough, and if I was so minded I could give you his name. But why you're on the dodge is as much a mystery to me as why he's whackin' the brush for you. Let's say I'm just sweating the game. The only enemies I've got in the world are Es-co-nella and his Apaches, and they're aplenty. I'm going to unload you a mile from Tucson, and how you got there is going to be your secret and mine. But if I meet you on the street, I'll bet I won't know you."

"Fair enough," Grif agreed. "But if you ever need a drink, a dollar, or a friend, Sig, I bet I'll know you."

8

THE PUEBLO LAY on the desert in a wedge of puckered hills. A river, the Santa Cruz, touched the town on the west, not far from the old wall. It was only a small stream in a piping of greenery, but where its waters had been carried in ditches, magic had been worked with the hardscrabble soil. Small orchards prospered and farms were dark patterns between the *acequias*. The town itself was a drab core within the wide belt of farms, in summer a foam of green, now, frostbitten, brown with dead growth.

A freight team had arrived that morning, so that the pueblo gave slight attention to the man who crossed Pennington Arroyo a little before noon. He stood on the bridge a moment, while he flexed his shoulder and gazed up the main street climbing gently away from the arroyo. Mentally, he took the town in his teeth to test it, like a doubtful gold piece. He had been here before, but Tucson was growing fast.

It had the appearance of a thriving town, but it was a rough one, dirty and careless of its appearance, like a bleary-eyed old man with food spilled on his vest. It was a town of church bells, crows, and rubbish, with little of beauty other than the tawniness of adobe walls against blue skies. Holbrook thought: He's been here an hour. Nobody ought to connect us by now.

He walked on. As he proceeded, anticipation began to throb in him. Thoughts of his little widow from Apache Pass tumbled headlong through his mind. Suppose they had raided the stage again—or there had been Indian trouble!

But he would level such possibilities with logic. Then he would picture her as they had talked beside the well that morning, her hair clean and bright, her eyes— He brought himself up. Twaddle! Mooning over adjectives was the stuff of adolescence. But—he had to chuckle—hadn't she flared up when he said she was fired? Spirited as a little mare in a mountain meadow!

As he walked on, he snapped his fingers and grinned, feeling as if a cork had been pulled somewhere in his breast and champagne bubbles were spilling all through him. Katie, Katie, he thought, they broke the mold after they made you.

He was in the town now, devoured by its smells and dust and bustle. He passed an open-air butcher shop where meat hung under a gently stirring mantle of flies. He winced at the foul breath of a mescal shop: *Las Garras del Infierno*—the jaws of Hell. He gazed respectfully at a new two-story structure on Calle Real, the main street. A two-story saloon and gambling house! The name painted on the white plaster front was *Congress Bar*. The town had now had the laying-on of hands.

Across the street from the saloon was the shop of Pie Allen, famous in the Territory for his dollar-a-throw pies, the best dried apple concoction in the West. Grif's mouth began to water as he anticipated a meal of about four of them some time soon. In front of Warner's general store, Sig Johnson was unloading before an audience of Mexicans, Papago Indians, and a few Americans.

A large man with a soiled beard stood on the awninged porch of the store. "How many cases of liquor did you break for me this time, Sig?"

Johnson made a playful cut at the merchant's boots with a bullwhip. "Not a dang bottle, old hoss!" Then he saw Grif watching him, and there was an instant when he hesitated; then he tossed the whip back up on the seat and went to the rear of the wagon. Grif moved on.

Beyond the wagons was a tall, wedge-shaped structure displaying a round *torreón*, like a silo half merged with one corner of the building. It dominated the nondescript, hustling street corner. The intersection formed a small plaza, with five streets converging, and horses, burros, and pedestrians coming and going with lazy turbulence. Above the door of the building a wooden sign swung gently: *Stage Depot—Tucson.*

Temporary indecision held Grif on the boardwalk a moment. His square fingertips rasped over whiskers a quarter-inch long. He glanced down at himself—dusty, muddy, his coat ripped by the sharp talons of cat-claw. Now, why did it matter what he looked like? he rebuked himself. But as he crossed the boardwalk to enter the depot, he reached up and adjusted the thick knot of his stock.

He entered a lofty room formed like a spraddled L. Waiting benches lined the wall on his left. Several passengers sat here; at the feet of one was a lunging sack from which came squawks of a tormented fowl. Facing the door was a partition rising from floor to ceiling and paralleling the outer walls; it broke away in a V-angle at the right, with a ticket-and-baggage window punched through at the angle.

Grif stood peering through the window and trying to find someone. The small cell behind the counter was empty. He could not see through the small door at the rear of it, which gave onto a rear chamber. As he stood here he heard a little cry from a door at his left. Suddenly he saw her standing in the entrance. She ran toward him, and Grif heard her say in a voice between tears and laughter: "Oh, Mr. Holbrook! Oh, I'm so glad—*so* glad—!"

She held both his hands. There was singing and a kind of irrationality in Grif Holbrook. "For what I been through," he said severely, "I sh'd think there'd be another of those kisses."

She laughed. "You think there isn't?" And she took him by the ears and smacked him on the cheek, loudly.

Grif forgot about the people in the waiting room. He took her in a bear-hug and kissed her on the mouth. His romancing had all been in the rough-and-tumble school, but it had, nevertheless, always been sufficient. She was little and soft as a kitten. She set fire to an exultation in him. Then he realized that she was struggling, only he was holding her so tight it was hard to tell. He let her go and she stepped back, flushed, with a hand to her lips.

"Why—why, Grif!" she said.

All his sureness fled. Stupid with embarrassment, he stood with his arms hanging. "I—pshaw, Katie, I don't know how I came to..."

She saw his confusion and took compassion. "In front of all those people!" she whispered.

She led him through a door to a tiny back room with a twelve-foot ceiling. Being in it was like standing at the bottom of a shaft. Light, splintered by wooden bars, slanted through a narrow window to warm the dry cold. The room held a desk, a safe, a letter-press, a couple of chairs, and a cuspidor. In a corner fireplace glowed a tiny jewel of warmth. Grif gravitated to it.

Kate had left the incident outside. She sat at the desk, leaning her chin in her cupped palms. "You still haven't told me how you got away from them."

Grif recited his saga, excising the part Sig Johnson had played. Kate listened intently. She had alert, facile features. "I hope Heydenfeldt didn't give you any trouble?" he said, when he had finished.

"I haven't even seen the man. He's supposed to be out cutting hay somewhere. According to the books, everyone else has been as short on feed as I was. But Johnny—that is, Mr. Broderick, the agent—has been wonderful."

"Never heard of him."

"Neither had I. He's been out for two days with a dozen men, trying to find you. He ought to have been back before now." She appeared a bit worried.

Grif rubbed his hands above a frosty-red bed of coals about the size of a sadiron. Sometime before spring, it seemed, it might bring the room temperature up to where ink would not freeze. A cowhide ledger lay open on the desk where Kate sat, exposing columns of caged figures. It had the look of sloppy bookkeeping. There were ink stains to be seen and what appeared to be spilled coffee.

"Had a chance to look them over yet?"

She turned the book. "They're in perfectly terrible shape. Shortages on every page! He's written 'To Balance' every time the discrepancies got too big. I don't know what he did about the auditors—he must have kept them drunk from the time they hit town until they left."

Grif watched her turn pages, scanning totals with pursed lips. She had, he observed, abandoned the short skirts in favor of a long gown, plain and dark except for some strategic tucks and rows of tiny buttons in the basque. In the weak sunlight her hair looked darker, brushed and parted and brought back to a smooth knot low on her neck.

Suddenly she looked about and caught him staring. She gave a quick, rather uncertain smile. Grif's heart thudded. There was something very personal about the instant, a quality as striking and unmistakable as a beam of sunlight shimmering in a dark room. He felt it as a fear of something he did not understand, as a force that was of him and yet stronger than he. A spark in him seemed to have been stirred, to be shedding its gray, insular cloak and coming to life.

Her voice came to him as from the end of a long corridor. "Grif, you—you look so strange."

The moment ended. Grif came to. "Do I? Matter of fact, I was thinking of something. Something about Heydenfeldt. We'll have to look into that boy, all right."

For a moment she let her gaze rest curiously on him. Then from beyond the window swept a clatter of hoofs muted by deep road dust. Grif got up quickly. Past the window, which opened on a little curving side street, flashed a file of horsemen. They were tawny with dust and rode with slickers tied behind the cantles and long noonday shadows depending from their hatbrims like masks. There was an end to the trampling of the horses, some loud conversation and laughter, and then confused sounds as though the party were breaking up. Someone came into the stage depot, his spurs chiming, the thud of his walk long-legged and stiff.

"Katie?" he shouted.

Kate Crocker stepped to the door. "In here, Johnny!"

Broderick could be heard vaulting the baggage counter and landing with a musical jar of silver tines. "Well, they either killed and buried the old hoot-owl or he's gone yellow and taken off. Not a sign of him. Found an old fire that might have—"

He stopped, staring at the large, inelegant man tipped back in the chair by the safe. "Who's that?"

"Why, it's Mr. Holbrook—Grif Holbrook!" Kate cried happily, with a woman's desperate desire to scotch incipient rancor with an excess of jollity.

Broderick stood there in surprise. He was tall and tight-built, dressed in a pony-skin jacket, black pants and a raw-edged brown Stetson. About him there was a look of young confidence, of rashness and good nature. Leonine: that was the word. Like a mountain lion in his smoothness, tawny coloring, and masculine grace. From long custom in rough times, Holbrook's eyes picked at him like a pawnbroker's fingers, searching for the flaw he would go for in a scrap. But Broderick's jaw was one for shaping anvils on, and his arms were long and the hands at the ends of them big-knuckled and capable, and if he had a vulnerable spot it did not show.

One of his hands extended slowly and he put on a tentative smile. "I—I was looking for a younger man, I guess—That is, I didn't know—" He blundered to an embarrassed stop.

It was the essence of tactlessness, so crude that Grif could smile inwardly. The kid was blushing. Grif shook his hand grimly. "Sorry you had yourself a wild goose chase, Broderick. I walked in."

Broderick turned away quickly and busied himself with a black *papel orozúz* cigarette, one of those concoctions young fellows smoked until they got tired of inhaling burned sugar and rose petals with their tobacco. "What happened?" he said. "We didn't miss a square rod between North Peak and Dunn Springs."

"Let's forget about it, son. They roughed me up a little, but here I am, wondering who you are and what became of old Harry Mason, that was station agent a year ago."

Broderick began fumbling among papers on the desk. ". . . There's a letter here someplace the Admiral gave me. I was working in Frisco. He—well, he took a shine to me for some reason and brought me down here last month. I'm supposed to help you."

In Grif's head, a shout of raucous laughter echoed: "*Help me!*"

Broderick lifted one shoulder. "Not implyin' that you need any help. But it's at least a two-man job here, from what I've seen."

Grif spoke with an awareness of being petty, and yet under a compulsion to avenge that remark. "Do I work under you," he asked, "or do you work under me?"

Broderick's eyes mocked him. "*I* work under *you*, Mr. Holbrook."

"Just so that's understood," Holbrook said. "I like a free hand."

Broderick, if he had been off balance, had landed on his feet. He removed the cigarette from his mouth, pinched a grain of tobacco from his tongue, and replaced the cigarette. "Just climb over me if I get in your way." His eyes came up to

Grif's. Mingled with their silent raillery seemed to be a pinch of disillusionment.

It had the effect of getting under Grif's armor like a thistle. He wished he had said less. He wished he could cancel some of it. He began to rub his hands together briskly, with a grin for Kate. "No use jawin' here when I could be getting my throat cut at a barber shop. Where do you get the hair clipped out of your ears, Johnny?" He got up, settling his hat on the side of his head; and then, in afterthought a bit over the right eye.

"Bay-Rum Brown's. He calls it the National Hair Dressing and Bathing Saloon, up on Cemetery Street. When he ain't drunk on hair tonic, he plows a pretty straight laceration."

Grif found his bag in a corner. Before leaving, he asked Kate: "Say, where are you staying?"

"With a Mrs. Ochoa. She's got a spare room she rents."

"Fixed up all right?"

"Fine! She's a good cook, too."

"Sure? I like my employees to be treated right."

Johnny blew smoke at the ceiling. "I wonder if I couldn't have a feather mattress on that cot of mine? I was the only child of a duke, and I swear I was bruised all the time from them putting peas under the mattress to see if I had enough padding!"

"Tell you what you do. Take four bits out of the cash drawer and buy yourself a shakedown of hay at the livery stable. If that don't work, we'll see about a fur-lined nightie."

Broderick laughed too loudly, swung down off the table, and sauntered out. Kate gave Grif a smile with a frown in it. "Do be easy on Johnny, Grif. He's such a kid. And the way he's been talking about working with Grif Holbrook has had everybody laughing. You'd think you were all the gunfighters and cattle drovers and stagecoach messengers in the West jammed into one pair of boots. Somebody said something about you he didn't like one day, and you know what he did? He threw him in the horse trough!"

It tickled Grif. "He do that?"

"*Did* he! He held him under for a full minute."

Grif felt a warmth growing where coolness had been before. "Oh, sure," he said. "Johnny and I'll get along all right. We're just kind of sizing each other up right now."

9

IN ONE OF the small cells behind the office, a concertina began to wheeze. Grif winced. "I gather he's musical, as well as handsome."

They listened to Broderick having trouble with *Camptown Races*. A horse pulled up at the small corral behind the station. A man could be heard opening the gate. Kate glanced out.

"That's Mr. Heydenfeldt now!"

Grif watched the man turn his horse in without unsaddling. He slogged, saddle-stiff, toward the building. He was a broad-shouldered man in fringed buckskin pants and an old Army shirt. He wore his belt low on his belly, apparently under the impression that it gave him more chest and less stomach. They heard him come into the station. He stopped at the door of Johnny Broderick's room. Broderick stopped playing the concertina and there was some conversation. Heydenfeldt laughed and came on, with Broderick behind him. He stopped in the doorway and looked at Holbrook, sitting on the windowsill. He tilted the low-crowned hat he wore to the back of his head. His sideburns came to the angles of his jaws, joining a mustache shaped like an oxbow that curved low and then up over his lip.

He said to Kate, whom he seemed to know from his duties as section boss: "Howdy, Mrs. Crocker. Company?"

Broderick made the introduction. "This is Grif Holbrook, Gus. Butterfield's right-hand man. Grif, meet Gus Heydenfeldt."

Heydenfeldt immediately assumed a hearty manner, advancing with his hand extended. "Mighty glad to know you, Grif. Just make yourself at home."

He had the uneasy grin and rumpled, slightly breathless air of a man interrupted at love-making. Grif shook hands with him. He asked about his haying excursion.

"No luck," Heydenfeldt grunted. He threw his hat over the letter-press. "Not an acre worth hayin' out there. Drought burnt everything off last summer."

"Came through plenty of hay on the way over. Anything wrong with the hay in Sulphur Springs Valley?"

Heydenfeldt scratched his head. "Why—nothing at all, if it ain't too thin. Looked kinda sorry to me, but if you say so I'll send a crew out today."

Grif walked to the desk where Kate sat and turned a page of the ledger. Heydenfeldt's attention was overconciliatory. He looked as though if Grif took out his pipe he would be right there with a match. "How are the accounts running?" Grif asked.

"Why—they could be better, could be better. Winter's always slack though."

"Especially in Tucson."

Heydenfeldt cleared his throat. "Don't quite get you."

"I mean in this particular office. Not to mention the whole danged Fourth Division. What's the matter with you, man? Don't you know they're tearing the line to pieces at Apache Pass?"

Heydenfeldt's eyes showed a pucker of truculence. "Ain't nothing any one man can do about that. I've done my best."

"What about the books? Done your best to keep them straight? Or do you just absorb any accidental profit?"

"No call for that sort of talk," the section boss declared.

"There's plenty of call for locking you up," Grif snapped. "But the Admiral's word was to pay you off and fire you, so that's the caper. Can you move your stuff out by noon?"

Heydenfeldt's face congested with surly blood. He scowled but did not look up. "Shore. But—"

"But what?"

"Well, it's mighty dull music to fire a man without rightful cause, and no notice."

Kate cut in tartly. "It seems to me you're being treated

better than you've treated the company."

Heydenfeldt's glance flicked. "Where do you come into this, *Missus* Crocker? You secretary to the president, or something, *Missus* Crocker?"

With his glance on Kate, Grif saw a small jolt of surprise widen her eyes, and then he saw color surge through her features as she turned angrily and went out to the ticket counter. There was an undercurrent here that he did not get. Broderick seemed to feel it, too. He piped a couple of notes on the concertina, regarding the section boss thoughtfully.

Anger came pumping up in Grif, but at the moment Heydenfeldt turned and began collecting various small belongings from the desk. "Hell of a note, that's all," he grunted.

Presently, his hat filled with odds and ends, he strode to the small room where he bunked.

Kate passed through to go to the storeroom. Broderick's eyes watched her pass. Nice, they said. He made a little run on the concertina. Grif's hackles rose, lying still again as he contemplated her himself. Nice, trim ankles; just the right amount of flare in back; a way of carrying herself that made you think she had had lessons in walking.

In the awkward wait, Grif and Johnny talked about how many wagons they would need for the haying, Broderick thought he knew where they could rent some. In the midst of this, they heard a sharp, concussive sound in back. Then there was the sound of Heydenfeldt's voice in rough laughter. Kate came back. She was pale. She stood looking at them a moment.

"What's the matter?" Grif asked.

She was breathing hard. "Nothing," she said suddenly. "I—I just don't like that man."

She went out front carrying some luggage labels.

A puzzled silence came to dwell in the room, ending when Heydenfeldt returned with a bag in his hand and a roll of blankets over his shoulder. He brought an odor of liquor. His face was redder than ever, except on the left cheek, where there was a rank of pallid stripes.

"All right, I'm getting out," he said. "I'll pick up my pay later." He turned, but paused to lean against the jamb. "She going to be your secretary or something?"

"Bookkeeper. Why?"

"Just wondering. Maybe it don't matter to you the kind of talk that goes on."

Grif let his chair rock back. "Why should any talk go on?"

Heydenfeldt lifted his shoulders. "It wouldn't be about you, so much, as Katie. Katie's pretty well known along the line. Funny thing, at that," he said, with a wink at Broderick. "Quite a change for Katie, keeping books. Up to now, it was always her that was kept. Well, so long, boys. I'll—"

He dropped the bag suddenly and let the blanket roll fall as both men started for him. "Now, wait a minute!" It was Broderick who was closer, so it was his fist that smashed into Heydenfeldt's cheekbone and sent him reeling through the door into the next room. Broderick was breathing through his nose like an angry bull. Grif grabbed his shoulder.

"Let me have him!"

Broderick struck his hand off and charged through the door. Grif heard the smack of a fist and looked through to see Johnny stumble aside. Heydenfeldt, a strapping, angry man with his small eyes choked in a face the color of fresh beef, was after him with chopping fists. He clipped the younger man behind the ear and Johnny went down. Heydenfeldt's boot drew back for a kick.

Broderick rolled aside and caught the foot that lashed at him. He gave a savage yank, blood seeping from his mouth in a sluggish dark rut. Startled, Heydenfeldt grabbed at a table, overturned it, and went down in a cascade of ink bottles and stationery. Johnny was on top of him like a puma. He brought his right fist down again and again. Heydenfeldt made guttural noises as he struggled beneath him.

Grif stood with a vast hunger in him, hearing Kate run into the room. Broderick was stealing the show. The damn young fireball! He had brought Kate here himself, and a pup like this had to . . . It made a man sick.

"Stop them!" he heard Kate cry. *"Stop them!"*

Grif stood stoically in the doorway watching Heydenfeldt suddenly roll over and slug Broderick on the ear. He heard the younger man grunt. Again Heydenfeldt's fist traveled. Johnny looked as though he were finished after that one, but as Heydenfeldt continued to club at his face, he turned his head and writhed partially out of his grasp. Grif wanted to shout advice. He saw the mistake Heydenfeldt was making—wearing himself out with frantic punches without half his shoulder behind them, looming over Broderick with his belly and neck totally unguarded—but Broderick seemed not to have the sense to take advantage of these things.

Then he saw Broderick glance up out of a puffing eye as Heydenfeldt paused to blow. His arm reached up and one stiff thumb prodded the soft, haired-over hollow at the base of the man's neck. Heydenfeldt leaped like a snake on a griddle. He got off Johnny in a hurry, grunting and gagging, but Johnny had his other hand behind Heydenfeldt's neck and went with him. Heydenfeldt's face was a turgid mauve. He floundered back, with Johnny coming to his knees and releasing him to drive a straight, hard punch to his face.

Grif heard himself shouting: "That's the tune, Johnny!"

Broderick doubled Heydenfeldt into a grunting horseshoe on the floor. He hunted an avenue to his chin, but the man had his face buried in his knees. Then he seemed to realize no more was needed. Heydenfeldt was in the throes of the sick, green, worse-than-death paralysis of a stomach blow.

Johnny got up. He looked at Grif and Kate. One eye was buried in puffy pink flesh; his mouth was bleeding. Some statement seemed to be required of him. He made a half-hearted gesture at the man on the floor. "He—I—!"

Grif let him sweat, knowing he dared not bring out what Heydenfeldt had said.

Kate cried, "I think you're both perfectly disgusting! Fighting like dogs, that's what! I should think you'd have had some respect for me."

Johnny Broderick had made the transition from Camelot to the gutter. He put on the girl a stare of bruised resentment, wiped blood from his mouth, and stalked from the room.

Grif lugged Gus Heydenfeldt onto the walk before the depot. He deposited his satchel and blankets beside him and took the precaution of extracting the loads from his Colt.

At the desk Kate was weeping silently, taking a prolonged, sniffling breath now and then. Grif stood behind her. He started to put his hands on her shoulders and then hesitated. A blanket of tenderness warm and moist as steam enveloped him. Finally he reached out to pat her shoulder.

"Katie, honey," he said, "you mustn't take it thisaway.

You didn't hear what started it, did you?"

She raised her head. "No. But I know what he said. He said I was a—I wasn't a good woman."

Grif was too startled to frame a lie. Kate turned quickly, her lashes damp. "That was it, wasn't it?"

His hand rubbed the rough fabric of his coat. "Something like that. But shoot! Letting a jimber-jawed ox like that bother you!"

Kate's eyes did not release him. "But—you see," she said, "it happens to be true. I wasn't married to Will Crocker, Grif. I just lived with him."

The impulse Grif had was to deny to himself that it had ever happened.

It was his failing, to be incapable of seeing shadows in the picture his mind painted of a friend. He turned the strong light of virtue on it, which admitted of no flaw. He had done a little more than that in the case of Kate Crocker. He had framed a picture with pink; when he peered closely, he could almost see himself beside her.

Suddenly she slipped from her chair and ran to where her handbag and hat lay atop the safe. She donned the wide-brimmed hat hastily, the ribbons falling across her shoulders. Grif lurched after her as she ran from the office.

"Katie!"

"Don't follow me! Just leave me alone!"

He watched her hurry across the street. A hurt sharper than any he had ever known was at his heart with its thin steel. He went back and sat in the dusty office. He smoked a pipe that tasted like corral sweepings. How, in a few days, could a woman come to dominate every pore of a man's life? Love had always been a mystery, like death, something to be understood only by experiencing it.

But if this were love, this feeling of having been hollowed out like a rotten stump, then nature took a hell of an unpleasant way of perpetuating the species. Sicken a man's heart, drain the strong juice from his veins, shackle him with a golden chain so fine he could not see it, yet so strong he could not break it.

He told himself it made no difference if she had been married to Crocker or not. If she had done anything wrong, she must have had a reason. But when he thought of her sharing the feverish, sweet ecstasy of the night with another man, languorous in the naked intimacy of love, he lunged from his chair and toured the office in agony.

It was not right to fasten this torment on a man unless he was pledged to a woman. But it began to come to him that he had been pledged to her in his heart ever since the first night in the stage station under the rough brow of the Chiricahuas. He had liked the prideful heart of her. He had seen the strength and weakness of her and loved them both.

Suddenly he decided to go after her. But when he reached the tumultuous street, choked with horses, wagons and ox teams, she was out of sight. The dark dress and wide-brimmed hat had vanished, and he had no idea where this Mrs. Ochoa lived.

Suddenly, as he stood there, the boardwalk jolted under his feet. A heavy, hollow roar overlaid the mélange of traffic, a thunderous clap of sound which sent him back a step. A sift of dust spattered down the adobe wall of the station.

There was a moment when everything seemed to pause and listen, everything except a horse which took to pitching with its swearing rider. The street traffic was frozen. He had the impression that a mine explosion had occurred.

The instant broke. As if on a signal, men again trod the boardwalks and horses and burros scuffed along in the powdery dust. A Mexican sitting with his back against the sun-warmed wall smiled at the man beside him.

"Oiga que los locos están tirando!"—The crazy ones are at it again.

Curiosity drew Grif from his misery. The crazy ones—the Territorials? It had been a cannon, sure as hell, and not far off. He asked the Mexican about it.

"Who's doing the shooting?"

"Los Territoriales, señor. Acerca del campo. Suficiente para velar los muertos, no?" —Over by the cemetery. Enough to wake the dead, the man thought.

Grif could see the humble belfry of the church above the low roofs across the street. He strolled unhurriedly down Cemetery Street, passing the tonsorial parlor of Bay-Rum Brown. Beyond the hotel a plaza opened up, a rough area dotted with manure of new and old vintage; rutted and pot-holed and dominated by a vast corral of mesquite poles. He saw animals which bore the OM brand of the Overland Mail tugging at heaps of loose hay. Streets slanted in here almost without plan—the Street of the Happy Maiden,

Street of the Sad Indian, crooked little trails of mud-and-pole *jacales* and ruined corrals and bake-ovens. Pigs scabbed with mud rooted in garbage heaps.

Beyond the corral was the little church of Guadalupe. Before it squatted a small, smoking six-pounder on a platform. A double line of men was forming beside it. He watched while they dressed up their ranks and a small, peppery man with a goatee and a potbelly strutted before them. "Column of twos—column right—maa—ch!" Booted, spurred; tall, short; fat and lean, they marched past the church and out a ragged hole in the old town wall.

Grif followed. A few houses lay on the desert. Several hundred yards away were the tottering crosses of the cemetery. To the left, the Territorials were preparing for target practice. They loaded and went into prone position. There was a prolonged, stuttering crash of fire. Puffs of dust popped from the wall as the bullets struck about paper targets.

Grif did not hear the man behind him until he spoke. "Do they look like a gang of hurrah-boys to you, Holbrook? They look more like the first Southern soldiers on Northern soil, to me!"

It was Senator Blaise Montgomery behind him, puffing from a brisk walk.

10

THE OFFICE OF THE *Tucsonian* was at the foot of Correo Street, near the canal. As they entered the building, they could hear the chattering of women washing clothes on the banks. Inside, a small Washington hand-press stood against a wall. At a type-font, an old man who was distributing type turned to squint at them. Montgomery walked through the litter of papers and spilled printer's furniture to his living quarters in the rear.

In a bare little room whose only prides were a few sticks of rosewood and a Winthrop desk, he set out brandy and cigars. There was the inescapable corner fireplace, giving off fumes and a small byproduct of heat. Portly but dapper in gray trousers, cream waistcoat of wadded silk and a claw-hammer coat, Montgomery chewed on his cigar and then sourly held it from him as if debating where to throw it.

"They grow more bald-faced every day. Man got into an argument with a Territorial in a bar last week. Five of them jumped him! Whipped him to a fare-thee-well! Last three weeks it's been target practice, target practice, target practice! Benteen strutting up and down like a banty rooster, telling men who could spot him forty yards how to hit the mark!" His pink wattles trembled with indignation.

When Grif, on the way down, had told him of his escape from the stage gang, he said: "I'm glad, Grif—can't tell you how glad. I gave you up. But don't be misled. You're not out on a pardon. You're on probation. Probation expires the day you bump into the wrong man on the street and find he's left a knife in you. Did you get a look at any of the men—

69

other than Prentiss and this fellow you killed?"

"Well, no. But if a certain young feller was to pass me on the street, I'd know him right now. He was the bandmaster. Talked as polite as though I was a lady. I reckon he'd have said 'Excuse me' after he shot me, like he'd belched. But what I remember about him is his eyes. Gray as lead. Dang near white. Hangman's eyes."

Montgomery grunted. He rolled his cigar between his fingers. "You could piroot around for months, but if we could hear every word that was said in that Congress Bar, we'd be 'way ahead of the game. Annie Benson runs it, a fine woman in many ways, but as Southern as cornpone. Now, what does a man do when he thinks he's put the big britches on somebody? Tells a woman about it. How he sold a blind horse or whipped someone in a fight. If we could know every brag that was ever made to those floosies of Annie's, the job would be finished tomorrow."

"If I thought I could fool anybody," Grif said, "I'd put on a short skirt and hang around Annie's for a while."

Montgomery stood up as Grif arose. "Or you could go about it in another way. Set your cap for Annie. The things she doesn't know about Tucson haven't happened yet. Maybe you could work a switch on the old game and get her to talk to you. Though she's nobody's fool."

Grif's smile was wry. "I've never got any place yet except by traveling in a straight line. Whenever I've set out traps, I've stepped in them myself."

Montgomery followed him into the warm reek of ink and grease. The thing that had been picking at Grif's conscious-ness for the last half hour became too strong to repress. As he opened the door, he asked casually, "Hope you took good care of our little lady on the trip?"

Montgomery looked puzzled. Then: "Oh! You mean Mrs. Crocker? Yes, she made out all right."

"Seems like a competent woman. I hated to turn her out. You knew she's going to keep books for me?"

There were small pinches of amusement beside the Senator's eyes. "I think she said something about it."

"You, uh—think she's as good a choice as any?"

Montgomery nodded gravely.

"We had to knock that feller Heydenfeldt around for something he said about her. Nice little woman like that!"

He watched the editor's expression narrowly, but Montgomery merely shook his head.

"Some fellows don't know where to draw the line."

"No." Grif cleared his throat. "I mean he ought to know better than to talk about a decent woman."

Montgomery chuckled. "Grif, if I knew anything derogatory about your lady, I wouldn't have the bad judgment to say so. However, as far as I know, the Widow Crocker is as well thought of as anybody around here."

Grif took a deep breath, unaware of what he had proved, but somehow stimulated. He shook Montgomery's hand. "Well, thanks, Senator. Thanks a lot."

He walked at a deep-lunged pace up the curving street toward the depot.

The road a man traveled could go along for years as level as a prairie, the little disappointments and achievements mere hummocks from which he took a brief, wider view. Then something would occur which rose up in his life like the Rocky Mountains. That was the way Kate Crocker had hit Grif.

He was so bound up in her that his brain felt hobbled.

There was this urge to put a sort of emotional glass bell over her, as though she were a Swiss clock which careless fingers might damage. Now at last he looked at it frankly. He was in love. It was a sweet, a sad, and a frightening thing.

He had loved before, but now he understood that those other seasons had been mere strolls through a hothouse. This time it was the full, raging solstice of the heart. The velvet was off the horns. He would marry in a minute.

He had secured his bag from the depot and taken a room at the little hotel next door to Brown's barber shop. His clothes unpacked, he sat at the window gazing out on the plaza, dusky in late afternoon. A wind was blowing, though there was hardly a tree to show it; only dust, and the streaming tails of horses. Dull burgundy stained the sky. The bell of Guadalupe church bonged mellowly, while women hurried along to vespers. Sadness of the dying day deepened his own misery.

Anesthesia for the soul was what he needed. On the way out, he caught a glimpse of himself in the mirror. A sight, that was for sure! Dirty, crusty, unshaven. The barber shop would be stop number one.

• • •

Bay-Rum Brown was shaving himself at a soapy mirror when Grif entered. He called: "Right with you, friend," and rinsed lather from his face in a brass washbowl. He turned, awling soap from his ear. He was a bald, florid little man with black mutton-chop whiskers. He wore a pink shirt with green sleeve-garters and a gold horseshoe in his tie.

"The works," Grif told him. "Bath, haircut, and shave."

Brown opened a booth in the back and glanced inside. "Water's still warm," he said. "Last gent left the towel clean as he found it. There's bull-taller soap if you're the greasy kind, reg'lar if you ain't." He offered his hand. "They call me Bay-Rum Brown, friend. Glad to form your acquaintance."

Grif latched the cloth frame door and stripped. With a vanity that smiled at itself, he made his belly muscles taut and gazed down at himself. Hard plates of muscle stood up under the hair of his chest. With thumb and forefinger he could glean a bare pinch of fat from his belly. He made a bicep. Hard. Age, he reckoned anew, was no more than a state of mind; and for some reason, as he let himself down into the barrel, he thought of Johnny Broderick.

In the soap-scummed barrel he dipped warm water over himself with a gourd. Laziness stole along his limbs in drugged surrender. It would be wonderful to go to sleep in this watery California that made problems seem like dreams. In this mood he was vaguely aware of someone entering the shop. The suave scraping of Brown's razor ceased.

"By Jeremy!" he exclaimed. "You been boycotting me, Jim? Ain't seen you all week."

A man let himself onto the bench with a sigh and stretched his legs. "I ought to boycott you. My last cut's just healing. Been down to Tubac, though. Benteen been in today?"

It was as though the water in the tub had chilled. Grif was standing up, a white, hairy-chested spectre.

It was the bland, deep-South voice of the man with gray eyes.

Brown said, "Doc? No, he was givin' us target practice this afternoon. With all that exercise, he must have gone over to Juan Burruel's for a therapeutic dose."

"I just came from there."

"Must be at Annie Benson's, then. He's tyin' it on somewhere, that's for shore."

The other's voice was crisp and concerned. "I've covered them all. Damn that little drunk! When you really want him, he's either stewed or got the shakes."

Grif, emerging dripping from the barrel, dried hastily and began to dress. Beyond the screen the outlaw must have asked something with his eyes, for Brown grunted:

"Traveler, I reckon. Getting the works between stages, prob'ly." Louder, he asked: "What do you want with Doc, Jim? You don't look sick."

"It's a friend of mine. Got him over at Annie's. Might be smallpox."

"Smallpox!" Brown screeched.

There was a shrug in the other's inflection. "Not much chance that it is, but we want to know. Annie's not going to put him up at the saloon if he's got the smallpox. Well, if you see Doc," he said, "send him over to Annie's. If he can't walk, carry him."

He was placing a soft gray Stetson on his head when Grif stepped from the booth. He was a tall and slender man with a loose grace to his body and a face too proud of itself. His hair was light brown, going gray, crisp with tight waves. He wore long sideburns which descended below his ears and made sharply slanting lines toward the corners of his mouth.

Grif gave him a bare nod. "Howdy." He faced the mirror and began adjusting his tie, but the focus of his attention was on the face of the man Brown had called Jim. He wanted to see if this man's nerves were as good as his. He could have shot him before leaving the booth, and yet he perceived that the man might be more useful as bait than as prey. "Who's next?" he queried.

Brown motioned him into the chair. Grif took a month-old St. Louis newspaper from the waiting bench and clambered into the chair. The other had not stirred. He stood there with his hand slowly curling the brim of his Stetson. Grif did not have to look at his face to understand the rabbity leaping of his thoughts.

Does he know me? Had I best force a fight and make sure?

Bay-Rum Brown paused in the act of pinning the apron around Grif's neck. "Sump'n?" he asked the other.

The man started. "No, I— You get what I said about

sending Doc over when he shows up?"

"Got it. Take care y'self, Jim."

The gray-eyed one left. His boots stepped away slowly and without much sureness down the walk.

Brown picked up scissors and comb, and swore. "Smallpox!"

"Good-looking young feller," Grif said.

The comb did not quite draw blood as Brown raked it aft. "That's Jim Maroon. Most of the seenyoritas think so. Grain dealer. Brings *panocha* up from Sonora and has it milled here. Does good."

Grif shook the tattered journal flat. "This Annie Benson's—" he said. "Is that a place I ought to know?"

Brown gave a lecherous chuckle. "Whether you *ought* to or not, I'll give you odds you will. Annie runs the Congress Bar. Good liquor. Watch the faro dealers though. No use telling you to watch the girls. If a man's pawing dirt, he'll brave hell for it, and cuss himself the minute he gets his breath."

"Parlor house, eh?"

Brown stood back to squint along the sideburns. "Yep. Lots more, too. City hall, sort of. We ain't got what you'd call a real municipal set-up in this pueblo. Year ago we were having all kinds o' hell. Shootin's and cuttin's till you dassn't poke your nose out at night. No sheriff, no prefect, no justice of the peace. Hell was sending them back! Wouldn't give a Tucson citizen room for fear of contributing to the delinquency of the damned.

"One day Annie moved in. Built the Congress Bar and freighted in everything from red curtains to the best whiskey this side o' St. Louis. First night she's open, couple jaspers go to the smoke over a sleeve card. Bango! Annie's got a corpse on her hands. She don't like it. She throws everybody out and shuts up for a week. Then she sends for all the big men in town, white or Mex, and shows them a badge she'd had a silversmith make.

"'Boys,' she says, 'we're going to have some government. This is the worst place I was ever in, and I come from Frisco. First office we're going to fill is the sheriff's. I nominate Pete Deuce.' Pete was elected, howling and pleadin'. 'Next,' says Annie, 'is justice of the peace. I nominate J. M. Holt. Any objections? Motion carried.' Then she elects a prefect and appoints some committees, including a standing posse. She pins that badge on Pete and shakes his hand, and pretty soon Peter steals a squint at it and rubs it with his sleeve . . . He's made a powerful good sheriff too, with the others to back him up. It's like a different town."

The scissors whispered beside Grif's ear. "They don't talk loose about Annie," Brown summed up. "They tip their hats to her on the street. By the way," he said, "when you go over there, don't ask for Annie, excepting you want to shake hands. Annie only runs the place."

In the little book he was keeping in his mind, Grif put another check beside Annie Benson's name. So she had elected all the town officers, and the Territorials ran wild and presumably had the blessing of some powerful citizens! Annie would do to get acquainted with, as the Senator had said.

A half hour later, his heavy plew of bear-brown hair pruned back, his jaws and neck still stinging from the scrape of unsharp steel, he left the shop. His legs carried him down the street at a straightforward gait. Love, for the time being, took a stool in the corner. He was on his way to a date with Sam Granjon.

He thought: Maybe I better grab Maroon while I can. But he could not forget that his job was to stop the raids and find the stages, not just knock over one or two of the men involved in them. It did not add up that Maroon was the leader.

When an army took the field, did the general ride in the van? If Jim Maroon were the head of this boa constrictor that had all but squeezed the Overland Mail in two, would he be leading the raids himself? It would, he thought, be damned peculiar if he did.

No. Maroon was a smart and aggressive man, but he was neither old enough nor smart enough to conceive a campaign like this, to load all the little political guns he would need and then run around shooting them. He would not, for instance, stick his neck out by hunting a doctor for the man who lay ill in Annie Benson's Congress Bar. For the sick man, if he had a pox at all, had one large scar in his right thigh about the size of a forty-four slug, and the fever he had would be the shouting madness of gangrene.

11

A STRONG PULSE OF life still throbbed along Calle Real in the cold windy dusk. Four troopers from Fort Buchanan jogged down the street. A man who might have been a successful merchant whirled from the alley behind the stage depot in a handsome turnout, drove half a block and stopped before the Congress Bar. Along the boardwalks bustled late pedestrians.

As he started across the street, Grif saw a woman turn in at the door of the depot. She was tall and well-formed, a handsome figure in a gray dress with a shawl hugging her shoulders against the cold. Something told him to slow down. He set his feet carefully on the walk beside the door and listened.

Johnny Broderick said something gruffly, and then the woman replied in a quick, emotional outburst:

"Then, for heaven's sake, will you tell me where he is? I've got to find him."

"I don't know where he is, Annie. He might be in a room at the hotel. He might be drunk. How should I know?"

There was a pause. "What's the matter with you, Johnny?" Annie Benson asked. "You look as though somebody'd taken a singletree to you. You don't have to take it out on me if you've had a squabble with someone."

"If I knew—"

"I think," Mrs. Benson said, "that you're going to be very, very sorry if you're putting me off. A man is dying at my place. A friend of Mr. Holbrook's. He's been asking for him. I don't think I'd take it on myself to deny a dying man the right to speak to an old friend."

76

Grif walked in. He halted, feigning surprise, and fetched off his hat. Mrs. Benson turned quickly.

"This is him," Broderick said. He turned sullenly, his face still puffy and bruised with the marks of battle, and went to the rear.

Annie Benson called after him. "Better come over and let Mike take care of that face, Johnny." She turned a grave smile on Grif, offering a gloved hand. "Mr. Holbrook, I'd almost given you up." She was a tall ash-blonde of about thirty-five, with the finest complexion he had ever seen. Tea-rose petals in lamplight. She wore her hair in a braided coronet; it was as clean and shining as pine shavings. He had the wit to observe that her eyes were just the color of the stones in the earrings she wore—the color of a mile of spring sky compressed and compressed until the whole depth and color of it were held in a tiny prismed teardrop.

Suddenly she lowered her eyes, a tinge of color coming to her face. "I—I didn't mean to stare so," she said. "But I've heard so much about you, Mr. Holbrook."

And she did something with her eyes, a quick veiling of long lashes and the downward glance again, as though she had overstepped. He had seen it done before, but never so well.

"Please to know you," he said. Her hand was firm and warm—the most personal hand he had ever shaken. He had to remind himself sharply of the things the Senator had told him about her.

She told him precisely what she had said to Johnny. He affected deep concern. He took her arm and they left the depot. On the walk, Mrs. Benson glanced up at him with a trace of resentment. "You and Johnny roughed up a friend of mine today, Mr. Holbrook. I don't like having my friends roughed up."

"I feel about the same way about my friends, Mrs. Benson. He sort of roughed up my secretary. And it wasn't us that cleaned his plow, but Johnny."

"The way I had it from Gus, you both jumped him."

"We probably will before we're through, but so far Johnny's had the honor... What about this sick man?" he asked her. "How'd he make it in, if he's so bad off?"

"They brought him in a wagon."

"Who's they?"

"I have a frightful memory for names. But if you were to visit my place some night, or commit some other indiscretion, I wouldn't likely remember yours either."

The street was dark. Like a lighthouse for the thirsty or lovelorn rose the dark bulk of the Congress Bar at the corner of Pennington and Main. Lamps burned in each window of its two stories. Mrs. Benson's hand was a warm pressure on his arm as they crossed to it. At the hitch-rack of the saloon stood the horses of the cavalrymen, humped against the cold breeze. The headlong dissonance of a piano reached them. She shook her head as he parted the slatted doors. "The side way."

Seventy-five feet from the corner was a narrow yellow door. Annie Benson preceded him, crossing a brief vestibule to a banistered stairway. Through a curtained doorway at the left came a gust of saloon noises. Thinly through the uproar slanted the bawdy, mincing voice of a singer.

Ascending, they reached a long bare hall. On the newel post balanced a cigar, faintly smoking. The hall ran a full forty feet and turned left. At intervals along the wall were numbered doors.

Mrs. Benson swept before him, her gown whispering along the floor. She had a grand, statuesque figure, the figure of a slender Venus de Milo, classic and deep-bosomed.

She opened a door and glanced in. "Awake, Sam?" she whispered.

A man groaned, grunted. "Oh—Annie! Yeah. Awake."

"I found Mr. Holbrook. Do you want to see him now?"

"Grif?" The voice was thin, shredded by pain. "Shore do!"

Annie stepped aside and smiled encouragingly at Grif. He hesitated. Almost, he was afraid to enter. Afraid of seeing the end result of what a bullet could do, and knowing it was his own bullet. He inhaled deeply and entered the room. The air was thick with odors of cosmetics and a sick fragrance of decay. It was obviously a girl's room. Feathers and flounces simpered on the costumes hanging on nails about the walls. On a dresser were saucers of carmine and mascara, a box of pearl face powder with a fluffy hare's foot, and assorted blond switches and rats.

Grif looked at the stage driver. Granjon lay on a wide cot. He had hauled himself up so that his back was against the wall. His long features were white as dead yucca blooms, with a thin burning on his cheekbones. His blond hair, that long yellow hair he prided himself on, was uncombed and looked dull in the dim light of a lamp turned low.

They stared at each other. Granjon's eyes were feverish black smudges. He had been long without a shave. Weight had sloughed off him until his shoulders were a bony rack. His mouth moved.

"Smell it?"

"Smell what?" But the stench of gangrenous flesh clogged the air and had Grif's stomach tugging at its moorings.

"My leg. You know what? Maggots get in you after so long. Ever seen maggots in a dead cow's belly? No worse than this. Look!"

He threw the blanket back. Grif had a sickening flash of a fetid thigh wound. The leg of Granjon's drawers had been slashed open and was matted with blood and matter.

"You done that, pardner. Proud? Do you wonder I wanted to see you?"

It was all off-key. There was no contrition in the stage driver, only a high flame of hatred that began to color his voice and brought his back from the wall behind him.

Yet even so Grif was caught completely off-guard. Granjon's left hand came from under the blanket. A blue spark flowed along the barrel of a Navy pistol. His chuckle was an exultant croak. "See you in hell, Grif! See you damned soon!"

Annie Benson screamed: *"Sam!"* In the same instant she gave Grif a push apparently meant to help him, but which sent him stumbling into the room. Granjon's gun leaped in his hand. The flashing thunder of the black-powder pulsed against the walls. The ball went through the doorway and whined off an adobe brick. Grif kept moving, sprawling to his knees, getting up and plowing straight forward at Sam Granjon as he fired again. This time Grif felt the ball whip his coat-tails, like Death plucking at a man's sleeve to say, *About time, pardner—about time!* Then he was falling across the injured man and clamping a hand on his wrist. He tore the gun loose and threw it on the floor. He stepped back and stood, breathing hard, at the side of the bed. Granjon cursed and turned his face away, stirring in slow agony while his lungs gasped.

Grif turned to stare at the woman who stood in the doorway. He said, "So Sam wanted to tell me something. You had a chance to tell me the same thing while my back was turned, Annie, but you'd better not try it now. You know what I was thinking on the way over here? I was thinking, This here is a pretty fine woman, for all she runs a stable of floosies. Shows you how wrong a man can be. What was your cut going to be—half of what I had in my pockets?"

Someone was on the steps, mounting fast and crossing the landing and mounting again. Annie Benson did not move from the door. She looked very steadily at him.

"Don't be dramatic," she said quietly. "You know very well I had nothing to do with this. I really believed that all he wanted was to shake your hand for the last time."

It was a moment for al kinds of sarcasm. The immediate situation was compromising and her social position was hardly one to encourage her to stamp her foot and say she had never been so insulted! But pride, in this woman, was something innate. He found himself reluctantly accepting her explanation, and, still more reluctantly, believing it.

A man came running down the hall. Annie turned and over her shoulder Grif saw the taut, pampered features of Jim Maroon. "I heard a shot!" Maroon exclaimed, trying to see into the room and encountering Grif's bulk at the side of the bed.

"There was a shot," Annie admitted. "Sam tried to kill this man."

Maroon entered. He looked at Grif. "I've seen you somewhere," he said closely. Then he snapped his fingers. "Brown's barber shop!"

"It's Grif Holbrook, Jim," Annie said. "You must know the name."

Maroon smiled. "Who doesn't? But I didn't know you were in Tucson, Grif."

"Just happened to be."

Annie was watching the long shape on the bed turn slowly in torture. "You and Sam hadn't had trouble, had you, Holbrook?" she asked.

"I'd call it trouble. It was me that got him his job with the Oxbow, but the way he showed his gratitude was to help shanghai me from a stagecoach. I got a crack at him later."

Maroon grunted. "Why, the damned fool! I found him

down near Tubac yesterday, riding on a load of chili. I don't know whether you knew it, but he was supposed to have been killed in a holdup himself."

"Is that right!" Grif stared curiously at Maroon. "Say— didn't I hear you tell Bay-Rum Brown it was smallpox he had?"

Maroon's eyes faltered. There was an instant of shock, and then Annie Benson was saying: "I told him to say that. I didn't want any trouble here in the house. If it were really a bullet wound, I wanted him moved out before we told Sheriff Deuce about it."

Another man could be heard on the stairs, moving without haste. Maroon lunged into the hall. "Doc! Will you shake it?"

A man came unhurriedly to lean in the doorway, a brown cowhide bag in one hand, regarding the room with myopic benevolence. "Hello, Annie! How's my girl?" he asked cheerfully.

Annie clenched her hands in vexation. "Doc, you old sot! Will you see if you can do anything for Sam? Can't you see he's dying?"

"Dying?" Benteen repeated. "Sam's dead! I wrote out the certificate myself. I'd recommend embalming for Sam, if he's still wandering about. Next case." He winked at Grif. A small but stocky man, he had the tilted brow and turned lip of the ironic drunk. He wore a gray chinbeard and a small mustache; his eyes shone soapily behind thick round spectacles. He wore a loose brown coat, hanging open; a vest, also open; a black tie, untied; and wrinkled black trousers, fortunately closed. And now, suddenly, Grif recalled him from this afternoon, leading the Territorials. The infamous Doctor Noah Benteen. A drunk.

Annie seized his arm and steered him to the bedside. Benteen sighed and began his examination. Grif watched his mouth. It pursed, relaxed, twisted, melting through a series of expressions. It was large and elastic. Granjon looked up at him.

"How'm I doing, Doc?"

Benteen straightened. "Are you especially attached to that leg?"

"Well, it's sort of attached to me," Granjon said. "It's got to come off?"

"Only chance. Why'n't you call me before?"

"I knew you didn't take cases out of the town limits," Granjon said. He was trying to be cheerful, but the impact of the judgment was in his eyes.

"How's 'at?"

"I and this big yokel had a ruckus in the hills. Over politics."

Benteen glanced at Annie. "Whiskey. Hurry it up."

"And a quart of black coffee," Annie said. "That's the one I'll *really* hurry up."

Benteen pulled a chair to the bedside. He sat with one elbow on one knee, chin propped on the heel of his hand, weaving only slightly. Grif stood at the foot of the bed. Maroon, motionless by a window, stared down into the darkening street.

Benteen said, "Politics, eh?" as if prompting.

"Slavery. Holbrook's one of the boys thinks one section of the country ought to be allowed to put the heel to another."

"I didn't know it was over slavery, Sam," Grif said. "I thought it was over a kidnapping and holding up a stage."

"You knew what was at the bottom of it. You know why you're out here. First Northern mercenary to set foot on Southern soil!"

Grif turned a chair and sat on it saddle-wise. He had heard that phrase before. He tried to recall where. "I don't know those things, Sam. I only know I work for the Overland Mail. So did you, till you got to confusing politics and duty. It wasn't states' rights nor anything so high-sounding that you and I fought over; it was the question of whether or not a man's got the right to ride a stagecoach without being shot at."

A barman came at a heavy walk down the hall. Granjon looked feverishly at Grif, anger in his face and yet a seed of confusion. "If we'd been taking them just for their value," he retorted, "we'd have sold some by now, wouldn't we? But there they—"

At the window, Jim Maroon turned.

The barman entered the room with a couple of bottles of whiskey under his arm and a pot of coffee in one hand, a thick china cup in the other. He said with heavy good humor:

"Well, Sammy, how's the boy? Furloughed from the grave, eh?"

"Just a three-day leave, Dave," Granjon grinned.

Grif sat there. "Settin' where, Sam?" he prompted.

Noah Benteen got up with a growl. "Less talk will do you good."

"One word won't hurt. You were saying—"

Granjon grinned, a measure of triumph having come his way. "I *was* saying. I ain't now."

The barman opened a bottle and gave it to Benteen. Benteen held it a moment. "This is one time that somebody's telling you to get drunk for your own good. Lap it up, Sam."

Granjon tilted the bottle. Benteen went to stand before Grif. His pouched, goateed face had lost its good nature.

"So you're a God-damned Abolitionist," he said.

"Just a plain one," Grif said.

"I suppose you think the wranglin' in Congress has been over slaves, eh?" Benteen's warped stare said he was going to have an argument. "Slaves! What about the wage slaves in Northern woolen mills and iron foundries? What about them? They don't eat as well as a slave on a Georgia cotton plantation. What about the blood-suckin' protective tariffs?"

"I was born with one leg in the South and one in the North," Grif said. He pushed Benteen out of his way and went to stand beside Sam Granjon. Granjon was taking the liquor down faster than any man could, and keep his sobriety long; time crowded. "A lot of men," Grif went on, "must be in this. And I reckon the pitch they're getting is about what Benteen's trying to give me. Okay—any man's got a right to vote the way he sees it. But he hasn't got the right to talk other fellers into dying so that he can get fat on their thieving. No, by God! And I say that whoever you've been working for, Doc Benteen or anybody else, is a copperbottom scoundrel that I'll see hung before I'm through!"

Granjon was getting dull and lethargic. At the same time, it was plain that he was disturbed.

"You're wrong, Grif. It's a holy war. Crusaders, not outlaws! We don't want money out of it. We want satisfaction."

"*You* don't want money! But the top nuts do."

Granjon looked in doubt at Benteen, then at Maroon, and finally at the ceiling. He closed his eyes. When he opened them, the light was out of them. "Can we git through it, Doc?"

Grif went out into the hall. He had failed. In the bedroom, in a thick silence, went on the grim prelude to horror, the silent drinking of a man about to undergo frontier surgery.

After some time Benteen went downstairs. Maroon came to lean in the doorway, smoking a twisted Mexican cigar. Benteen returned with two men from the saloon. One of them had a dish towel tucked under his belt as an apron, a massive-jawed man with a massaged, fleshy face and yellowish eyes. The other man was Gus Heydenfeldt, big, hard-jawed, florid, in his buckskin pants and tight Army shirt. A skilled hand had been at his wounds, reducing the swelling under his right eye, pulling a split lip together with a sliver of tape under that oxbow-shaped mustache he affected. He looked at Grif and said, "Hello, heavy," and went by him into the room with its fetid stench. Grif followed him.

Benteen came in, rubbing his hands. He had the bartender, Ollie McCardle, lay a fire in the hearth and deposit a pair of sadirons in the flames for cauterizing. Granjon lay in a stupor. Benteen arranged four lamps about the bed, took off his coat and rolled up his sleeves.

"Anybody that's got on his best bib-an'-tucker better strip. This is going to make a shambles look like a Dutch kitchen."

He produced a butcher knife and saw, stropped the knife on the upper of his boot and wiped it on the seat of his pants. He had cut away the leg of Granjon's drawers and now stood in melancholy contemplation of the wound. Of a sudden he began to shake. His face underwent a convulsion. Maroon handed him the fresh quart of whiskey.

"If I ever get off the mescal and back on the whiskey," Benteen panted, "I'll lick em! . . . All right. Catch holt, now!"

There was an instant when Sam Granjon opened his eyes and looked dumbly up at them. It was like a corpse looking up from his casket. Grif had thought he was beyond speech, but now he heard his mouth saying in thick, slow-witted wonder:

"We—done right—didn't we, Jim?"

Maroon and Grif looked at each other. Maroon's careful features appeared startled, and then unhappy. He looked down. "Crazy drunk," he murmured. "Let's go, Doc."

Benteen brought the knife across the leg, much like a butcher cutting a steak. Granjon's body arched itself and he screamed—a scream they must have heard in the depot. Blood fountained from the wound and a stream of scarlet shot across the bed and struck the lamp chimney; the heated glass shattered. McCardle, the bartender, choked and became sick. Benteen did not look up.

"Get sick if you want to, but if you quit, dammit, I'll cut off your head while you're out!"

He continued to cut.

It was not entirely new to Holbrook. He had seen it in the Mexican War. He hated it but had the power to endure it. Benteen finished cutting and grabbed the saw. It was all four men could do to keep Granjon on the bed.

Benteen was snorting like a horse. He ran to the fireplace, returning with a smoking sadiron.

With all his weight on Granjon's arm, Grif panted: "He's doin' better, Doc—ain't bleeding so much."

Benteen started. He peered at the patient and reached for his wrist. He straightened.

"All right, boys. Meet you downstairs. It ain't hurting Sam any more, so cheer up." He peered wistfully into Granjon's face and reached out to rumple his hair. "Sorry, Sam. Best I could do—even for a good Tennessee Democrat!"

12

THEY STRAGGLED DOWN the steps. Mrs. Benson was in the cramped vestibule at the bottom. Benteen had washed up and was in a dogged mood, the splintered end of his drunk prodding him. He grunted at Mrs. Benson: "He's dead this time, by grabs."

Gus Heydenfeldt put an arm about Mrs. Benson's shoulders and gave her a gravely tender smile, which to Holbrook resembled the soft-boiled sentiment of an elderly drunk. "Don't you be worrying your head about it, Annie. You done all you could. We'll send somebody up for the body."

Annie appeared uncomfortable, and deftly moved out of his embrace. "Thank you, Gus."

A girl in a short skirt and feather-trimmed bodice parted the curtain and came from the saloon, moving with pert hips and laughing back at someone. She had red hair and wore lace stockings; her bosom was crowded fantastically by the bodice. She stopped laughing when she saw them.

"Helen," said Mrs. Benson, "tell Mike to set them up, will you? Sam's dead."

The girl ran back. "Will you drink with them?" Annie asked Grif.

"Why not?"

Benteen stopped to stare at him and then walked on with Heydenfeldt and Maroon. Annie touched Grif's arm. "I'm sorry he pulled the gun on you. But let's be charitable. Let's say he was delirious."

"Sure. If I'm mad at anybody, it's not at Sam. It's at the boys who got him into this. Want to tell me who sent him out there?"

Her eyes were steady. "Do you think I could tell you that?"

"I think you could tell me about anything you wanted to, Mrs. Benson."

"Perhaps I could. But I don't know this time, truly. And I'm not going to guess."

He passed her. He was still feeling the green sickness of the operation and tasting his frustration. The saloon was high-ceilinged and wide, with a bar down the east wall, a piano and dancing enclosure near the back, and game tables grouped in an alcove in the rear. Heavy chandeliers, suspended on chains, held clusters of beef-tallow candles, fat as stalagmites. Quiet spread through the room. The foolish chuttering of the keno goose ceased. The roulette wheel ran down and the piano went silent. The hurdy-gurdy girls and their dollar-a-dance partners slowed down.

The front door opened briefly on the night. Jim Maroon went out with Ollie McCardle, the bartender, who had doffed his apron. He still looked green. Benteen walked to the bar.

"Boys, one of the best of them went over the divide tonight," he said. "Sam Granjon. You drank to him once before, but this time is for good. Fill 'em up, boys. This is for Sam Granjon and all he stood for."

The crowd was slow to understand what had happened, but Benteen dominated them with his belligerent gravity. They drank in a heavy, maudlin silence. Gus Heydenfeldt stood with the doctor. Benteen turned and his eyes found Grif beside the faro table.

"Not drinking, Holbrook?"

"Not to that toast. I'll drink to Sam; you drink to what he stood for."

A breath of resentment passed over the thronged bar. Through the hostile silence, Holbrook walked up and waited for a drink. He drank the whiskey in a gulp. After a moment the doctor drank his liquor. But there was a malicious glint in his eye as he refilled the glasses.

"This one," he said, "is for the man who killed Sam. I give you Grif Holbrook."

Grif set his drink on the bar and seized Benteen's soiled stock. He twisted it so that the cravat cut deeply into his white flesh. "I wish you were ten years younger and six hours soberer," he snapped. "But that don't keep you from telling them why I killed Sam, and what happened upstairs."

Heydenfeldt lurched against him. He placed his palm against Grif's chest and held his fist cocked, and there was a look of intemperate fury in his eyes, as though his resentment toward him had fermented in his brain until it went sour. "I ain't on your payroll any more, Holbrook. I can call a windbag a windbag now. Make your manners to the doctor, or get out."

Without releasing Noah Benteen, Holbrook suddenly smashed Heydenfeldt across the nose with the back of his free hand. When the big man stumbled, throwing a punch wildly, Grif brought a hand-axing blow down on the bridge of his nose. The sound of it was like a hand laid heavily on a quarter of beef.

Heydenfeldt stumbled back. Grif abruptly sensed that he had overplayed his hand. Other men were falling out of line at the bar, moving in on him, and Benteen, beginning to thresh, yelled across the rising uproar: "Move in, you Territorials! Do you need an invitation?"

Grif gave him a shove that lifted him onto the bar and halfway across it. He grabbed a pair of bottles and turned his back to the bar. Standing that way, he saw the figure in the rear doorway. There was a look of angry alarm on Annie Benson's face. He saw her seize a beer schooner from a table and throw it against the wall. The splintering crash laid a quiet on the saloon.

"That's enough!" she cried. "Doc, I've never seen a more cowardly thing. I'm ashamed of you too, Gus."

Heydenfeldt hung his head. He muttered: "Maybe you're right, Annie. We were carried away."

It surprised Grif. When, he wondered, had Heydenfeldt become Annie Benson's spaniel? Before he lost his job, or after? If he were looking for a berth as her right-hand man, he seemed to know how to go about it. But Noah Benteen was still resentful. His countenance was that of a dissipated, defeated old ram. "This is a man's argument, Annie."

"There's only one man *I* can see. Tell them, Doc, exactly what happened."

Benteen sulked a while longer. "Sam was in that stage doings," he said. "Holbrook claims he shot him in self-defense. He took Sam in the leg and it got infected. Upstairs, I had to cut. I lost him."

"That's better," Annie said. "You boys all know how I feel about Black Republicans. I'm as far from being a blue-nosed Northerner as any of you. But I haven't even heard this man mention his politics. I only know that he seems to have more fight in him than a whole roomful of Territorials."

She looked them over, and there was not a man to raise his voice. "I'm closing for the night," she said. "Get out, the whole pack of you. From now on, any man who mentions politics in my place will go out of here feet first. Grif, I hope you'll come back. It won't happen again."

She departed. A croupier at the roulette table said, "Last play was black on seventeen, boys."

Drinks were hastily finished. A barman appeared with a pushbroom and started at the back wall, working front. Grif had the impression that an imperial edict had just been issued. He smiled, set his bottles down, and drifted out with the crowd.

He was surprised to discover that complete darkness had invaded the pueblo, scattering the last of the traffic. A moment he stood drinking the chilly air, letting its astringent bite heal the sickness left by Granjon's death. A breath of unease touched him.

He tried to isolate it, gazing up and down the street. A few Mexicans hurried along with sarapes pulled up to their eyes, bent on getting out of the poisonous night air. A little crowd of American cowboys jogged up Pennington from the river. A cart rumbled across the bridge. Solomon Warner's big store was dark. Except in the stage depot, hardly a light showed.

Everything under control. Everything buttoned up. Then why did he have that impulse to go back into the saloon? *"You're on probation. Probation expires the night you bump into the wrong man on the street...."* A calming thought, from Senator Montgomery's book.

He began to walk. The saloon evictees dispersed, some walking, others tugging at latigos of racked horses. And yet it seemed to him that he was the only man on the street, that eyes peered behind every drawn blind.

He started across the street. Just ahead, on the right, an alley separated the post office and a store. Suddenly he stopped and faced the alley. A man stood straight as a post just inside it. A pulse awoke in his throat. He swallowed and got his breath and swore softly.

God A'mighty, man! Get out of the trade, if you're going to let every Mexican in an alley goose you into hysterics. But he found himself wondering why Jim Maroon had left without drinking.

Turning back, he paced diagonally toward the stage depot. Suddenly his head jerked toward Warner's store, on his left. A shadow stirred among deeper shadows on the roofed porch. A puncheon that was not a puncheon. A corner post that wore a hat and moved with the prudent care of a man raising a rifle for a shot at a lynx poised to spring.

Holbrook stopped dead. He reached back to his gun, at the same time flinging another look at the alley. The man standing there had moved. He now leaned hipshot against the building—left shoulder against the bricks, right elbow extended, head hunched. As familiar a stance as a rifleman could take.

Holbrook's heart leaped. He dived headlong at the street. He was late. The man in the alley had taken up the last ounce of trigger slack and a firing pin had fallen. A scarlet rose bloomed in the darkness. An explosion tore the night apart, sending a wild horde of echoes roaring along the street. Something stung his back and knocked the wind from him. He landed on his belly with a grunt and wriggled about to set his gun against his shoulder, left arm extended in the dirt to steady him. He fired back at the man in the alley, hearing a crash of gunfire behind him from the gunman on the porch of the store. The bullet tore through the loose street dust.

The street was going crazy, horses bucking and men sprawling into store entrances and sprinting around corners. Someone was shouting hysterical curses as he ran toward the Congress Bar.

The man in the alley did not like being shot at. He moved back several paces and yanked at the loading lever of his gun. He fired again. Grif got off his second shot, trying to forget the man at his back, focusing his whole attention on the slender dark target in the alley who would be Jim Maroon.

Maroon, who knew Sam Granjon had spilled the soup and was trying to square things in the way he understood best.

Maroon, if it were he, jerked spasmodically as his hat rose from his head. An inch too high... Grif dropped his sights for the next; and now he hunched his shoulders and clutched the earth as Maroon pumped off three shots as fast as he could fire the heavy sporting rifle. The bullets whipped and sang about Grif. An undisturbed portion of his mind thought, Where'd he get a repeater like that? I could use such a gun. Maybe I'm going to have one...

Maroon had emptied the gun. The thunder of his shots rolled along the street like a giant's chuckling. Grif could feel the burning of the wound in his back. He steadied himself over his gun, and saw Maroon turn and race down the alley. He fired once, saw Maroon swerve but catch himself and run on.

He squirmed to hunt for the other man. The darkness seemed less thick now. There was something familiar about the blunt-shouldered look of the man on the porch. He carried no rifle, but he had two revolvers, each of which he was firing, but neither of which disturbed Holbrook particularly. The man was no gunfighter. He didn't know you couldn't kill a man with noise. He didn't know you were only half as wide from the side as you were head-on.

Suddenly through with firing, he ran from the porch and lunged into the alley between the store and the depot. Grif let his shot roar away. He cocked and briefly aimed and fired again. The man did not stop running.

Quiet flowed back into the street. A horse was still pitching, grunting each time it struck the road. A window scraped in the second story of the Congress, and Annie Benson shrilled: "What in heaven are you crazy fools doing down there? Stop it this instant!"

Grif came to his knees. He called up: "Sorry, Annie. Send a lantern down, will you?"

13

HE HAD BEEN certain he had hit the neurotic gunman with the revolvers. When they entered the alley, he saw that he was right. The man lay against the foundation of the stage station, writhing slowly in dumb agony. The lantern's glow burned on the face of Ollie McCardle.

Someone said, "Big night for you, Holbrook." It was Benteen.

Grif was shocked beyond replying. The barkeeper, still alive, was unconscious, moving with the spasmodic jerking of a rabbit with a gut full of buckshot. His eyes were glassy and he kept making retching mouths. Grif could not watch. He pivoted and shouldered through the crowd in the alley.

"I'll be at that cantina down the street if the sheriff wants me," he said. "I guess you all saw it. Say a good word for me, if it comes to that."

As he passed the door of the stage station, Broderick plunged out and collided with him. "What's going on? Who got it?"

"Man named McCardle, from Annie Benson's."

"McCardle!" Broderick's eyes widened. "You mean— you and him?"

"And Jim Maroon . . . Stop blinking, boy, and see if I got shot or scratched, there on my back."

Broderick steered Grif into the station and had him remove his coat and shirt and drop his underwear to the waist. He had him lie on a bench and held a lamp over him. "Uh!" he said. "A groove, but deep."

He got medicines, a basin of water, and a clean handkerchief. He began cleaning the bloody trough across Grif's shoulder blade. "What happened?"

Grif told him. "I'll be damned!" Broderick finished washing the wound and looked over his remedies, a dusty dozen patent medicines. "Wonder what'd be good? Here's some Perry Davis Vegetable Pain Killer. Better have a slug. I guess this blue vitriol'd be as good as anything to cauterize it. Holt on, now."

The crystals seemed to sear Grif from neck to buttocks. "Jesus God, man!"

Broderick chuckled. "Be glad I'm not Benteen."

Grif dressed again. "I told them I'd wait for Pete Deuce at Juan Burruel's. I'd better get down there before they get out a warrant."

"I'll go with you." Outside, he said, "Let's take a look at Ollie."

"Once is enough for me."

"What's the difference between a dead man and a dead horse?" Broderick snorted.

"Plenty, when you've killed him."

Just inside the wall, on Alameda, not far from the mud box of a jail, was the mescal shop of Juan Burruel. The ceiling was barely higher than a tall man's head, and the bar was about twelve feet long and painted green. It was a peon's dive. The smells and talk were not a white man's, but it was quiet and mescal was strong, and Grif preferred it to an American place tonight. He found himself thinking broodingly of Katie Crocker. He was glad she hadn't been in the stage station. Something in him gave a sick lurch as he speculated on her connecting the shooting with the trouble that morning. Would she jump to the conclusion that he had killed McCardle over some remark of his about her?

He began to sweat. The way she had laced Johnny up and down for fighting over her! All the women he'd known had kind of rubbed up against you after you'd cleaned a man's plow over her. Not Katie.

Johnny Broderick's thinking was right with him. He rubbed the bruise under one eye and grinned. "Wonder what Katie'll have to say about this? Bet you'll be the fair-haired boy around the office." Grif grunted.

Deuce did not come and Grif began to stew. "What's the matter?" Broderick grinned. "Ollie haunting you already?"

Grif pondered. "Haunting is all in a man's mind. I saw Granjon die tonight. Nobody ever died having less fun. He died because of the ball I put in his leg. Then I put a shot in McCardle. I guess he's done, too. He reminded me of a rabbit that almost made its hole, laying there kicking its life out and squealing like a pig. Death ain't pretty, Johnny. It ain't like going to sleep. It's big. Bigger than life, because people keep getting born, but nobody ever comes back carrying his coffin and brushin' off the dirt. I've killed men in my time, and once in a while one walks in still, showing me the hole in his breast and saying, 'You done that, pardner. Don't forget to tell God.'"

Broderick's mouth smirked. He drank the mescal, priding himself on not blinking. "How old did you say you were?" he asked.

Holbrook's lips firmed. "You call yourself to be a pretty hard hombre, don't you?"

"I didn't get where I am by bowing and scraping."

"Where are you?"

"I was shoveling manure out of a stable two years ago. I'm making a hundred and twenty-five a month now, just cleaning my fingernails on John Butterfield's time."

"An armadillo is hard too," Grif speculated. "But under that armor of his he's tender as Southern fried chicken. I got a notion something like a killing might shuck you out of that twenty-three-year-old shell of yours pretty fast too. But give me twenty-four hours and I'll have McCardle put in his place. I wouldn't take even money you could do the same."

They heard hoofs thud briskly up the road and then the hard jangle of a man's spurs as he dismounted. A bulky, blue-jowled man parted the doors and stood with his lowering eyes searching the murky room. Johnny signaled him.

"Here's the prisoner, Pete! Sit down."

Pete Deuce came in, pulling off buckskin gloves and staring narrowly at Grif. He was a big, dark-browed, simple-looking man with a head like a buffalo, a belly cut by a beaded belt, and guns that pronged from his hips like the horns of a Texas steer. A silver star shone on the pocket of his brown sack coat. He removed his hat and laid it on the table. His hair was black, lustreless and as close as that of a cat.

He accepted a drink. The glass was a thimble in his scarred paw. He drank, shuddered, and frowned. "About the time I get the burrs curried out of this town's hide," he said, "another one drops in. Two killin's a day about your average, Holbrook?"

"I try to hold it to one."

Deuce chomped on a pair of cheap vulcanite plates like a horse chewing a bit. Any moment, Grif expected him to whinny or break wind. He began taking things from his pockets and laying them on the table.

"The story seems to be that McCardle throwed down on you, and some other galoot in the alley cut loose at the same time. But all I could find was McCardle."

"I'm guessing the other was Jim Maroon. If he's around in the morning, I'll admit I was wrong."

Among the things the sheriff had taken from the bartender's pockets was a printed leaflet. He unfolded it and scowled at the heavy black printing while he pondered.

"I reckon we won't have to put it to a trial. Everybody seems agreed you didn't start it. I'd have to freight you clean over to the county seat at Mesilla, and that would mean a week away from my butcher shop and only a dollar a day expenses. You and McCardle had any trouble?"

"No. But Maroon and I had. He was in that last stage holdup. Sam Granjon spilled it when he was dying."

"Maroon done that? Why, they don't come any finer than Jim Maroon."

"And they don't leave much faster. I'll buy the rope if you catch him. Or maybe shooting stage drivers isn't a capital offense here?"

Deuce shook his head. "It's going to put you in mighty bad with the Territorials if you swear out a warrant for him."

"I'll risk it."

Deuce rubbed his palms slowly on his heavy thighs. "All right. You're the character Butterfield sent out to purify Arizona, ain't you? Well, the betting's five to one ag'in you, and no takers. Now, personally, I'm back of you. But if I was you I wouldn't claim any more than my rightful space at the bar. This here is no Baptist stronghold, and I can't run around holding an umbrella over you so you won't get sunburned."

"I never yet went looking for trouble," Grif remarked.

"I'm going to get my business done the best way I can, but if I have to step on anybody's toes they'll buy their own cornplasters."

"Then all I can do is write on the death certificate, 'Victim warned, as per instructions.'"

He got out a piece of paper and pencil and began listing the articles on the table. He paused and shoved the printed leaflet across to Grif. "Read it. Might do you good."

He finished listing the articles and stood up, sighing heavily. "For two bucks and a stage ticket, I'd clear out myself. Tucson's changed me, the color of my skin, and my name. My real name's Dusenberg. A good name, some places. But these johnnies cut it down to Deuce. Too hard to remember. I suppose they'd call the Lord the late J. C. It's like any Spik town. Saps your stren'th. Well, good luck!"

At the door, he turned back. "By the way—the buryin's are for two o'clock. You might like to lock yourself in your room during the ceremony. Ollie McCardle was pretty well liked. Poured the straightest shot in town."

He lay sick with fatigue on the hotel cot. The lees of the day's failures turned sourly in his belly. A rat was running up and down the roof in pointless rushes. It was like the neurotic jumping of his thoughts, leaping this way and that, but always coming back to the main bait: Katie . . . *"We weren't married. We just lived together."*

He had an impulse to do something to show her it did not matter what she had done. But that was a lie. It mattered enough to make him sick when he thought of her and Will Crocker in the bedroom at Apache Pass. Only it didn't matter enough to release him from his love for her.

He sat on the edge of the cot. In the candlelight he read the leaflet the sheriff had handed him. It was all rant and bluster.

!ATTENTION——TUCSONIANS!

You are invited to a rally of the Fraternal and Benevolent Order of Territorials, Tuesday night the Eleventh. Barbecued beef and beer will be the order of the evening and there will be a talk by the distinguished Dr. Noah Benteen.

The Territorials have no political axes to grind, unlike the butt-headed Republican administration at

Santa Fe. We are a social organization dedicated to Prosperity for Arizona; to Separate Territorial Organization for Arizona; and as such we welcome you if you have, like us, become tired of being hind titmen of the political farrow.

There is no reason why Arizona should be in slavery to political mad dogs five hundred miles distant, getting no military protection nor other benefits but having the last dollar leached out of her for taxes to fatten the pockets of Republican politicians. The purpose of the society is, however, primarily social.

Primarily social! The entrance fee will be one Republican scalp. But he read the thing again, vaguely disturbed by a feeling that he was missing a point somewhere. "... Hind titmen of the political farrow ... political mad dogs...." It had a familiar ring, but it was not the voice of Benteen he heard, somehow. Maroon? He shrugged, snuffed out the candle, and undressed.

14

In the morning he ate elderly eggs and salty ham at the Shoo-Fly Restaurant and then walked back to Brown's. It was a fine, shining morning, the birds setting up a mighty twittering, the smell of charcoal fires sweet on the air, a hundred women and girls hurrying up and down the street with ollas balanced on their shoulders, engaged in morning water-carrying. But for him the edge was off everything.

There was a stage around noon for California. Would she be at the depot to take it? If he could just get her alone for a while— But what could he build out of the materials of a rough-and-ready vocabulary like his?

Bay-Rum Brown had just finished shaving himself. He gave Grif a close look and whipped the apron from the chair. "They tell me you put in a pretty busy evening."

Grif picked up a paper and settled himself. He said nothing for a while, finally grunted "Yeah," and let the barber know he was not primed for talk.

Brown worked silently. He finished clipping and shaving, raised a suffocating fog of powder, and handed Holbrook a mirror. He squinted into it. In shape, his neck and head were not unlike those of a bear, sturdy and thick, the ears set close. His brows were heavy, his mouth too wide, and a couple of old fractures had not improved the topography of his nose. Holbrook, he thought, you're nobody's pretty boy. It's a sorry face to take courting, but it'll have to do.

"How about clipping the hairs out of my ears?" he said, returning the mirror.

Brown snipped delicately. "Somebody," he said, "is goin' courtin'."

"They get to interfering with my hearing."

Brown gave a wheezy, tonic-laden laugh. "They ain't bothered you up to now! Well, take 'er easy."

Grif went down to the depot. Broderick had a pot of coffee on the coals in the office and was drinking alone and tootling the concertina. Grif poured himself a cup.

"Seen Kate?"

Broderick frowned. "She was down for a while last night. Dang fool kid. Picked up her things and said she's leaving for California—today."

A terrible alarm stroked sonorously in Grif's head. Suddenly he knew he must see her. "Where's this Mrs. Ochoa live?"

"Out on India Triste. The Street of the Sad Indian," Johnny said wryly. "And a couple of sad stablehands. Think you can talk her out of it?"

"Got to. Secretaries are hard to come by."

Broderick regarded him coolly. "Yeah."

Grif left. He walked slowly south toward the arroyo. Doubts beset him. The chill was out of the air, but a rind of ice lurked in his stomach. Yet the heat of a belated fire in his heart kept him moving until he reached a small house with a brush-thatched porch and a front yard fenced with fluted green cactus. While he was trying to decide whether this was it, Kate's head appeared in a window. Her hair was done up in a bandana.

"Were you looking for me?" The voice was prim as a prayer book.

"Can I come in?"

"Well—I'm awfully busy. Packing," she added.

"That's what I wanted to see you about."

"I'll come out," she said after a moment.

They walked toward the river. She had removed the bandana, and her hair, caught back with a red ribbon, lay glistening on her shoulders. In tacit defiance, she wore the shirtwaist and short skirt she had worn at Apache Pass. They passed a ruined corral and entered the winding path beside the canal.

"I suppose you want me to say it was all a lie," she said suddenly.

"I don't want you to say anything. If you did anything wrong—well, I reckon you had a reason."

She gave him a melancholy smile. "A friend of yours could steal every cent you had, just so he had a good reason."

"It'd better be a danged good reason," Grif grunted. "Katie, I don't want you to tell me anything, but I want to tell you something."

"But I want to tell you," she said in sudden warmth. "It wasn't true, Grif! I don't know why I let you think it was, except I was so ashamed. I—I wanted to hurt myself, and you too. It was true that I lived with Will Crocker, but—not the way you think."

A bubble of joy burst in him.

There was a cottonwood stump by the canal. She stopped and let him lift her onto it. She patted the space beside her. He sat down but didn't trust himself to look at her, merely staring down at the slow swirl of brown water below them.

"Yes, I lived in the station with Will. I did all the things a wife does except—be a wife. By the grace of God and a strong lock on my door, I'm still a good woman."

Grif heard himself saying: "You don't have to tell me this, Katie, but—why did you let him get you in that spot?"

"I got myself in it. My Uncle Dick—Dick Nolan—had the station before Will. I'd come out to be with him, but he'd left. He never stuck to a job more than a year, and after my aunt died he told me there was only five hundred dollars of my parents' money left and I'd better be thinking of marrying or making my own way. Uncle Dick and Aunt Martha raised me from the time I was nine. I had a crazy idea that I could be a dancer. Uncle Dick enrolled me with a French dancing master in New Orleans. Then he took the stage contract and disappeared. It lasted about six months. Maître Danton suddenly told me that if I wanted to finish my lessons I'd have to go East with him; he was leaving to teach in New York. Naturally we wouldn't go as teacher and pupil."

Grif made a bear-like rumble in his throat.

"I put everything I had left into a ticket to Apache Pass. When I got there, Uncle Dick had gone to California. I didn't have a penny. I offered to stay with Crocker as a helper until I could earn fare. He was willing to have help, but he said that if I didn't want to be talked about we'd better announce we were married. And now," she said, "I find that they talked anyway."

Grif patted her hand.

"And that," she said, "is why I'm leaving Tucson. I won't be talked about as your mistress, the way I must have been as Crocker's. For your sake as much as my own. They'd be calling me the sweetheart of the Great Southern Overland next."

He held her other hand. "Nobody's going to talk about you, Katie. You're staying, but anybody that says a word about Katie Crocker will answer to me."

"How would you go about beating a woman who slandered me?"

"Would they slander you if we were married?"

For a moment her face was expressionless. Her glance hurried to his mouth as if looking for the key to the joke. Then her lips formed a puzzled little smile. She gave a laugh with a gasp in it.

"Why—Grif! Are you proposing to me?"

He stood before her, his hands moving up to her shoulders, the hunger for her dislodging all sham and artificiality. "Katie, honey, I know I'm ugly as galvanized sin. I'm older than God, too, but—"

"Silly! You're not old. Just—mature."

"I've got some of the virtues of my years, but I hope I don't chomp my plates and cup my hand behind my ear yet. I'm steady, and I've got seventy-two hundred dollars in a bank. And I'm not much of a hand to drink, not what you'd call a real booze-fighter anyhow, and as far as women go—"

Her finger on his lips arrested the declaration. "Grif, dear, I've never been so flattered. But you don't love me. You can't, after only—how many days?"

"All my life!" he said fervently. "Most fellers my age have wives and fourteen kids. But I've been waiting. And the day I saw you at the stage station, I said to myself: 'That's her. That's Mrs. Grif Holbrook.'"

His hands traveled caressingly down her arms. "I don't ask you to say you love me. But say you won't try to keep from loving me. Because I'll do everything any man ever did to make a woman happy."

There were tears in her eyes, and her smile was the caressing, yet sad, smile of a mother trying to reason with a son about to elope with his teacher.

"Loving is just a step from admiring, and there's nothing about you I don't admire. But—" She hesitated, her teeth taking her lower lip as she looked away.

"Will you, Katie?" he pressed her. "Will you do it?"

Suddenly she slipped from the stump. "Let's walk back," she said. "Don't say a word until we get there."

It was a fifteen-minute ordeal, that walk back to Mrs. Ochoa's. His bones were broken, individually; his heart was removed and cut into small bits; and finally he was reassembled, in torment, afraid to hear her answer but afraid not to.

She stopped in front of the house, opened the gate and went inside. Closing it, she leaned across it and kissed him lightly on the lips.

"Of course I will! If I don't love you now, not really, I know I will, because you're so fine. But it will have to be in a month or two. If you really love me, you'll want to wait."

He had stripped a ring from his finger, a large yellow-gold lion's head ring with a two-carat diamond in its mouth, and he pressed it against her palm. She tried it on. Finally she made it stay on her thumb, laughing.

"We'll have it made smaller. Won't their eyes pop when they see it on my finger?"

She ran in. Clouds like pink froth scuffed about Grif's feet as he walked back to the stage depot.

15

Broderick was still in the office. Grif went back through the chain of cell-like rooms. Broderick, tilted back against the wall, took one look at him and let his chair thump down on the floor.

"What've you done?" he demanded. "Caught the he-coon?"

"Better'n that!" said Grif. And then, feeling the remark had been in bad taste: "Well, in a way. Two months from today, my boy, I'm marrying Katie Crocker."

Broderick slowly rose from the chair. "Did you say marrying, or adopting?"

A rush of anger dinned through Grif. He crossed the space between them in a stride and caught Broderick by the front of his buckskin shirt. "You damn young pup! When you're my age you still won't have sense enough to pound sand down a rat hole. You got some idea that a man's blood dries up after he passes thirty?"

Broderick's features were like bone and the young eyes were smoky. "Just let me have my little joke, Wild Bill," he said. "That was my way of congratulating you."

Holbrook shoved him away, only vaguely aware that he had acted in fear rather than in anger; only half conscious that he hated Broderick for an offense greater than any his mouth could give: the intolerable offense of being twenty years younger.

"See if you can't find a better way of saying it than that," he suggested.

"Many happy returns. That ain't so good either, is it?

103

Let's say, 'Mr. John Broderick wishes Mr. Grif Holbrook great happiness in his coming matrimonial venture.'"

Grif's shoulders moved in a settling shrug. As Broderick started out, he said: "Wait a minute. If you aren't too busy, Mr. Broderick, we can get down to business. There's no use fooling around town wondering about hay when we can be out cutting it. See if you can find some wagons and get a line on any hay that's closer than the Sulphur Spring Valley. Tomorrow morning wouldn't be too early to leave."

"All right."

The biggest man at the funeral of Sam Granjon and Ollie McCardle was the Senator.

He was chief pallbearer, and, after the procession left the church and wound out through the east wall to the cemetery, he delivered a sort of double eulogy that combined the virtues of the two men neatly and worked in a couple of plugs for separate territorial status for Arizona, a subject Grif had noticed got a cheer whenever it was mentioned. Conscious of the figure he made—white hair tousled by the breeze, claw-hammer coat brushed and trousers pressed—he stood at the head of the twin slots in the earth and talked for an hour.

Grif stood by himself. Uneasily, he kept his eye on the crowd of about forty men who wore mourning rings of bent shoeing nails and black rosettes in their hats. They had come in a bloc and done some plain and fancy drill, under the soprano piping of goateed Noah Benteen, before the funeral. It occurred to Grif that he might have the whole devil's kitchen of his opposition under his eye—not counting Jim Maroon. Or perhaps it was merely a portion of it. And if this were his opposition, was the grim file body the brains and belly of the creature?

He studied Benteen. Doc was shaking. An hour on his feet and nothing to drink. The snake's den in his belly would be crawling. Call him a hothead or a saber rattler. But could he be a schemer? The mind that ramrodded the stage gang did not seem to be that of a drunk.

Heydenfeldt was in the mob too, standing with Benteen as an officer of some kind. Physically, he could be danger-ous, but the menace he offered did not seem to go beyond this.

Grif's glance traveled to Mrs. Benson, tall and

handsome, with something wistful in her face as she stood with a dozen of her girls. A cool stream of logic awoke in his brain. Could a woman ramrod a crowd like that? Perhaps a woman with a man's ruthlessness. To be in her business, she couldn't be too buttery around the heart either. The mortality among the lassies must be pretty high. The wear and tear on customers was a factor to wreck the repose of some women too. A good customer today; complaining of a slight misery on Saturday. Definitely off the active list in a week. An on-and-offer from then on, until finally he was getting around on two canes and cadging drinks. No—it wasn't for the average female.

He thought that of all the people he had met since he left El Paso, Mrs. Benson had the shrewdest mind, the coolest nerve, and the greatest flexibility of temper.

Senator Montgomery, his voice breaking with emotion or hoarseness, extended his arms and let the first clods thump onto the coffins. Tears were streaming down his cheeks as he turned away and joined Grif. He stood close to him, wiping his nose with a handkerchief as big as a pillowslip, and muttering in a voice altogether cold: "So long, Sam. You son of a bitch. I hope you stay dead, this time. I'll get rheumatism from about one more of these!"

On the way back Grif got to noticing his boots. They were scandalous. Each toe had its own little pocket of comfort. They fitted like gloves, but there were other bulges and creases which connoted nothing but age.

On Alameda Street he found a *zapatería*. In a dusk of weak light and fumes of poor leather, he selected a boot popular with Mexican dandies, the toe coming to a sadiron point. They were fashioned of tan leather so blond it might have been called yellow. They reached a price and achieved a fitting. Grif went on to the depot.

Johnny came in around four. He had information.

"The army cut hay up the San Pedro a couple of years ago, in Babocomari Valley. Sig Johnson says he hauled it for them. He'll guide us in and haul it out for seventy-five a ton."

'How soon can he take us?"

"I told him tomorrow morning. He said all right. I'll go down to Warner's and order the grub."

Kate was at the desk. As Johnny started out, she asked in

mock petulance: "Aren't you going to congratulate us?"

"Why, sure," Johnny said. "Congratulations." He went out.

They looked at each other. "Funny kid," Grif said. "When I told him about it he looked like I'd said the Oxbow had folded up."

He laughed, but Kate's eyes were grave and he noticed that she was some time getting back to her work.

At sunup next day, twelve of Sig Johnson's wagons lined up before the depot. Grif climbed up beside Johnson. The freighter spat tobacco on the rump of a mule and sent his long whip out in a stinging crack. "Catch up! Stretch out!"

Grif looked back once, knowing that Katie had not come down yet but wanting to be sure. There was no sign of her at the door. He saw Johnny Broderick hunched on the seat of a following wagon with one of those tarnal Mexican cigarettes in his mouth.

They swung south along the canal road through hordes of women carrying water jugs. A mile along, they turned east toward the *Rincóns.*

They reached Babocomari Valley, on the San Pedro, on the afternoon of the third day. About them the plain was locked with rocky palisades. Giant saguarocacti broke the valley's flatness with their green, many-branched candelabra. There was abundant water. Desert cedar spread its tattered purplish lace above the springs and small branches flowing down from the snow-frosted ramparts.

Grif rubbed his hands like a pawnbroker. There was hay everywhere. North was a barbered section the Army had hayed over, but for the most part fat white grama and side oats stood hub-high to the wagons and made a rich rustling under the breeze. They camped beneath a basaltic ledge on the north side of the valley. On the following day the haying teams went out, scythes and forks flashing with a clean steel glitter. The shoulders of the harvesters rolled steadily through the morning. By afternoon a thick alley had been cut into the tilted field and there was hay to be trussed and stacked.

Johnson liked to cook, and provided a great iron kettle of beans for dinner, with small, toothsome steaks of an antelope they had shot on the way out. At night the darkness and cold drew them close to the campfire; there was whiskey and the music of Broderick's concertina to ease their weariness.

In the morning, Johnny threw a saddle on one of the horses they had brought along and rode east into the tapering wedge of the valley to scout how far they could cut. Not long before noon, Grif saw him coming down the creek at a high lope.

Broderick passed the cutters to approach him, pulling the horse around harshly and leaning on the swell. There was a keen anticipation on his face.

"Grif—by God!" he said. "Wagon tracks two miles ahead! Not hay wagons, either. Stagecoaches, or I'm blind!"

"How old?" Grif demanded.

Broderick scratched his neck. "Couldn't tell, but—"

"Wasn't there any horse sign?"

Broderick seemed put out that his news did not set fire to him. "I don't know, but for hell's sake does it matter? What were stagecoaches doing out here, twenty miles from the stage road?"

"That's what we'll have to find out. It might tell us a little about what to expect, if we knew whether they went by last night or six months ago. I'll get a horse."

He saddled, tucked a carbine in the boot, and rode with Broderick up the stream.

The mountains piled higher and more abruptly on their left, stair-stepped with rimrock and bare of vegetation. Shadows lay gauntly in the clefts and pockets. It was a rough pile of masonry, looking as though a giant stone mason had practised here, gouging and hammering and leaving steeples and thumbs of stone along the eaves of the range. It did not look like stagecoach country.

They came upon the tracks quite suddenly. Broderick reined in. Through the deep stand of hay wound the twin grooves. They left a scalloped trail curving toward a high notch in the mountains. Grif swung down and examined the ruts. The grass had come fully from them, but the edges were still fairly sharp. They followed them a quarter mile until they found manure between the ruts. It could not have been over a month old, probably less. Broderick struck one gauntleted fist into the other. Excitement glistened rashly in his face.

"Let's get 'em, Grif!"

He had his toe in the stirrup when Grif said curiously: "You mean you'd ride on up there just like we are?"

Broderick looked blankly at him. "You mean we ought to go back for the others?" He sounded disappointed.

"For the others?" Grif laughed. "Son, we don't know what we're going to run into up there. Certainly more than two men, if this is the cache we've been talking about. What've we got to fight 'em with? A couple of dozen jackasses, three horses, and a gang of mule-skinners. And liker'n not they'd lead us into a box. No, sir. This is a job for fellers as know how. I'm going back to Fort Buchanan for a detail."

Broderick left his horse and stood with his fists on his hips. "It'll take four days to get a detail."

Grif had a feeling of inevitability, a sullen joy rising in him. "A man stays dead longer than four days. If those coaches are in the mountains, they're going to come out the same way they went in. No toll roads around here that I know of. You and the others will camp on their front door till I get back."

Broderick let his arms hang. He stared at Grif in unvarnished contempt. "I'll—be—God—damned!"

"You will if you don't simmer down."

"I'm licked!" Broderick breathed. "Butterfield told me I'd be working with a ring-tailed roarer. But all I've seen you do is tiptoe around town holding hands with Kate Crocker and sniffling over shooting a man."

"That right?"

Broderick's big hands worked and he let his mouth turn sardonically. "If you ever saw trouble you wouldn't recognize it for all the dust you'd be raising. The Admiral said you were brought up on blood and powder smoke. You act to me like you were weaned on poke salads and pizzle grease. I'll be danged if you're any better'n a cut-proud old billy goat!"

There was a red explosion in Grif's head. He went after Broderick with his right hand cocked and his left reaching. Broderick went back a step. He bumped into his horse and jerked aside. Grif's haymaker missed him and hit the stirrup leathers. Grinning, Broderick took an instant to measure and let the gathered power of his shoulder travel with his fist to the side of Grif's head.

Grif was down.

He was on hands and knees with his head wagging. His ear rang like a church bell. His mind was focused on the pebbly earth beneath him, cognizant of nothing beyond it. Then with a jolt it came back to him, all the anger and urgency of it, and his head raised to see Broderick looking down at him with an odd expression of satisfaction and wonder. The kid stood just as he had struck him, stooped a little, fists made and held hip-high.

Holbrook reached for the stirrup and hauled himself up. Broderick lunged in again. This time he missed. Grif got in a lick. A small cut opened in the stubbly hairs of Broderick's eyebrow and he shook his head. He covered up while Grif moved heavily after him. Then he let the left go again. It was light and fast, but it toughened when it hit, still driving. While Grif was blinking off the stunning blow to his ear, the left found his cheekbone again. Stung to rashness, he bored in with both arms swinging. Broderick took a single crushing jolt on the brisket and began to back up. Grif kept swinging but couldn't reach him again.

Balked, he waited. "Anybody kin run," he challenged.

Broderick, grinning but pale, shuffled back, a big man whose bigness was aliveness and rashness as well. They circled, and then Broderick let another go and it hit high on Holbrook's forehead like a rock. He went back and sat down.

Broderick said, "The great Holbrook, that mighty man." He laughed in his throat.

Grif took four deep-lunged breaths, extracting everything from them, sucking them dry of their wine, holding himself down until he knew he could get up without staggering. And now he put his right hand behind him and shoved himself off his rump and onto his heels, and hunkered that way an instant to get his balance. He knew what had to be done. There was no stopping those fists. They had the darting swiftness of dragonflies. He had not fought a man like Broderick in years, and he knew now that he was no longer the man he had been then. He had spent some of the biggest coins of youth without knowing it.

He came up too fast, slipped and went to one knee, but lunged up again to crash against Broderick. He hammered one deep into his belly. He felt it lift the kid off his feet and heard his tortured gasp. He thrust him away and chopped at his face with desperate savagery.

Broderick started backing. Grif kept crowding him until he forgot all about offense and merely pushed at him. Cuffing, slashing, Grif bloodied his nose and split his lip; he was almost sick with the joy the letting of the blood gave him. A brittle-bush caught Broderick's spur and spilled him. He rolled over and rested a moment on all fours, blood dripping warm and slow from his nose onto the ground. Then he got onto his feet again and swerved with blind and desperate swiftness into Holbrook. He stopped cold and swayed an instant. An ache spread through Grif's hand and up his forearm; he saw the white impression of his knuckles on the cleft point of Johnny Broderick's chin. He heard him make a low snoring noise in his throat. He watched him go into a slow twisting fall to the ground.

Grif walked over and held onto the horn of the saddle. He felt himself getting sick, and doubled over with hands gripping his knees. In too much anger, as in a surfeit of wine, there was sickness.

When Broderick came around, Grif was talking to Sig Johnson. He had lashed a small sack of food to the cantle of a saddle. Broderick caught a canteen a Mexican tossed him. He drank, poured the rest of the water over his head, and stood up. He reeled toward one of the wagons, stopping to say thickly:

"Nobody's licked me since I was four years old. Nobody's goin' to lick me again, either, not even you. Butterfield was half right. You got guts, if you only knew what they were for."

16

HOLBROOK CAME UPON the pueblo in early night. Lights burned in the many small *jacales* and the buildings of Calle Real. In the filtered desert air, lamps burned clean and clear as stars.

He was tired, hungry, and discouraged. On the way in, he had visited Fort Buchanan, six miles below Tucson. Captain Ewell, a little woodpecker of a man with the South in his voice, had refused to aid him. He was undermanned already. And a glint in the Captain's eye said he was satisfied with things just about as they were.

Grif jogged into town. It had been nearly two weeks since he had left El Paso. Two weeks! The way the days slipped through your fingers when they really counted. Butterfield shouting that war was as sure as rain. Find those coaches! Get ready to move.

But he had achieved precisely nothing, beyond killing someone who didn't matter and getting engaged to someone who did. Still, the Babocomari Valley thing might sprout into a harvest. In a way it made him think he had an honest scent. It put a frame around his lost-stage-valley notion—an arsenal where the stolen coaches and animals were hidden, along with God-knew-how-much else in the way of arms. But it was a flimsy frame that was constructed of a single set of wagon tracks.

Since the funeral, an idea had been blowing about in his mind like a rag of paper. Now he took it up and examined it, and it said: Why not take a leaf from Benteen's book? Organize the first chapter of Butterfield's Regulars right here! Barbecues, turkey shoots and parades—the whole shooting match!

He had been wondering why, with over a hundred white men in town, only forty belonged to the lodge. There were few enough recreations in the pueblo that a man should jump at a thing like the Territorials.

He thought of two reasons why a man might abstain. Because his politics didn't come wrapped in Southern ribbon, for one thing. Or because he did not like the noisy little sachem of the lodge, Noah Benteen. What Tucson needed was a nonpolitical outfit that stressed plenty of beer and good beef, with a little marksmanship thrown in.

Absolutely nonpolitical, boys! he would tell them. (But no banty rooster of a Buchanan Democrat is going to tell us which side of the street we can walk on. No more five-to-one fist fights in bars after this.) So that when the time came, he might have some strength to call on. But the time was now, and it would take some jockeying to get together a gang to go out to Babocomari Valley with him.

He rode two blocks out of his way to pass Mrs. Ochoa's, but Kate was still at the depot. All the way in, then, he thought of her. But, annoyingly, Johnny Broderick kept sidling in between them.

". . . No better'n a cut-proud old billy goat!" They called an animal that when an emasculation was only half effectual. He became as ridiculous as an old rake laughing in a high, cracked voice and pinching the girls. But Broderick didn't know the Holbrooks. They hadn't shoveled dirt in Grandpa Ed Holbrook's face until he was eighty-seven. His youngest child had been six.

There was a good week-night crowd at Annie Benson's. The gaming tables in the rear were crowded and all the girls had partners. Private card games were going on at some tables, while at others men were drinking. There was one empty table near the piano. Grif decided on a couple of drinks while he sorted his thoughts. What he had in mind would first have to be cleared with Annie. As he passed a table he heard Benteen's voice in a half-shout. "I say the South ain't had a square shake! Discrimination! Chicanery!"

The doctor sat with four other men at a game table. Cards and chips sprawled about. Heydenfeldt hunched over a stack, soberly absorbing the Territorialist's bluser. Bay-Rum Brown, drunkenly slouched on one elbow, nodded grave approval. "Y'r right. Y'r absolutely right."

There also sat Senator Montgomery, pink, goateed and frowning, and at his right, tilted back in a chair with his hands meshed over his vest, a fifth man. A quirk of humor softened his mouth. He was a tall, bearded, sad-eyed old man who looked like a tired field marshal revisiting a forgotten battlefield.

"But Noah," he said, "wasn't the Kansas-Nebraska Act a pretty fair shake for the South? It certainly didn't favor the North. Gave you—them, I say, every chance for new slave territory."

Benteen screeched: "Will you quit talking slavery? Slavery's no more the issue than the right of a man to whittle with his left hand! It's the right of a farmer to raise a crop, sell it where he wants and spend the money the way he chooses."

"Trade the crop to England for manufactured goods and stuff the money in John Bull's pants; and let our Northern manufacturers fail because they can't compete with cheap foreign goods! We've got to have that protective tariff, Noah, if this country is ever to be more than a race of one-mule croppers."

Gus Heydenfeldt's eyes raised, found Grif and darkened his whole face with their irritation. He stood. "By God, you've got your guts, coming back here!"

Grif carried a chair over. He struck the Senator on the back, ignored the others, and sat down between the bearded man and Benteen. He liked the sound and the look of the man. "Thought I might run into some friends here," he said. He glanced at the lean, bearded man beside him. "Don't think we've met."

Senator Montgomery put a hand on the other man's shoulder. "Time you did, then. Holbrook, this is Sylvester Mowry, next to Annie Benson our most important citizen. We're sending Sylvester back to Washington to find out why Arizona continues to be New Mexico's chore boy. Syl, shake hands with Grif Holbrook, one of the Butterfield people."

Mowry had a warm, strong grip, not an old man's handshake, and the lines in his face were strong lines. He smiled. "You're just in time to sign Doc's petition."

Benteen regarded them out of lowering eyes. He shoved a

wrinkled paper before Grif. "If I get enough names, this is going along with him to Washington. It's all right to ask for favors, but a petition is the strong way to do the thing. This demands that Arizona be set up as a separate territory, with the option of slavery every man's own matter."

Grif shoved it back. "I'm not much of a joiner."

"Do you believe in justice?" Benteen demanded.

"There's some merit in the idea."

"Then you've got to admit—"

"I don't admit anything. As a matter of fact, I'm here to do some petitioning of my own. I'm going to get up a lodge."

Montgomery chuckled. "A lodge!"

"Sort of patterned after yours, Doc, only nonpolitical. The only local option will be whether you like your beef rare or well done. Parades and shooting matches and all the rest."

Benteen's stare was close and suspicious. "What are you going to offer that we don't?"

"Nothing. But I'm not going to offer one thing that you do: petitions. I thought I'd make the boys a little speech and kind of leave it to them whether we need it or not."

Heydenfeldt shook his head. "We aren't running this place as a convention hall. Use the street."

"We?" Grif said.

Surly blood colored Heydenfeldt's face. Mowry chuckled and Bay-Rum Brown laughed windily. "Gus has been like a stud hoss in April ever since you canned him. Don't know whether he's in love with Annie or her saloon!"

Heydenfeldt's palm took him across the mouth. The barber fell sideways against the Senator. Heydenfeldt's eyes challenged anyone else to laugh. His attention came back to Grif; he seemed for an instant to gather his forces, and somehow what Grif noticed was the way his hand nervously lingered near his holstered gun.

"You've blowed your bugle enough around here," he said, "If you want to drink, drink. If you want to make a speech, go outside. Annie's hired me as her manager. What I'm saying she'll back up."

"I'd like to hear her back that up," Grif said.

Heydenfeldt's breathing was loud through his nose. "Drink up or get out."

Grif was not unaware of the attention of the barmen, nor of a somber houseman who stood among the gaming tables.

He had the impression of a preconceived plan beginning to operate. He regarded Heydenfeldt a moment longer and stood up. Heydenfeldt moved back.

Heydenfeldt watched him leave the table. Holbrook walked through the tables to the aisle before the bar. He sauntered to the rear. A girl slipped in beside him and took his arm, a smiling little black-haired girl with a short skirt and bare arms, who looked too cold to be gay. "I'll bet you can dance the legs right off a girl," she said.

"I'll bet I can too." He pinched her cheek and kept walking. At the door to the rear vestibule, he turned. Heydenfeldt had turned to watch him and the saloon men had not lost him, but their hands were above the bar. He parted the curtain and went through.

It was chilly in the vestibule. From above came sounds of conversation and laughter. "Annie!" he shouted.

After a moment her voice answered. "Yes?"

"Holbrook. I want to talk to you."

She came down hurriedly, holding her skirt as she descended the stairs. Her hair was clean and shining and there was vitality in her face. She gave him her hand and the warmth of her eyes.

"Your manager and I can't reach an agreement about a speech I want to make," he told her. "He says I make it in the street and I say I make it in here. What do you say?"

"Let's talk to Gus."

They went to the table. All the men bounced up as Annie approached. Heydenfeldt waited in surly tension. "What's the matter, Gus?" Annie asked him. "Why shouldn't he make a speech if he wants to?"

"We don't want to turn our place into a danged convention hall!"

Annie's tranquil features were amused. "'Our'?"

Heydenfeldt shrugged. "If I'm going to manage it for you, I've got a right to take an interest in it."

"That's fine, Gus; but I think we'll let him talk this time."

Benteen shook a finger at her. "And lose the trade of the Territorials? I'll boycott you! Not a man of mine will drink in your place if I give the word!"

"You make a speech every night, Doc. Why shouldn't Grif?" She took Grif's arm. "Will the bar suit you for a pulpit?"

By now the whole saloon knew what was going on, and he did not have to shout for attention. He sat on the varnished pine bar with his coat-tails flipped back and his fists on his hips.

"Boys," he said, "I'd like to buy you all a drink. Drink all you want, but don't get drunk until I've talked to you for five minutes. How many of you would be interested in a lodge that offered free beer seven days a week?"

It appeared that even the girls were in favor of it. "Now, that's the kind of a lodge I'm planning. I'm having some beer checks stamped. Any time you feel the need of a beer, just drop in at the depot and call for one. Spend it where you please and we'll redeem it. John Butterfield will. So we'll honor him a little by calling it Butterfield's Regulars. Dues will be a dollar a month. As far as politics go, we haven't got any. We welcome Whigs, Democrats, Free Soilers, Republicans—you name it. There's just one plank in our platform. Since Butterfield's buying the beer, we'll give him a little boost now and again, if he needs it."

Now they were suspicious; it was Benteen who put it into words. "And get our gizzards shot out for a couple of free beers?"

Grif hesitated. This was the teetering plank over the chasm.

"I didn't say that. You might say my politics are this: everything for Arizona. Tucson was a hog wallow before Butterfield gave it a stage line. Now you get St. Louis papers only two weeks old. The population has jumped; it will keep right on jumping, unless people get the idea they're isolated out here. Without the stage line, it'd still be every man for himself outside the city limits."

"Ain't it so right now?" Benteen yelled.

Grif leveled a finger at him. "You named it, Doc! Somebody—let's be polite and not point—is out to wreck us. If Butterfield goes under, Tucson and Arizona go under. You say you're sending Syl Mowry to Washington. How are you going to send him if the Oxbow fails? On a jackass? What's he going to say? That Tucson is two weeks from St. Louis—three days from El Paso—eleven days from Frisco? And that she's part of the Union and getting too big to be administered from Santa Fe? Or that he comes from a burg where the jackass is king and the population is half what it was last year?"

Sylvester Mowry said, "You're talking sense, man. But what to you mean by risk?"

"It's my notion I may find those lost stages one of these days. I'll need a posse to help bring them in."

Mowry considered. ". . . That's fair enough. How does a man join up?"

"Just by drinking my liquor. We'll sign the roster later."

Mowry approached the bar. He poured himself a drink. Bay-Rum Brown lurched after him. Senator Montgomery said pompously. "Boys, he's got something." With his and Mowry's official seals on it, the others came along. Grif counted eighteen drinkers. He wiped his face with a bandana.

"There *is* one thing—" he admitted. "I may have a line on those stages already! There's a trail leading into the Galiuro Mountains. My pardner and Sig Johnson are blocking it while they wait for me. I hoped for a detail from the fort. Since I can't get it, it looks like I've got to draft a few of you. Anybody that's game for it?"

Benteen gave a laugh of harsh triumph. "*Now*, do you savvy him?"

Holbrook leveled a finger at him angrily. "Is what I said any less true now than it was two minutes ago? You know it ain't! How about it, boys? Or have I just organized an elderly females' society instead of a shooting club? Free chow, free ammunition, and maybe a chance to make a hero of yourself!"

There was a prolonged silence. Senator Montgomery cleared his throat. "I don't want to influence anyone else, but prior engagements will keep me in town."

Grif recalled a moment two weeks ago, when the Senator had declined to sit atop a stage going through Apache Pass because of what he called a cold in the eyeballs or something. Was there a small streak of jaundice in the man? He could have strangled him for it at this moment of balance, but in the next moment he heard bearded Syl Mowry saying roughly: "Don't know about you, Blaise, but I'm for it. Has it got to be tonight?"

"Dawn will do. Anybody else?"

Mowry said, "They'll all go, or I don't know a Tucsonian from a chuckawalla. Drink and git, for we'll all need sleep."

Annie was waiting in back, beaming. The piano was banging away again, the hurdy-gurdy girls in their scandalous costumes brassily hunting partners at a dollar a throw. "Can't thank you enough, Annie," Grif said.

"Why, I was glad to help. Do you still think I'm a rebel?"

"If you lean," Grif grinned, "it ain't toward Dixie." He hesitated an instant before saying: "Annie, if you wanted to give a lady something to show her you thought she was—all right, you know...what kind of a gimcrack would it be?"

Annie's face began to turn pink. "Why—it all depends on the lady. What's she like?"

"She's—oh, you know who I'm talking about!"

It was shyness in her eyes, madam though she was, and it was like the shyness of a fifteen-year-old virgin. "I—I didn't, really! But I have an idea she'd like some perfume. Sig Johnson brought some up from Mexico last month and left it with me to sell to anybody who wanted to please one of the girls especially. It's behind the bar."

"Great! The biggest bottle you've got! Send somebody over to the depot with it in the morning, will you? and just say: 'To Katie, from she knows who.'"

A change took place in Annie's face that involved a deepening of the lines beside her mouth and quenched the glow in her eyes. Tears stood in the gray-blue eyes and she caught her lip angrily with her teeth. She said in a tight, controlled voice: "You're stupid, Grif, and you're homely as a skinned mule, and I wish I'd never seen you. If you want any perfume taken to anybody, you can take it yourself. Good night!"

She was gone, just the swirl of the curtain to remind him that it had happened. And he thought, as a ray of intuition tardily struck him: My Lord! She didn't think I meant *her!* An old bat like Annie? Why, she must be about thirty-five!

But he was sorry it had happened, and he conjectured, as he left, about how to smooth it over. He hated to hurt anyone; and besides he might need her help.

17

ELEVEN REGULARS WENT out with Holbrook at dawn. They
rode hard that day, making thirty miles, and traversed a
flinty run of hills the following morning to descend into the
San Pedro Valley. For an hour he had watched the sky
ahead, puzzled by an amber light about the sun. Now they
came into full view of the valley and he saw a thin yellowish
haze rising from the floor. There were oaths from the riders.
Grif sat rigidly, studying what lay below.

Fire had swept the whole valley south of the creek,
lapping up into the canyon where the haying party had last
camped. It had burned itself out only recently, it appeared,
the smoke still rising from the sea of burned grasses. But a
half mile east of the burned area, a column of smoke fluted
high into the air: the cook fire.

"Could be Apaches," Mowry speculated.

"Or it could be the second cousin of a Territorial." Grif
swung his pony down the slope through giant black rocks.

They followed a dry stream bed, feeling the sultry warmth
of the burned fields. When they had put it behind them, they
rode up a shelving bank onto the flat. Grif saw the camp a
quarter mile ahead. He went in at a lope; the dozen-odd
workers scrambled up. Broderick came out with a tin cup of
coffee steaming in his hand. He was grimed with smoke and
sweat rivulets had cut his face grotesquely. His eyebrows
were scorched.

"Some dang fool knock his pipe out on a rock?" Grif
demanded.

"Some dang fool crept down out of those hills and started

it just after dark. We put in one hell of a night. I had to draw off everybody from the gap, yonder, to save the wagons and hay. Now there's new tracks. I scouted them but I can tell you we're going to have a picnic following them far. Those flats make a trail like an ant leaves on a rock."

"Anybody following them?"

"One of the teamsters. But the bird's flew the coop now; that's for sure."

Grif peered up the rugged slope that merged with the giant carcass of the mountains. The gap where the wagons had entered was as sharp and narrow as a trench. It would be a perilous entry. He turned back and spoke to Mowry.

"Got any ideas?"

Mowry had been in the cavalry and had a number of ideas. One thing he did not want to do was to try to bull it through the gap. "They'd cut us to dog-meat, if there was anybody up there. Better to quarter around both sides of it. May mean footwork."

Grif glanced at Broderick. Broderick, hearing expert verification of Holbrook's tactics, only brooded over his coffee and regarded the hills.

"Well, let's git at it," Grif said suddenly. "There's one thing: If any more coaches are up there and they decide to make a run for it, they could leave us clean behind. A stagecoach on a decent road can always outrun a horse. For a ways, anyhow. I'm going to drive one of the wagons up there and block the road while the rest of you bore in."

Mowry stared at him. "You'll get your behind shot off too."

"I'm not going far. Just till I find a bottleneck."

Mowry and Sig Johnson led the divided strength of the camp up the slope, Mowry riding west, Johnson east. They would try to follow the road in a general way, scouting ahead for the camp. As Grif shook up his mules, Broderick jumped onto the wagon. "This was the way I wanted to go in all the time," he said. "You're not going to make me go with the scouts, are you, General?"

Grif shrugged. He put the string of mules up the almost obscured wagon tracks. The land began to shatter into boulders and clumps of yucca. They saw where the tracks of at least one coach broke east, worked down through the rocks, and vanished into a now burned-over area. Something began to tremble in Grif. He was like a hound with a scent. There was now no doubt that he was approaching at least a holding-station of the raiders. Broderick seemed to feel it too, tensing forward on the seat with his Colt's sporting rifle across his knees.

Subtly the gap began to enclose them, enticing them up a trough that gradually narrowed. The ground at each side mounted to low ridges. Yet there was still room for a coach to pass, and they went on. Mowry and the others were out of sight. The valley was hidden from view. The terrain was now definitely unfavorable, yet to quit too soon would be to have accomplished nothing. They kept going, the mules trudging along cheerfully. Grif kept wanting to look behind.

They labored through slow turns. Low-growing oaks flanked the road; the slopes at each side were steep and gouged with hollows. They were in a canyon now, shallow but fairly wide. Halfway through a blind turn, Grif grunted.

"This ought to do it. We'll work 'er around slanch-wise and cut the mules loose."

He ran the mules up the hillside. He was on the point of backing them when Broderick sat up straight. "Did you hear that?"

Grif's back tingled. He listened. Undoubtedly he heard it—the scuff of shoes on sand! He started to climb down, but at that instant a high yell came to them and he heard wheels roll and horses break from a walk into a lope. Broderick leaped from the wagon and went into the rocks as a lurching Concord stage broke into view. Grif was caught on the right side, so that as the team raced through the turn he must either jump among the horses or stand his ground. He had a flashing glimpse of a rocking Concord, of six wild-eyed horses heading into his mule team in an effort to miss the wagon. The driver seemed to loom six feet above him. The man was busy, fighting to jockey the team past the mules and onto the slope of the hill.

He saw Grif and transferred all the ribbons to one hand, so that his right hand was free to raise a carbine from his lap. He threw an unstudied shot at Grif. He was a big, hatless, sandy-haired man in a black coat buttoned to the neck, and looked as wild as his team. He dropped all the ribbons and worked the loading lever of the carbine. The horses were hopelessly tangled with the mules, rearing to strike at them as the mules shied.

Grif said through his teeth: "All right, brother!" He was way ahead of the man, but something made him hesitate. Among the rocks, Broderick was kneeling with his gun to his shoulder. Grif held his shot but waited to see what the kid could do.

A gun blasted. The driver went to one knee, groped blindly and was hurled from the stagecoach as the horses rocked it crazily. Grif waited to see what came out of the coach. He saw Broderick work around to the left and put a shot through the panels.

"Hold your fire, dammit!" he shouted. "That's a twenty-five-hundred-dollar Concord you're shooting up!"

Cautiously they circled the coach, examined the rear boot, and finally persuaded themselves that it was unoccupied. They went back and looked at the wounded man. Grif's glance stayed on Broderick. He was staring in awe at the wreck he had made of the man's head. The driver had been dead before he hit the ground. His face was a red ruin. Broderick suddenly made a sound in his throat and turned away. He stood among the rocks, hands gripping his knees, vomiting.

Grif said lightly: "I always say, Johnny, there ain't any real difference between a dead man and a dead horse. Ain't that right?"

In about an hour, Sylvester Mowry, Sig Johnson, and the rest of the men came down the canyon to join them. They had heard the shooting. "Camp seems to have been about a mile above," Mowry declared. "Nothing left but a few bales of hay. Know this feller?"

"Never saw him before. Any of you others?"

They looked at him and shook their heads. "A foreign import," Grif said. "You know, he had guts. He knew he wasn't going to get out with that coach. He probably had trouble last night and couldn't get out before you boys slammed the door. But he was game enough to try it."

Within the coach were blankets, some food, a bundle which Grif unwrapped to find a stack of printed leaflets. They bore no organizational signature, but were as inflammatory as a bird's-eye match. He and Mowry read them. They shouted of unfairness and cheating, of fat New England manufacturers and Georgia cotton farmers coddling their slaves. Grif made a pile of them and set fire to them on the sand, retaining one copy as a souvenir.

Late that afternoon, Johnson's man returned from attempting to follow the coaches. "Plumb lost them," he said. "They split up and I only found one trail coming out of the burned land. Lost in the malpais. I'd say, though, that there weren't over three stages got out."

Then, Grif speculated, they must have them spotted in little caches all over Arizona. And unless they too read the handwriting on the wall and were regrouping for a grand race through Sonora and Chihuahua to Texas, they were not in much danger of immediate capture. It was a disconsolate thought to take back with him.

A letter was waiting for him from John Butterfield.

"Friend Grif:
    It has now been two weeks since our talk, and I daresay things are shaping up nicely. I must tell you matters look dark indeed at this end. Most of the Southerners in Congress have now been recalled and are apparently sitting in the Confederacy.
    We had thought of California as secure, but there are some hotheads in the southern part of the state who are raising trouble. We cannot count on Los Angeles at all.
    For this reason, Grif, I am asking you not to take the coaches west through California. I have given instructions along the line to rush all coaches, stock and cash to Tucson upon word of the outbreak of hostilities. It will then be up to you to take them north by some other route."

Some other route! Grif balled the letter and fired it at the hearth. They had spent a solid year chipping out one route, and now he said—just casually—to find some other route! Just ford the Grand Canyon, old man. Take them across Pike's Peak, but don't overwork the horses.

In this mood of desperation he thought of the Senator. He took his hat from the table; he hesitated. He told

Broderick, "I guess you ought to be in on this. I'm going down to Montgomery's for a powwow."

Broderick flipped a cigarette away and rose. Katie turned from the desk. She looked closely at Grif. "I'll bet you haven't shaved in a week!" she chided.

"Only six days."

She laughed. "You'd better shave before I see you again. Or no more kisses. Besides I've got a surprise for you."

Broderick made a sound in his throat and left the room with a face like stone. Kate's eyes followed him.

"A surprise, eh?"

"I'll tell you about it this evening, when you take me home."

Exhilarated, Grif went after Johnny. The kid had nothing to say as they walked down Correo Street to the print-shop. Senator Montgomery was operating the old hand-press. He flipped a wet sheet from the bed and waved them in. "How'd things go, boys? You both look healthy enough."

"Healthy but mad," Grif said. He told him of Butterfield's letter. "So how do I get to California without going through Los Angeles?"

Montgomery wiped his hands on a rag and took them to his back room. He had a map of the Western territories and states on the wall. He studied it a while. "Anythin' the matter with Beale's wagon road?"

"That crosses the Mojave, doesn't it?" Broderick observed.

"Yes, but one needn't follow it all the way. Cut no'th to Lee's Ferry, on the Colorado, and you're practically in Utah. After that you'll be in the City of the Saints in a week's time."

"Salt Lake City, eh?" Grif stood before the map. "But if the ferry-keeper happens to hail from Tennessee, we're not going to get far. He could cut his cable and we'd be licked."

"Well, then—Santa Fe trail! Detour through the Black Mountains to avoid Mesilla. You'll come out on the Rio. Straight up the trail, then, to Santa Fe and on to Cheyenne."

"That's long and risky. But so's Lee's Ferry risky. One thing's sure. The minute I get word she's busted loose, I'll have to send all our cash and papers along to Mesilla. Can't risk them in this hotbed."

Broderick left the map and stood at the window, watching the Mexican women washing clothes at the canal. "Maybe you better do a little asking around before you try to decide."

They talked a while longer before Grif made up his mind to leave. "You think the Santa Fe route would be too long, eh?" Montgomery said.

"Can't say. Too many factors."

Montgomery walked to the door with them. "Let me know if you do decide to go by Santa Fe. I've got friends there. Might do a little to smooth things over for you."

About three that afternoon the cannon before Guadalupe church rolled its thunder over the pueblo. From the door of the depot, Grif saw the Territorials hurrying along to make the formation. Benteen's poodles. Ready at the snap of a finger.

There was an idea in it. All at once he strode back into the office for a pencil and a piece of paper. He went to his hotel. From the window of his room, he could see them lining up. The cannoneer replaced his ramrod in the church and hurried to his place. Noah Benteen called roll. "Heydenfeldt! Maroon—still absent, eh? Brown. Rubio . . ."

He got most of the names. One of these days he was going to want to know just which of the Territorials were around, and he thought he now had the means of finding out.

18

THEY STARTED UP Main Street, after locking the office. Grif
had picked up his new boots at the *zapateria* that afternoon.
They fitted like gloves—new, unstretched gloves—and were
a bright tan; you might say a chrome yellow. They were
gorgeous things, with their high, pointed toes, and he did not
mind the pinching of them as they walked down the street.

"What's this surprise?" he demanded.

"You wait."

Kate did not turn at India Triste, but led him on to where
the street began to merge with the mesquite forest. At the
corner of a pair of ruts called Jackson Street she halted. A
small adobe house with a ruined corral but a sound roof
occupied the northeast corner. Beside the door an ocotillo,
like a cat-o'-nine-tails planted lashes up, hissed in the breeze.

"What do you think of it?"

"Kinda wrecked, ain't it?" He was puzzled.

"Yes, but for fifty dollars it could be fixed up."

"What for?"

"For us."

"A—a house?"

She trilled a little laugh. "We aren't going to live at the
hotel, I hope!"

"We may not be here long, honey. I thought a couple of
rooms at the hotel would do until we can leave."

"That—pig sty? How many white women in this town live
in hotels? I haven't learned the price of this, but I don't think
we'd have to pay over two or three hundred dollars. I simply
can't wait to start hanging curtains."

He still stood somberly, weighing it. He had not speculated much on the mechanics of domesticity. And the house was a fright.

"Grif-fy!" she said. "You're not going to make me live in that old hotel?"

He rose staunchly. "Not if you don't like it. Well—we'll find out who owns the thing."

When they reached India Triste, she suddenly exclaimed in dismay: "Pshaw! I forgot to close the books."

"Close them tomorrow. They'll keep."

She shook her head. "I couldn't sleep tonight if I thought of them untotaled. We collected on a lot of overdue accounts today and sold some tickets. No, I've got to go back. It won't take long."

They walked back. Grif saw her to the door. Then, thinking of dinner, he started across the street. He thought he heard her come back into the doorway, and turned to see her standing there with her face as white as cloth. Suddenly she covered her face with her hands and her shoulders began to shake. He ran back.

"Katie, honey! What's the matter?"

"He—he's got a girl in there! A saloon girl!"

"Who has?"

"Johnny. They—I started into the office, and—and they were in there. They didn't see me. Oh, Grif—!"

Grif strode by her. He walked straight back through the chain of small rooms to the office, standing a moment in stolid contemplation of the man and girl at the desk. The girl wore the costume of a hurdy-gurdy girl. Grif remembered her from Annie's—Helen, the strawberry blonde. She was attired in the short skirt, silk bodice and lace stockings she wore on duty, with bits of feathers fluffing out here and there. Helen sat on the desk while Broderick occupied the chair. She was leaning forward with her hands at either side of his head and her lips against his upturned face. She released him and he affected a loud sigh, as though he had partaken of straight whiskey. "Baby, I got to see more of you!"

"Honey," she told him, "you is going to!" She slipped from the desk and stood there tousling his hair. "Got to get over to the saloon, Johnny. Going to come and see me?"

Then her eyes raised to the man shadowed in the doorway. She slowly straightened, while Broderick chuckled. "At a dollar a shake, I'm going to need a whole sack of sawbucks for all the things I've got to say to you!" Then he too sensed Grif's presence and turned.

Grif said to the girl: "Get on out."

She approached with a saucy swing of her body. She stopped and flipped a finger under his nose. "That preaching the other night kind of got into your blood, didn't it, Reverend?"

"You can run around in nothing but gloves and high-button shoes at the saloon," he told her, "but if you come back here, be dressed like a lady."

She laughed and went by with a scent of rose-water.

Broderick waited, his hard young face sullen. It came to Grif that the things he had been about to say were out of order. Broderick was grown up. He had a right to all the women he wanted, of whatever kind.

"Kind of keep your lady friends out of the office, will you? Kate just walked in here and saw you ... Lock up when you get through."

All the way back, Kate kept trying to speak and choking up. It finally got on Grif's nerves. "Suppose he did have a girl with him! Any young buck his age is apt to. Only of course he's got to keep them out of the office after this."

"It made me see how—how cheap I must have looked to other people, that's all!"

"Look here," Grif said sternly, "that's all past. We're not thinking about it any more, are we?"

Her face was tear-streaked and forlorn. "No ... Oh, Grif! Let's do it soon! Let's get married as soon as the house is ready!"

He picked her up and kissed her. "Now you're talking! We'll get at it the day I come back."

"Come back? From where?"

"Can you keep a secret? Butterfield's told me to take the stages north by a new route, I've been back and forth over it and I can't see any way but the Grand Canyon. Across Lee's Ferry and on to Salt Lake City. But I've got to sound out that ferryman first. I want to know when we can get across and how he feels about Republicans. If he's a Reb, I'll knock him over before we try to talk business. I may be gone a month," he said. "Can I trust you?"

Her laugh was brief and breathless. "There isn't another man in the world."

19

It was a month before he returned to Tucson. It was a period of fretting and stewing. *Days, not weeks!* Butterfield's war-cry hammered at him. But he had made sure of a crossing of Lee's Ferry, and he felt better about taking the coaches north.

The ferryman was a keg-shaped little man with a brow like an iron bar and a direct manner of thought and speech. "You'll have to be across before the thaw," he warned. "Can you gimme a date?"

"I'd guess before the thaw. It might be later though."

"Well, it'll have to be before the thaw or a month later. I can handle them. I'll see you as far as Little Salt Lake. You work out of Tucson, eh? You ought to know Senator Blaise Montgomery then."

"Anybody that doesn't?"

"Great speaker," said Jury. "I heard him give a eulogy when I was down one time. Choked a man up, I can tell you."

They shook hands on the deal and Grif left.

The desert was ablaze with spring when he returned. Flame tipped the scraggly branches of the ocotillo, mats of wildflowers clung to the earth and the spreading arms of the saguaro held clusters of waxy white blooms too delicate for the giant cactus. He thought of Kate as he rode into town, of how she would look, how he would come up behind her to drop a kiss in her hair. In his veins, the lusty sap of spring ran strongly. It was the time of sweet fever. It was marrying time.

Tired from fifteen miles on the trail, he went to the hotel early. He was in a deep, drugged sleep when a hand shook him rudely awake.

"Snap out of it!"

He sat up, his gun magically in his hand. Neither he, nor the man by the bed, seemed to know where it had come from. But the visitor, moving back a step, exclaimed: "Easy!" It was Broderick. "They've knocked over another one!"

"Another what?" Sleep lay soddenly on Grif's mind.

"Stagecoach, dammit! The shotgun messenger just rode in. They killed Pat Coleman, the driver, and took the stage out near Pointer Mountain. The passengers are waiting at the station there. I've sent a buckboard out to pick them up."

"That the best you could do?"

"No. I've got ten new Concords in the stage barn, but I'm saving them for the King of England's party... I don't know what you can do now," he said, "but I knew you'd beller if I didn't tell you and probably if I did."

Grif sat with his head in his hands, trying to wake up. "All right, kid. Thanks. Go back to bed."

Broderick was at the door when Grif's head snapped up. "By grabs!" Broderick waited. Grif padded to the bureau, lit a candle, and rummaged through a drawer. He came up with a wrinkled fold of paper. "Yes, sir! Know how to load and fire a cannon, Johnny?"

"What are you doing now? Recruiting for the artillery?"

"The Tucson light artillery. Wait till I get my britches on..."

They left the silent hotel. The night was cool. In the stage corral, horses moved restlessly or lay on the ground. In all the pueblo there were no sounds but the distant yapping of dogs. They skirted the corral to cross the plaza and approach the church. The Territorials' little brass six-pounder sat on its pedestal like a muzzled watchdog.

"There's a ramrod inside the church, and probably powder and wadding. I wonder if they lock it?"

They did not. A small keg of powder rested in an alcove just inside the door. There was a ramrod like a mop, and a coil of fuse. Grif found a tin can and got a scoop of powder. They inserted the fuse, rammed home a charge, and Grif took time to explain.

"I've got a roster of those tin soldiers of Benteen's. The cannon will bring them on the run. Benteen may not be in town to call the roll, so it's going to be up to you. Check the ones that are absent. They'd all know me, but if you yell loud enough and keep your hat pulled down, they may not stop to ask questions. When you get through, start them through the gate on the double. Then cut for the stage depot."

Broderick thought about it, grinned, and groped for matches. "Sometimes," he said, "I think the Admiral was right."

He touched flame to the tip of the fuse.

The fuse sputtered down, a little fountain of fire erupted from the fuse hole. The fieldpiece belched a cloud of blazing gases as big as the church. The shattering roar of it barreled over the town. There was a resounding silence, an instant of tense waiting, and then lights began to come on. Grif ran back to the church. Broderick stood by the gun.

In about five minutes the first of them appeared, pulling on coats and buttoning trousers as they ran. "Fall in!" Broderick walked a little way off and pretended to watch for the rest. They came straggling from all points, some, from the saloons, moving not too steadily. The voice of Bay-Rum Brown came plaintively.

"What's the matter, Doc?"

"Doc ain't here," Broderick snapped. He produced the roster, held it to catch the silvery frost of moonlight, and began to call the roll. Heydenfeldt was absent. Maroon, of course, was not present, and four other men did not answer to their names. Broderick replaced the roster in his pocket. Men were beginning to stir and ask questions.

"Dress up those lines!" Broderick shouted.

They got into a semblance of military formation. "Column of twos—column right—march!"

By sheer weight of authority, he managed to carry it. He fired another order and they cut through the hole in the wall. "On the double—march!" They broke into a shuffling run. Broderick turned and darted back to the church. He and Grif plunged into the alley behind Pennington Street and returned to the depot. Johnny broke into a laugh. "Wonder how far those monkeys will go before they stop!"

But Grif looked at the clock and pensively filled his pipe. "You can go back to bed," he said. "I'm going over to Annie's. There's a theory that a man who's been in a scrape gets a hunger for two things: liquor and women. I'm betting those boys will come back to town tonight. The way it looks, I'd guess they left the coach somewhere for the others to pick up, and cut back to town. If they come back, they aren't going to have a cup of cocoa and go to bed with a hot brick. They're going to have a bellyful of whiskey and go to bed with a floosy. But when they come in that door, I'm going to be waiting for them."

He got his pipe going and went to the door. After a moment, Broderick extinguished the lamp. He went out with him.

It was twelve-fifteen, but things were still lively at Annie's. At the faro tables, the case-keepers hunched over their boxes. The professor's white, raucous fingers thumped the piano and the girls behind the rope danced or sat on the bench making eyes at woman-hungry patrons. The smells were of tobacco and beer and dust from the packed earth floor. For a moment Grif stood within the doorway, his eyes questing through the room. No sign of Gus Heydenfeldt; no sound of Benteen.

They stood at the bar a half hour, nursing beers, before they could get a table. As they went to claim it, Grif said, "Here's the caper. We tell them we're holding them till they can explain to Pete Deuce where they've been. If they go for their guns, all we can do is the same."

The table was close to the piano and it was too noisy to converse. They played can-can, drank beer, and watched the doors. Through a slit in the curtain, Grif could see the rear vestibule. Broderick watched the front.

By one o'clock, they were sick of can-can and warm beer. The girls were getting more haggard-looking. A couple had gone out and others came to take their places. The edge was off the fun, but girls and patrons kept playing because they had things to forget or wanted something to remember. A burly cavalryman tossed his partner like a doll.

All at once Grif laid down his cards. The curtain had stirred; there was a brief view of a man slapping his Stetson against his leg to beat the dust from it. He started up the stairs, and another man who followed him paused to glance through the curtain into the saloon. By luck, he looked straight into the attentive face of Holbrook. It was Ira Prentiss. Prentiss, the pimp and would-be killer. He literally fell back from the curtain, tried to duck through the side door and banged into someone entering, leaped for the stairway then and disappeared.

Grif was around the table, barging through the crowd and jumping the rope to plunge across the crowded dance floor. He heard Johnny's spurs jingling behind him. The vestibule was empty, but it held still the echoes of men climbing the stairs. He mounted, the muzzle of his Dragoon Colt going first. He stopped on the landing; at once the gun flashed and set his shoulder back. A shot came from above, ricocheted with a howl from the wall. The men above ran on.

Grif followed more carefully. On the second floor, a girl cried shrilly and a door opened. Her cry ended as a door banged. He ran up the steps three at a time, letting himself sprawl at the top. A shot filled the hall with its thunder and the hanging lamps blinked, sent up rings of smoke, and flared again. Two men huddled at the end of the hall. Prentiss was holding the little bootleg pistol Grif remembered from Mesilla. He looked at it in dumb panic, trying to make it fire. The other man was Noah Benteen. He was unarmed and stood with his back against the wall and his fingertips almost touching the ceiling.

"Don't shoot, man! Ira—drop that thing!"

Prentiss dropped it. Its charges had either fouled or not been replaced since the stage holdup that night. He looked like a slightly seedy weasel trapped in the corner of a hen-house. His pallid, skinny face was whiskered with a spare stubble.

Annie Benson appeared from the other leg of the corridor, wearing a negligee and with her hair up in papers. She carried a pistol approximately the size of a man's thigh. "All of you . . . !" she cried. "Drop your guns!"

Grif said tautly: "Sorry, Annie. But I've flushed a honker this time, and I'm not letting him get away. They killed another of my drivers tonight. I've got reason to think the men who did it are up here. Hold that gun on Doc and this other man. Did you recognize the girl who screamed?"

Annie stood there, not understanding it but grimly determined not to be outmaneuvered. After a moment she turned the gun on the doctor and Prentiss. "It sounded like Rose. Number Eight is hers."

Grif found Number Eight just beyond where he stood. As he approached it, he heard a muffled screaming. He turned the knob, kicked the door open, and waited beside it. The cries were profane, angry and terrified, and accompanied by a wild threshing. He was about to glance inside when Broderick lunged past him into the room. Grif expected a gun to blast him into eternity. But there was no sound, and he followed him. In the light of a table lamp, he saw a girl crawling from beneath the bed.

"I'll kill them! What kind of doings is that? Breaking into a girl's room, hitting her on the jaw and kicking her under the bed! Where are they? I'll scratch their ...!"

The room was empty, but the window above the street was open. Broderick and Grif stood at it, staring down into the street. Below was a wooden awning over the sidewalk. In the dark street boots thudded rapidly, and then a vague shape lurched from under the awning. A gun flashed. They dug back. A bullet popped through the oiled rawhide of the raised panes. Johnny edged up to the open lower section again and fired across the street. There was a burst of return fire. By the time he and Grif were ready to chance another look, there came the muffled staccato of running horses.

Grif stood an instant swallowing his gall. So close! He could send the Regulars out after them, he guessed, but on the dark open desert it would be difficult to find a freight wagon, let alone mounted, hard-riding men.

"Who were they?" he demanded.

Rose was pulling a green silk kimono about her and scanning her bruised jaw in a mirror. "The dirty, lousy ...! There were two of them. Gus Heydenfeldt and that Jim Maroon. What was the matter with them? Jim's always been sweet as pie to me. I'm going to have a lump like an egg on my jaw."

20

ANNIE BENSON'S apartment was decorated in what Grif supposed would be considered good taste. There were flowered rugs, some decent armchairs, deep-framed photographs on the walls, a glass-shaded lamp on a flimsy-looking table. There was even a small harpsichord—a virginal. It all seemed too pink and cluttered to him. He sat in an armchair that threatened to engulf him, and listened to Annie talking intensely to Noah Benteen. Pete Deuce had gone with Prentiss to the little mud jail on the plaza. The obscene, defiant little fox had had nothing to say.

"If you'd just lay off the liquor, Doc," Annie pleaded, "you wouldn't get mixed up in things like this! What in heaven's name persuaded you to help kill that man?"

Benteen sat with his elbows on his knees and his fingers linked, gloomily contemplating a vase of flowers in the rug. "I told you I wasn't with them. I just ran into them on the road."

"Do you ride much at night?" Grif inquired.

"Too much—whenever somebody's sick. Vicente Calcadillos came for me about seven. He said his wife was dying of asthma. Hell! Nobody ever dies of asthma. They only wish they could. But I went out with him."

"And it took you five and a half hours to make the trip?"

"After I got through I went to Ramon Blanco's cantina, on the Tubac road. Gus and Jim and Prentiss came in just as I was leaving. How should I have known where they'd been! Maroon said it was a lie about him trying to kill you, but he was staying out of town until you quit gunning for him. He

135

was just sneaking in with Gus for a drink."

"Then why did you sprint upstairs with them when Prentiss saw me starting for you?"

Benteen's rutted face turned ironic. "What would you do, with everybody pulling guns and yelling. 'Let's get out of here!' I thought it was an Indian raid."

Grif shook his head. "How do I know you went to Blanco's after you left Calcadillos? Maybe you rode up to Pointer Mountain afterwards. I've been watching you a long time, Doc. I knew you'd slip sooner or later. I didn't know how many of your crowd were in the stage gang, but I know now. Broderick and I assembled them and called the roll tonight. I was surprised there weren't more. I suppose the rest of your pack stays in the hills, eh?"

Benteen said: "Now you're talking like a Republican again. I tell you my politics are all above the board. If they're wrecking a Northern stage line, that's all to the good, but I don't approve of the way they're doing it, and I wouldn't lay hand to it myself."

"I wouldn't bet Judge Meyer would swallow that."

Benteen winced. Charlie Meyer was a druggist by profession and a jurist by avocation; he was short on legal knowledge but long on dispatch, and he was popular with the citizens because he was three hundred miles closer than the county courthouse and had a fondness for scaffolds.

"Holbrook," Benteen said levelly, "if you put me in jail you're going to have sixteen kinds of hell on your hands. Whatever you think of me, the Territorials are behind me a hundred per cent. They'll break your jail apart and set fire to the depot. Sure, you can lock me up. But Tucson will never be the same."

Annie gave Grif a verifying nod. "Why don't you bind Doc over to me for probation? I believe him, Grif. Every scrape he's ever got into has been because of liquor. I'll see to it that he stays off whiskey for a while."

"Mescal," Benteen corrected. "I can carry my whiskey as well as the next man. It's this damned Mexican slop! On whiskey," he said, "a man can write poetry or reduce fractures; at least until a hundred proof ain't strong enough. Back in Tennessee I was doing both. But people in cities don't like doctors who hiccup. So I came West. Where I found mescal. But what do I try when the mescal quits working?"

"The wagon," Annie said. "You'll report to me three times a day: ten, four, and ten."

Grif had a feeling that Benteen could do what he said, and he accepted the terms.

Benteen got out of the chair. On the way to the door, he paused to examine a decanter of brandy. "Liquor!" he murmured fondly. "A fine, God-anointed idea. But faulty, like every other invention of the All-Wise. There's no apple so fine you can't find a bruise on it. Sunsets . . . either they're over too soon and leave you hungry, or they last too long and you see there was too much red in them. Excuse me, Annie," he said. "It's the fumes of the mescal I've drunk rising again. But someday I'll get off it, and these hands will be as steady as Holbrook's." He laughed. "Yes, and when Benteen gets off the mescal it will be because they've run out of it!"

Annie smiled sadly. "Poor Doc! Sometimes it makes me sick that I should be in a business that leads men to that. At least I don't sell mescal."

Grif started to get up, but she said, "Don't go. I want to talk to you. Even with all these people around, I get lonesome. Lonesome for somebody who thinks the way I do."

She poured brandy for him but took none herself. "You hurt me the other night. Did you know that?"

"I know, Annie. But what I meant—"

"I know what you meant. And why should I have expected that you would dream of buying perfume for a—a saloon madam?"

He saw that she was getting sentimental. He felt uncomfortable, and took a quick bracer of brandy. "Anyhow, you're different. You could pass for a dressmaker if you wanted."

"Tell me something," Annie said. "How does a man feel about a woman in my business?"

"That's a straight question. I reckon a man kind of wonders how she can sleep nights, for worrying about her girls. Not to mention the customers."

"I don't worry about the girls, because I won't take one who hasn't been at it on her own. And the customers can worry about themselves. They don't worry about us, do they?"

"I keep thinking that you're in the wrong line, anyway. That you ought to be running a boardinghouse or something."

"Well, I didn't pick this work because I liked it. I was just another miner's wife in Grass Valley ten years ago. Then my husband was killed in an explosion. I had to make a living somehow, and someone told me the miners in Washington Territory were paying three hundred dollars apiece for brides. I could see there was a need. I got together a dozen girls in Sacramento and took them up the coast. The work sort of came naturally. But of course you know I—I mean—"

"That was the first thing Bay-Rum Brown told me about you," Grif said.

Her eyes decorously evaded his. She picked up a book that lay under the lamp and opened it. "Do you like poetry, Grif? It's just about all I have of beauty out here. A woman named Browning wrote this. I think it's beautiful.

How do I love thee? Let me count the ways.
I love thee to the depth and breadth and height
My soul can reach, when feeling out of sight
For the ends of Being and ideal Grace
I love thee...."

The words had a music, a flow, and he found himself lulled, though somehow stimulated. Suddenly she stopped reading and looked up at him. "Shore is pretty," he agreed. He ran his fingers through the thick mane of his hair. "But it's not getting any earlier. Thanks for the brandy, Annie."

He stood. Annie Benson rose and came to him, her eyes holding him, and standing that way in the softening rays of the lamp she seemed small and dainty and desirable. He experienced a tingle.

"Grif," she said, "that poem was me talking to you. Maybe you've got to be a woman to feel it, particularly a woman at my time of life. Not young and not yet old. My last chance for love."

He stood stiffly, wanting to touch her, on the very point of possessing her, but thinking with his conscience of

Katie... He groped. "I reckon you'll find somebody one of these days."

"I have found somebody. Only he can't seem to find me." Her hands came to his shoulders and she gave him a little shake, while her lips smiled poignantly. "What's the matter with me, Grif, that you can't see me for my thirty-six years? They say I'm strong. They think that flatters me. But, oh, how I want to be weak!"

He searched for the words. "Ain't nothing wrong with you, Annie. But you know about me and Katie. We're getting married as soon as our house is ready."

Annie shook her head. "Are you really going to do that to those kids? Can't you see they're in love with each other?"

"Katie in love with Broderick?" He gave a loud guffaw. "Why, she hates the young idiot!"

"The way Frankie hated Johnny. She hates him with all her heart, and it's breaking right in two. You're not going to marry that child, Grif, because of what it would do to them—to you."

Snatching his hat, he started in blind, speechless rage for the door. She clutched his arm. "Grif, listen to me! If you never look at me again don't do it! Stop and think! Why, when she's forty, you'll be seventy. When she's sixty—"

"Shut up!" he roared. "A woman in your line ought to know love when she sees it."

"But you see, I know infatuation too. I've always said that boys should play with dolls just like girls, because too many of them get to yearning for a doll after they reach middle age."

He faced around, wanting to hurt her, himself hurt with the aching knife of doubt and jealousy she had thrust into his bowels. "When you talk about love, I reckon you and I are thinking of two different things. With you, love comes wrapped in a two-dollar bill."

He saw her face break up into crying lines. He closed the door and went out. A clammy emptiness in him robbed him of the victory he had won.

21

THE TRIAL OF Ira Prentiss was a brief affair solemnized only by Charlie Meyer's gavel. On the druggist's desk rested his legal library: a volume on *Materia Medica* and a treatise on fractured bones. In broken German-English he shouted questions at Prentiss, rode down his attempts to cavil, and sentenced him to hang in a month.

Grif took Pete Deuce aside. "I've put the screws on this prisoner of yours to tell me who ramrods the gang he ran with. I said I'd turn him loose if he would talk. He won't. Now, since he's got to hang anyway, would you have any objection to me building the scaffold right away?"

Deuce did not object.

"I'm going to build a scaffold Tucson can be proud of. Trapdoor and everything. But we don't want any slip-ups, so that's why I'd like to start stretching the rope as soon as it's built. I've seen them drop and the rope stretch till they were standing on the ground! In a month we'll have all the give yanked out of that hemp."

Deuce chuckled. "And most of it out of Prentiss' nerves, eh?"

Grif's grin was hard with the dregs of his soul-sickness. He had not been able to tear the rotten shreds of jealousy from his eyes all night. He had invited his soul to its ease, setting out the memories of all that had passed between him and Katie. But on all of them he could read the label: gratitude. Gratitude for giving her a job, for putting a frame of respectability around her. It was not the kind of love he wanted. He hated the spiteful tongue of Annie Benson and hoped she had passed a night like his.

He took a crew of Mexicans over to set up the scaffolding, bossing the work himself. Four stout poles to support the platform. Two tall ones with a crosspiece for the rope. A simple trapdoor with a sliding bolt. They had it done by sundown. He brought a sack of sand from the depot and as he tied the rope and gave the lever a yank, sending the sack into a dead, lurching drop, he could see Prentiss' small white face at the window of the box-like jail. The new rope made a little cry as the strands squealed.

He put two men on it that night. They were to drop the sack once every fifteen minutes.

In the morning, the sheriff reported that the prisoner had walked the floor most of the night. Yet he was not ready to talk, even for his freedom. It was not sturdiness of soul, Grif realized. He had thirty days in which to be liberated, one way or another, whereas if he talked and went free he might never get out of town before the Territorials exacted vengeance.

Holbrook's bottled jealousy would not stay under pressure any longer. When he walked Kate home that night, he put it bluntly.

"Annie Benson thinks you and Johnny are in love."

She stared at him, then her laugh tinkled. "That's all Annie Benson knows! He's too cocky to love anyone. And as far as my loving him goes—" She dismissed it with a sniff.

"Why did you cry when you caught him and Helen together, then?"

"Grif, I told you before. It made me realize I must have looked as cheap to other people as she did to me. Now, stop tormenting yourself."

He might have been wrong. But her shortness with him seemed to stem more from uncertainty of herself than from impatience with a jealous lover. He could not warm himself against this chilliness in the atmosphere of his Indian summer.

He found a recent copy of a St. Louis paper in the restaurant that night and gloomily read the political news. A fist fight on the floor of Congress. Some business about South Carolina demanding that Fort Sumter be evacuated: an insult to Southerners to have guns held over them.

He had a feeling of things rushing to a climax. War was on the march, sure as fate. One of these days stagecoaches would be racing west, consigned to a miracle man known as Grif Holbrook, who would have a dozen other Concords ready to throw into the caravan, provisions for the hegira, and all information on the safest route to California. Or was it merely a cut-proud stud whinnying ridiculously after a filly, too lost in sick dreaming to follow the main target?

He went over to the jail in the morning, primed for business. A broken, saw-tooth edge of temper was in him. Deuce let him in. Prentiss' cell was littered with pipe dottle and old newspapers. Prentiss stood at the east window, from which he could see the cemetery rather than the scaffold. In the plaza, the trapdoor creaked and the sack hit the end of the rope with a thud. Prentiss started. He turned, showing Holbrook a face he hardly knew. Loops of loose skin hung beneath his eyes. The flesh of his face had withered into wrinkles.

Grif sat on the cot. "That's going on for another twenty-eight days," he said. "Unpleasant, ain't it?"

Prentiss looked out the window again.

"I'll make a deal any time you say the word," Holbrook continued.

Prentiss spat on the floor. It somehow enraged Grif. He crossed the floor and spun the man about. His fist collided with Prentiss' mouth. Prentiss went back onto the wall. Men did strange things when they were frightened. Prentiss' eyes filled with tears and he looked as though he would cry.

"We'll just add this to your diet—" Grif panted. "One trouncing after the morning meal." He yanked him close and smashed him again in the face. Prentiss covered his mouth with one hand and sobbed.

"Who is it?" Grif snapped.

Prentiss shook his head. Something had broken loose in Holbrook. Prentiss was merely the whipping boy, the target. Grif caught him by the stock and began to slap him, bringing the blood to his cheeks, snapping his head about and finally driving his fist again into the little man's face. Ira Prentiss fell across the cot.

Grif loomed over him. "I don't tire quick," he said. "I think we'll make that three times a day. And we'll cut your food down to tortillas and water. I'm kind of worried there won't be enough left of you to hang, though."

Prentiss lay there trembling. Grif walked to the door. "It's a funny thing," he said. "If I were in your shoes, I'd talk. Then I'd stay here until night. Right after dark the cell door would come unlocked and more'n likely there would be a fast pony behind the jail. I'd cut out that east wall, and I'll bet nobody would know I was gone until I was forty miles on my way to the Coast. In two months I'd be raising hell with Aimee, on the Barbary Coast."

Prentiss sat up. The bloody, stricken look of him twisted through Grif, shaming him. "Are you lyin'?" he whispered.

"I'm talking straight at you. As far as you're concerned, the game's over. The best you can hope for is to get out with a whole hide. This is your last chance. Don't get the idea anybody's going to rescue you, because I've got the lid on the Territorials right now."

Prentiss came to him. He looked out the barred door. He said in a whisper: "You ain't going to believe this. There's only a dozen of us know. It's your old pard, the Senator!"

Holbrook stood there, receiving the impact of it.

"You don't look so surprised," Prentiss said. He sounded disappointed.

"It could be. It shore could be!" Grif murmured.

He was back in the plaza at Mesilla, being schooled in what to expect by the pompous old Senator. *"A lot of us are tired of being hind titmen at the chewed dugs of the ship of state!"* He was at Apache Pass in a cold, foggy dawn, hearing him say: *"I'll be blessed if Ah'll sit up there. Get a most frightful pain...."* An hour later, the coach had overturned. And he was recalling his refusal to ride to the Babocomari Valley fight; and reading once more a leaflet taken from a dead man's body! *"... no political axes to grind... welcome you if you have, like us, become tired of being hind titmen of the political farrow."*

It could, with no taxing of the imagination, be the dear old Senator.

"What about the stages?" he demanded. "Where are they keeping them?"

Prentiss' eyes pleaded for acceptance. "I don't know. Honest to God! Some place in the Dragoons, I think. They moved them last month after you jumped that bunch at Stone Corral Spring. That was only three or four of them. The rest were spotted in the Galiuros, but the Senator was afraid you'd scout that area too close. He sent me over to Pointer Mountain to wait for the word to jump the next. He was getting leery of Apache Pass, too."

He seemed beyond dissimulation. The spigot of truth was turned on and he could not stop it.

"I'm not going to lock this door when I go out," Grif told him. "I'll send a horse over with saddlebags full of grub. You can leave any time you want. Personally, I'd wait till it's dark."

Prentiss said humbly: "Thanks, Grif. I—I'm sorry about it all. But you get into these things, you know. Aimee wanted to hit the high spots, and this looked like a quick way to get some money. But all I've got out of it was board and found, and a hell of a scare."

Holbrook went back to the depot and picked up Johnny."Hang on, kid! Prentiss says the he-boar is Senator Montgomery. We're going down and see him."

Broderick walked beside him with his typical swagger. "It's about time. I've been watching him for a month. Heydenfeldt's been down there every day. I found tracks behind the print shop this morning where four horses had been tethered last night. But somebody'd driven Prentiss' nag down to the canal."

22

THE SUN WAS over their heads, yellow and heatless, throwing sharp shadows as they strolled down Correo Street. Two Mexicans went by beating a rawhide drum and blowing a horn, advertising a *baile*. The pueblo went about its business as if nothing had changed. But something had. The guns of destiny were on full cock.

The office of the *Tucsonian* was deserted. A note on the door said: *Back at two p.m.* Grif tried the door. It opened, and he entered quietly and crossed the shop floor to open the door of the Senator's apartment. He was not there. A cool tingling ran down Grif's back as he walked out.

"Well, we can't rush it. I'll get him talking and then put the bite on him before he knows it's happened. We'll have to keep an eye on the place from the saloon until he comes back. Johnny, you don't know what this means to me! To get out of this hell-hole! All of a sudden I feel like I couldn't stand another twenty-four hours of it. I don't know what it is. It's brought me good luck, but it's brought me plenty of bad."

"It's brought me," Johnny said, "a pain in the neck. What do you aim to do after you get him?"

"Try to find out from him where the stages are. If I can, I'll take the Regulars out there and recover them. Then set down and wait for things to pop. If war don't come in another month, I'll write the Admiral that everything's under control and tell him to send out another man, because I'm quitting. Or, shoot! Maybe you'd like the job?"

Broderick shook his head. "No. If you get your loop on

him, I'll get out tomorrow on the eastbound. I'm sick of the place myself."

Looking at him, Grif thought of the contrast between him now and the way he had first seen him, tromping manfully into the stage depot as if he could lick any man alive and kiss any girl in the world. Cocky as all git-out and full of fun. He reflected that he had hardly seen him smile in a month; that when he played his concertina at all, it was something like "The Letter Edged in Black," or "Little Joe, the Wrangler": sad songs to make a cowboy cry.

There was only one soil that would nurture such a weed of gloom, and that was a young man's heart. Again he thought of night before last, at Annie's. *"Don't do it to them, Grif!"* Her lying, jealous tongue! But she had left a drop of gall in his soul, and because it was still sour on his tongue he decided to make a test.

"Well, if you don't want it," he said. "But it's a chance to get established, you know. Some day you'll want to get married, and the money will matter."

Johnny spat.

"You don't seem to be much for the ladies, do you?" Grif speculated. "Ain't a better way of passing the time than in a girl's arms, though. By Ganny! Katie's a lovin' one when you get her in the mood. Kisses like a French dancer!"

Only by a sharp bulge of jaw muscles did Broderick react.

Grif chuckled to himself. "Other night we went over to the house on Jackson to measure it for rugs. There's an old cot there. We sat down for a minute and I bit her on the ear. By grabs, Johnny, she like to went up in smoke! I swore I'd have to rush her right over to a preacher to make an honest woman of her. Some are like that. Some could set next to an iceberg and make it shiver. But others, like Katie—wheew!"

Broderick swung around, gray-faced, eyes black as old coals. "Will you shut your lecherous mouth? She's no chippy, for that kind of talk."

Sleek satisfaction moved over Holbrook. "Why, Johnny! What's she to you?"

Broderick's face worked, then he turned and went on up the road. Grif paced him. "In love with her too, aren't you?"

"So I am—what of it? You've got her. You haven't seen me mooning around over her, have you? Why, you'd go into hysterics if she so much as let it slip that she thought Romeo had anything you haven't. Besides money," he added.

"She's marrying me for money, is she?"

"Why else? You're twice her age. There was me around if she'd wanted love."

"Oh! She's in love with you, now!"

"I wouldn't be surprised. Lots of them have been. I was making pretty good headway till you came along."

"I didn't come with a bankbook in my hand. The way I figure it, some women like solid gold and some like tinplate."

"And Katie," Broderick snapped, "seems to like tinplate. Well, she's yours, and welcome. I'm taking off tomorrow. You don't have to cry any alligator tears for me, either. Couple of nights with one of those El Paso *chamacas* and I'd have to look in my address book to remember Kate Crocker's name."

Grif hunched over a beer in the half-empty Congress Bar. Through the window he could glimpse the hitch-rack behind the print shop, down near the canal. His mind stayed on Broderick. He was a little sorry about it. Johnny wasn't a bad kid. He would make a pretty fair man, when he got around to growing up. But, since somebody's heart had to be broken, it might as well be his.

Sex, he decided, was a powerful, sweet, and dangerous thing. He flicked a fly out of the foam of his beer and wondered what would happen if, say, all of a sudden there wasn't any sex. What would happen to the perfume people? Ruined! And the people who made hoop skirts and jewelry and women's hats? Yes, and tight boots like these which were strangling his feet right now. It began to seem as though sex had been invented for the personal profit of the manufacturers.

But on the credit side were an end to murders and a lot of excessive drinking. But, by and large, it was all worth it. It was like living with a bomb, but a thoroughly wonderful and stimulating time bomb.

The afternoon wore slowly away, but he did not leave the table. Stiff and bored, he decided to chance a run down to the depot.

He found Kate alone. "Listen, don't do anything about those curtains! We're getting out before long."

"What's happened?"

"We'll just say that the trout's about to rise to the bait. But my guess is that in a month we can leave. We'll be dickering for a ranch in Los Angeles by spring."

"Wonderful!"

At the door he turned, keeping his eyes on her face. "By the way—make out a pass for Johnny, will you?"

A quick brightness of interest warmed in her face. "Oh? Are you sending him somewhere?"

"No. Johnny's quitting, Katie. He says I don't need him any more, and there's nothing to hold him here. Kind of miss him, won't we?"

She started to speak, but didn't; she moistened her lips and continued to stare at him. "That—that's too bad..."

He went back, suddenly gripped by the same sadistic anger that possessed him when Prentiss defied him. He had her arm. "You don't have to lie to me," he snapped. "If you love him, you can say so."

She flung away from him. "Grif, if you ever ask me that again, I'll tell you I do just to hurt you! Now stop it! Or, if you've tired of *me* already, why you can just say so and I'll—"

He pulled her close. He wanted to say something tender, but the words weren't there. He just held her against him until she signified by moving that she wished to be released. She looked up, tears shining in her eyes but smiling again.

"Let's not talk about Johnny any more, or Annie Benson, or anybody but us. I don't like to argue with you, and there's no sense in it, feeling the way we do."

He patted her cheek. "It's going to be all right," he murmured, "just as soon as we get out of this town. It does something to people. Nobody seems very happy around here."

Afterwards he remembered his bargain with Ira Prentiss and filled a saddlebag with food, which he fixed behind the saddle of a long-legged dun. He led it over to the jail. Deuce was not there. He paused under the window to say: "Any time, pardner."

People did not seem very happy in the Congress saloon that afternoon, coming and going as aimlessly as the irritable wind rushing up and down the street. Sig Johnson came in at dusk from a short haul to Cienega Springs. He was tired and dusty. The blocky-shouldered Swede brought a rough

freshness with him, however. He had a couple of drinks with
Grif, and was proposing another when Grif sat back against
the chair.

Down the winding street, limned against the darkness of
sunset fields beyond, a rider jogged across the canal and up
to the print-shop. Here he dismounted and, after a glance
about, walked out of view down the alley between the shop
and the next building. Grif got up hastily. "Excuse me, Sig."

Johnson belched. "What's the matter? Ain't I—?"

In the street it was chilly. Dark clouds massed over the
pueblo. The night wind pressed the ragged mesquite bushes
flat. In the streets, everyone hurried along as if he must be
indoors before dark, while far down the street a woman
stood in a doorway and screeched at a child. Grif crossed the
street and started down the arroyo to the back of the newspaper office.

He saw no light in the office when he reached it. He
glanced at the pony, which was a blue roan powdered with
dust and carrying a wooden saddle. He did not recognize it
nor the brand. He walked through the alley and around to
the front. A moment he stood, regarding the lightless front
of the building. Curtains drawn in the Senator's apartment.
No light behind the other window. No sound, no smoke
from the chimney, but a man was in there.

Grif went up and knocked. Getting no answer, he pushed
the door open. Now he had a brief glimpse, through the
crack of the door, of a man pressing against the wall behind
the door. He started through—abruptly to lunge against the
door and drive it hard against the man who stood there. He
heard a startled grunt as the man was crushed against the
wall, and he flung it back, then, and smashed at the man's
face without waiting to see who it was. He felt the good ache
of that blow in his forearm and drew back for another, and
then he knew the man who stood there, and held it in
surprise.

23

HE FLIPPED THE man's gun out of its basket-weave holster and turned it on him. He was just coming out of the daze of that unanticipated blow to the jaw. It was Bill Jury, the ferryman from Lee's Ferry, the bar-browed little barrel of a man who was going to be of such help in getting those Concords to Salt Lake City. He shook his head and rubbed his jaw, beginning to talk fast.

"Golhorn you, Holbrook! You drunk? That's a nice way to treat a feller, as is going to help you!"

"The Senator," Grif said, "has what I'd call a wide circle of acquaintances."

Jury fumbled. "I—sure, I know the Senator. Everybody does. I used to live here, you know. I just hauled in. Thought I'd shake hands with him."

"Do you always hide behind doors to shake hands?"

Jury spat; there was blood in the spittle. "Well, I never knew who it was knocking, and I kind of—"

"Light the lamp," Grif snapped.

Jury went past him and touched a match to the wick of a lamp on the composing bench. Grif drifted in. It was wicked, what had to be done, but it was no more wicked than what had been happening to a lot of good Northerners around here. The gun-barrel fell silently, and Bill Jury made a long, tongueless "Aghhhhh!" in his throat and slipped down.

Grif muttered: "Yes, you'd shake hands with your old friend and tip him off to whichaway I was going, eh? You lay there, you barrel-chested little demon, till I decide what to do with you!"

He could kill him, but that seemed extreme and unwise. On the other hand, he couldn't keep him locked up forever, and once he got loose that busy mouth of his was going to babble all the things he knew about the Oxbow. He could plant an ambuscade at every turn between here and the City of the Saints. It was a cranky thing to decide, and it was like a breath of fresh air suddenly to remember Sig Johnson.

Johnson was still puzzled at having been deserted. But he let himself be taken aside and listened to what Grif had to say.

"Sig, you want to make a hundred dollars quick?"

"I always want to make a hundred dollars quick. But I'd rather make a hundred and fifty quick. If you're mixed up in it, I'd have lead balls tickling my back before I'm done."

"Aw, now! This is just a quick little trip to Sonora. I thought maybe I could talk you into picking up a cargo of hardware or something around here and running down to Hermosillo for a swap in wheat. Wheat's high, you know."

"Yes, and the Yaquis are hungry for yellow scalps like mine. Peddle that to somebody else."

Grif's stomach knotted. He thought of Jury lying there on the floor, perhaps coming to; perhaps already being tended by the Senator, and talking a mile a minute. But there was a strange thing. When he had searched the place for a cord, he had found the back rooms in a state of uproar, the desk emptied and a brick pried out of the hearth. There was every indication that the bird had flown the coop. But why? He couldn't have known, this soon, that Prentiss had talked. But it was an odd thing, and tightened a feeling of pressure about Grif.

"I'd be a low-assay coyote if I asked another favor of you," he said humbly.

Johnson's pale blue eyes watched him. "Yep. You would."

"Then that's what I am, because I'm asking it. I've got somebody I want packed out of town pronto. No, not dead. Too danged lively! Believe me, Sig—you're a Regular, and I think you feel the way I do about things—I've got my sights on a big one this time! But if this feller I'm speaking of starts talking, all the work you and I have done will be spoiled. I've got to freight him out of town before he gets loose on the street. I can't kill him, and I can't keep him locked up long.

So I thought if you could wrap him nice and snug in a tarp and take him along with you, it'd be about the finest thing a man had ever done for me."

Sig Johnson's gaze roved about the saloon. "Make it three hundred," he said.

Grif whistled. "Your loyalty comes higher all the time."

"This scalp of mine is practically irreplaceable."

Johnson rounded up his crew quickly. Work was not so plentiful that men could complain about going out the day after they came in. Just after dark Johnson drove a wagon down Correo Street and they went in and lugged Jury's trussed, gagged body out. Johnson told Grif he would camp five miles out of town and let his boys come back. But in the morning they would start, sure.

They shook hands again, liking and respecting each other, and Grif said: "Look out for them señoritas down there. They'll set a man's blood afire."

He went back into the office. Johnson's wagon rumbled off. Now the vague feeling of things being out of joint attacked him again. Again he went over the whole place and persuaded himself that Montgomery had hauled out. For good? For a trip? But there was no stage until tomorrow morning, and a man of the Senator's bulk did not ride far. It was apparent that he had left hurriedly, and this was the thing which disturbed him, for it seemed to indicate that Montgomery had some information that Grif did not—something which had sent him rushing from the town without even locking his door.

He pondered it as he strode through the early night back to the depot. Kate would be closing up. He swung into the station. Standing in the musty gloom, he heard voices faintly in the rear. Gooseflesh stole up his back. He was getting edgy, fancying spies behind every closed door. Yet he sensed emotion in the indistinct run of conversation, and he walked around the baggage counter and approached the office from the other entrance.

He listened. Someone was crying, a woman. And a man said, roughly but gently: "Well, what do you think it's going to do to me? But what else can I do? If I cut my finger, Katie, I get blood, not ice water."

Sobbingly, she said: "But I can't stand it alone! And you'll be after every girl in Texas just to spite me. I think that hurts worse than losing you."

The world rolled and thundered about him. He stood there. This was the apocalypse of the soul. This was the black chasm opening under his feet.

"Then maybe you can savvy what I felt every time I saw you kiss him... Wanting to kill him! Wanting to kill you! And yet loving you till—" He choked off. "And liking the big ox like a brother. God's got a hell of a sense of humor, honey. Set two men, alike as peàs in a pod, down by the same woman; two men wound up the same and ticking the same, and bound to fall in love with her. And then let them go it!"

She whispered, but Grif could hear it. "I'll never forget you, Johnny! Never!"

He turned blindly. He bumped against the counter and someone exclaimed, inside the office. As he passed through the door, he heard Katie cry: *"Grif!"*

At the hotel, he dug his chamois moneybag out of the straw pallet. He had three hundred and fifty dollars in gold. That would buy a party in any man's town. That would get him and all the girls he could get both arms around drunk as fools.

24

ANNIE BENSON REGARDED him suspiciously. Things were not busy yet and she had been sitting there in an isolated corner working on her accounts. The frost of their last conversation was still in her eyes. "A party? What kind of a party? You can buy all the whiskey you want right at the bar, if you want a party."

He spread his arms, driven to a kind of frantic, senseless humor. "I mean one that big! Girls! Whiskey! Dancing! And me in the middle of it."

She tapped her teeth with the pencil. "Grif, are you sick?"

Sick? He was dead. He shook a handful of goldpieces under her nose. "I want about four girls, a nice quiet room, and a table full of bottles. I've been working too hard. I'm going to relax. I'm going to dance the legs off those girls and when I get through drinking you won't know for two days whether I'm drunk or dead."

The gray-blue eyes pinched. They saw him steadily and saw him entire, and for an instant a quick, responsive sorrow was in them. Then she looked down. "You know I don't go in for that sort of thing, Grif."

"All right, the devil with you! They go in for it other places."

He started off, but Annie called: "Any way you want it. I'll tell some of the girls they're wanted. They don't generally come down this early, you know. Have a couple while they dress."

He could see himself in the backbar. Were those things eyes, or holes in his head? He moved farther along to where

154

there was no mirror. Mike, the huge, black-Irish bartender, poured the first. Number one of a series ending at infinity. He grabbed the bottle out of Mike's hand and finished pouring it himself. Mike looked at him in irritation, saw something in his face which checked his tongue, and moved off. Grif put the bourbon down quickly, neither tasting nor feeling it. In a dark room in his mind a maniac was screaming.

It could have been an hour later when the door swung in and Johnny Broderick stepped inside. He had a tense, worried look about him; in the doorway he stood looking the room over, tall, wide-shouldered; his thong-edged Stetson pulled down on his brow, a kind of lofty arrogance in his bearing. He saw Grif just as Grif saw him.

Joy leaped like a flame. Grif took one step away from the bar, whipped back the skirt of his box coat and found the trigger guard of his Colt. Johnny stood rigidly. Something struck soddenly in the face, clammy and blinding. He fought it off, had a glimpse of Mike standing with his arm pointing straight at Broderick and shouting one word:

"Out!"

Broderick was gone when Grif snatched the wet bar-towel from his face and got at his gun. Mike came to lean before him by his elbows, a big, calm, steady-eyed man. "I don't know what kind of a drunk you're starting, but I don't think we want it here. Now, if you want a real quick one, and cheap, I'll just tap you behind the ear with a bung starter. Otherwise—git."

Meekly, Holbrook said, "Annie's getting a room fixed up for me. I'm having a little party tonight. I won't be on your hands."

Mike was an understanding man, his sympathy not quite blinded by the cataracts of cynicism. He shook his head slowly. "Mr. Holbrook, you shouldn't do things like this. Whiskey ain't no good when you got a sorry. No good a-tall. Take my advice and go for a long ride; go huntin', or something. If you want to shake a rug, take it outside. Same thing with your mind. Take it out and air it."

Annie came quietly from the rear. She wore the false pleasantry of a physician putting a prognosis negative into a cheery lie. "All set! You're going to have your party in my room. Would you like that?"

The whiskey had already knocked the edge off his acuteness, but it had not found the broken razor-edged thing in his breast. He thought about it a moment. "Why, sure, Annie, if you don't mind getting your furniture broke up. Lead me to it."

Helen was there in her feathers and lace stockings and carmine. She had even added a beauty spot for the occasion. Rose was there with only a shadow of the bruise Maroon had given her on the jaw; she wore a green silk dress which exposed three-fourths of her bosom and made him hold his breath every time she took one. Myrtle, a henna'd beauty with a suspicion of Creole in her face, and a little blonde called Eunice, filled out the roster. Annie stayed around a while, getting things moving. She poured everyone a drink, placing one on the miniature harpsichord.

"Helen, play something for Grif on the virginal," she said.

Grif chuckled. "Annie, you had a sense of humor when you bought that."

Helen played in a tinkling fashion and presently Annie sang, "Oh, Willie, We Have Missed You." It all seemed extremely sad, and he had to blow his nose twice during the song. The room should have been rocking by now, but it was perfectly steady. He hadn't stopped drinking since he entered the place, but it had only given tears to a formerly dry grief. Suddenly he stared into his glass. He flung it into a corner with a roar and the music stopped. "Somebody's been cutting my likker! By God, if I ketch anybody cutting my likker—!"

Annie winced when she looked at the splotch on her rug. She brought another glass and a fresh bottle and let him pour it himself. "Nobody's been cutting your liquor. We want you to have a good time."

She left. He drank with growing terror. The whiskey was not touching it. It was not blurring the pictures that rose up before him.

"Mr. Holbrook, you're the sweetest man I've ever known. I'm going to kiss you . . . If I don't love you now, not really, I know I will, because admiring is only a step from loving . . ." And then: *"I'll never forget you, Johnny. Never!"*

He acquired a need to go downstairs. The backhouse was in the rear, under the steps. When he came out he saw a bunch of men at the bar talking with Pete Deuce. Deuce looked gray and shaken. Grif went up to him. "You need a drink," he said. "You look like hell."

Deuce did indeed look like hell, his face the color of an old canvas tarp. "I had to kill a man," he said. "I never killed a man before."

Benteen was there, the goateed fixture of the place. He was drinking beer. "Don't let it throw you, Pete. Who was it?"

Deuce frowned, trying to work himself back into a self-righteous mood. "Oh, he had it coming, all right. I only did my duty. You see, he wouldn't stop when I yelled halt. He kept right on riding, and I dropped him."

"Who?" Benteen demanded.

"Ira Prentiss. Somebody unlocked his cell and brought him a horse and grub. He was almost to the wall when I saw him."

It sank dully through his blunted senses. Prentiss shot, trying to escape. Then a great cry of horror rang in him; a fist squeezed his heart. He had forgotten to tell Pete about the arrangement! He had looked for him this morning... or yesterday morning—when the hell was it?—but he had not found him. He had taken a horse over and left it there.

Deuce placed both hands on the bar and seemed to stare at a face on it. "It was the way he went. He was shot through the lungs, but he kept trying to talk. 'We had a deal, we had a deal!' He kept saying that."

Benteen grunted. "That's plain enough. He was trying to confess. He wanted to say him and somebody else had a deal to knock over those stages. Ain't that how you figger it, Holbrook?"

It was somehow worse that Prentiss had died this way than that men had died trying to save their stages. A rabbit-souled man whose word was nothing had made a deal with a man he had thought too big, too far above him, to trick him. But he had walked right into it. I wonder if he'll tell God on me, Grif thought. Then he recollected that Prentiss would not likely be seeing God anyway. Little fella, he thought, I'd trade places with you.

He said, "That's the way I figger it."

He returned to Annie's room. He kept drinking, more and more grimly, but getting crazier all the time. He insisted on dancing with the busty girl called Rose, clumping like a fool and shouting his laughter in her face. She kept saying, "Mr. Holbrook, you be*have*!" Scared, but trying to handle him. He was aware of all these things with a part of his brain that was cold sober, but he was lurching about a warm, reeling, pink room in which nothing was real but a sharp, steel pain in his breast.

Once Prentiss came in. He plucked at his shoulder until he saw him, and whined: "We had a deal! Did you forget?"

Grif shouted: "Get out of here!" and Prentiss disappeared. The girls looked at each other. Myrtle tried to sneak out, but he caught her and whirled her into a dance.

It was not so much like experiencing all these things as trying to remember them. Once, it seemed, he had sat down and clapped both hands to his head, bellowing: "Where are they?"

"Where are what?"

"My horns!" Then he laughed, but they looked frightened, not getting it, not knowing about cuckolds having horns maybe, or maybe not even knowing they were dancing with a cuckold. An old cuckold wearing tight yellow boots.

And another time he and Annie were sitting on the sofa together. "Did they hurt you, Grif?" she asked him, with those gray mother's eyes of hers.

"Nobody hurts Grif Holbrook! They try to hurt me, I'll—"

She held both his hands and tried to look into his eyes. "*I* love you, Grif. Doesn't that matter?"

It was the first solid ground under him in a century; the world for an instant ceased to have bedsprings under it. There was what approached importance in that fact: Annie loved him. Then he recalled that he did not love her. "Nope. Don't matter."

But from this point things began rapidly to expand, rushing away from that spot in his breast which was like a clutching vulture's beak. All at once there was release; the whiskey was not the amber water it had been but a fountain tossing up visions of beautiful girls, gusts of melody, and causing him to shake with mirth at secret jokes. Then the fountain began to darken, and when he leaned over to see what it was trying to hide he lost his balance and toppled in, and, falling a long distance, he heard the music and laughter dying out behind him, and knew all at once that he was tired. Tired; dead; asleep. They were all the same. They were all night, and night was good.

But they would not let him rest.

They pulled and shrieked at him, and the loudest, most annoying voice of all was that of Broderick.

"Grif! Grif! Grif! Grif!"

The voice went on and on, rising and falling, and then there was a douche of ice water in his face and he lunged up with a grunt. Where the devil—! He sank back, the lees of ruin stirring in him. Still in Annie's room, but they were all gone, his houris. Nothing left but empty bottles, a fragrance of rose water and cigar smoke.

Then when he knew it was really Broderick—Broderick, with Noah Benteen and Annie Benson—he came up with a snarl and fumbled for the gun that wasn't there. But he knew in a moment he didn't want the gun. He merely wanted to obliterate Broderick and Katie from his life and his memory. He pushed him away with an oath. The room reeled.

Benteen was putting a glass in his hand. "Drink up," he said.

It went down at a gulp. His stomach rejected it, but his throat was adamant. "Wha' wazzat?"

"A little concoction of my own. Elixir of cigar ash. How do you feel?"

He felt sick, violently and suddenly sick. Broderick half carried him to the lavatory. The cigar ash brought up most of what he had drunk in the last hour of his sortie into purgatory. When he was through, white, limp, exhausted, he stumbled back. The floor was buckling under them, yet Broderick anticipated its lurches and kept him on his feet. He sat him down and stood over him in disgust.

"If I had a mold that looked like a man, I'd pour you into it. Try to get this, now: I've got a letter from the Admiral. A courier brought it a half hour ago. It's war! They've started the fighting!"

"Who's fightin'?"

"Oh, God!" Broderick groaned. "*This* is what's going to save the Union!"

25

WHEN HE TRIED to slip down and sleep, Benteen jerked him upright and slapped him back and forth across the face. He sat and took it, and because it was funny to see such excitement and concentration on the pudgy ram's face, he started laughing, deep haw-hawing laughter without a mind behind it.

Benteen poured coffee into him. "Straighten out, man! I'm supposed to be the drunk, not you. Don't you savvy now why the Senator lit out? He'd had word of it! He's going to run those stages to hell-and-gone before you ever catch up with him! You've got to snap out of it and find them."

Back they crept in a nasty little horde, all the anxieties and frustrations of the last two months. His mind flinched from them, but they raked their small, sharp teeth into him and held on.

Broderick made him drink some more coffee. "What are we going to do? How are we going to find them?"

He tapped Johnny on the chest. "You've got the girl; now you can have the job. But I'll make a deal with you. Gimme twelve hours' sleep and I'll come up with something."

"You'll come up with something now! It's a matter of hours, not days. Some place they may be hitching up right now, getting ready for the swing south. We've got to get out there. What did Prentiss tell you? Any idea where they were?"

Prentiss. Another thorn to fumble at and drive deeper. He sat in dumb misery, thinking about Prentiss.

With a groan, Johnny turned away. "What are we going to do, Doc?"

"Walk him."

They reeled down the stairway to the empty saloon, all dark except for one candle burning in a chandelier. The tables were covered with cloths and the bar was for once dry and shiny. Outside, it was perfectly quiet. The stars were lost behind clouds. A cold mist peppered his face; they walked into it and felt its sting and the astringent chill of cold desert air.

He began to recover a little. He muttered, "I kinda remember something—"

They whirled on him. "Remember what?"

"I remember that day we asked the Senator about a different route north. He kept asking what we were going to do, and I didn't tell him, but I said one thing was sure, that when we got the word we'd ship all the cash and important papers ahead of everything else, to get them out of town. He'd probably want that cash, wouldn't he?"

"Right! So we send a stageful of Regulars out with it, and when they jump us—"

Grif sighed. "When they jump us, all we got is them. We don't get any stagecoaches. So that won't work."

They walked gloomily into the mist.

The stage office was cold. A handful of fire burned dispiritedly on the hearth. There was Benteen, Broderick, Grif and Katie to soak up its warmth. Grif sat slumped before the fire, now relatively sober, but sick. Katie sat close to him and held his hand.

"Grif, dear, there's no use lying to ourselves any more. You don't love me either, you know. It never would have lasted. But I don't want it to end this way."

"Then shut up," Grif snapped. He jerked his hand away.

She arose tartly and walked out. Grif glanced at Benteen. "How do you get in on this conference?"

Benteen frowned. "I'll get out if you say so. But I've had the laying-on of hands since that Pointer Mountain fracas. It was knowing Jim Maroon could seem so square and be so Injun-cruel. And Heydenfeldt and the rest. They let me make an ass of myself, recruiting men into the Territorials so that they could sound them for possibilities. I don't know how many men they've got out there in the hills, but I do know of eight or ten men that have moved out of Tucson in the last six months. Just packed up and drifted. Why? Because they'd had the call. They were wanted."

Grif watched him from under knotted brows and let him pace and talk.

"For the principles of our beloved South! Principles! They've got no more principles than a ruttin' buck. Some of them, yes. But not Montgomery and Maroon and Heydenfeldt. It's my guess they'll hide those stages again when they get them across the Mississippi and hang big price tags on them, and it won't be Confederate money they'll take, but gold they can spend anywhere. Maybe I'm wrong. Maybe Blaise Montgomery has more integrity than I give him credit for. But I do know he's shrewd, and that he's the man to beat."

Grif grinned with one side of his mouth. "Doc, you're an idealist. Only an idealist could drink as hard as you do and talk as pretty."

"Whatever I am, I'm with you this far—I'll toll off the Territorials I'm sure of and take them into whatever game you decide on."

Grif found it less difficult to accept him now. They had something in common. There was something wrong with the soul of each of them, something that Benteen tried to drown in liquor and something Grif might be a long time drowning too, and in the way of a man in a hospital studying his companions, he wondered what had brought Benteen to his knees.

"Well, if you've got to have a star to shoot at," he said, "you can borrow mine for a while."

He heard Kate come back into the room. He watched the ebb and surge of coals. "You know, there's something in that stagecoach angle. They'll be watching for it. What will they do when they run it down? Haul it away with them. What if we decide to follow it?"

"That's going to be hard," Broderick remarked. "Apt to be weather. Rain won't make tracks any easier to follow, not a hard rain."

"What if it rains iron washers?"

Broderick studied him frowningly. "Give him some more of that cigar ash, Doc."

"Of course it ain't going to rain washers unless somebody makes it. That'll be either you or me, kid, hiding in the boot

under a blanket. After they take the coach, they'll search it
for the money. That'll be in the safe—they'll figure—and too
heavy to carry on horseback because they've got no way of
opening it. Now, they may go through the boot thorough, or
they may not. If they do, whoever's in the back will get his
right then and there. If they don't, he won't get it until they
reach the holding ground. Then he's sure to. But all along the
way, he'll toss out a washer every so often to mark the trail.
We'll dump them in that yellow wheel paint and he can fish
them out as he needs them. We'll see them, all right."

Their faces lighted, and they watched him with respect as
he chewed the idea some more. "That's the caper," he
decided. "Thing is, the one that goes out is just liable to be a
dead man twenty-four hours from now, so we want to be fair
about how we pick him." He glanced at Kate. "Say, there's a
job for you! *You* can pick him."

He saw her elbows hug her sides. Her face twisted. "How
can you be so—!"

He leaned back in the chair. Broderick's face was like
stone. "Why, honey," Grif said, "you mustn't let sentiment
stand in the way of logic. Send the old man out! He's a pretty
sorry old hoss, but he can still throw an iron washer with the
best of them."

She sobbed and ran from the room. Grif stood up. "I'm
going to the hotel for some truck. Wake up Jim Cheek and
tell him he's to drive. He boards somewhere over on Warner.
He ain't to make a fight of it, though. Drop the lines when he
sees them. You fellows empty the safe, lock it and load it
inside the coach. I'll be back in an hour. Doc, you round up
all the boys you can and turn them over to Johnny. You'll go
out an hour after we do, so you won't be spotted."

He anticipated the adventure like a bath after a desert
crossing, a bath of danger, action and perhaps blood. Now
that he had done it, he was sorry he had hurt Katie. If she
loved Johnny, it wasn't her fault. Yet he had the tingle of a
soldier going to battle at the idea of her worrying over him.

He had acquired an extra cylinder for his Colt from
Bosburg, the gunsmith. He drew all the loads from both
cylinders and replaced them. He tested the powder in his
flask by pouring a charge on the floor and touching it off
with a match. Thinking of the wind flapping through a stage
boot, he donned two suits of heavy underwear. He wound

his watch. He sat down, pulled off the tight yellow boots and drew on his old ones. He had forgotten how comfortable feet could be.

Forty-five minutes had elapsed since he left the depot. A misty dawn had started. He heard the shattering roar of Benteen's cannon. He took a few minutes longer to stop by Annie Benson's and buy a pint of whiskey and a stack of tortillas from the night watchman. In that dim, gloomy room he lingered to fish a stub of pencil from his pocket and write on one of the cardboard-like tortillas:

Annie, you're okay. Set them up for me some night. Here's a double-eagle. And here's the best, from
                                                                Grif

He left it on the bar. As he went out, Noah Benteen rode by on a lumbering white gelding, about the kind of horse you would expect him to own, a horse for Don Quixote. He saw Grif and shouted: "Those danged tin soldiers of mine! They won't come to heel any more, since you fired the cannon the other night. I'll have to round them up by hand."

Grif chuckled. "I'll go over with you. We'll keep firing her till they do show up."

It took four salvos to arouse the lodge members. Then there were only eight. Grif left Benteen strutting up and down before them, shouting imprecations. He hurried along, aware that he was late; turning up the alley between the depot and Solomon Warner's, he reached the stage yard and stood there looking for the stage. But only a Mexican hostler was in sight. There were fresh tracks of iron tires, but no stage.

"Where is she?" he shouted.

The Mexican stood still, saraped, sombreroed, sandaled, not understanding. Then: "Ze es-stage? *Ave María Purísima*, shees alraddy go! Shees go an hour ago, *patrón*. Señor Cheek sad eet was time to leaf."

Grif shouted a curse at him. "But that crazy Broderick *zoquete* wasn't supposed to go! I was!"

"Señor Broadereek? He's not come back from the hotel, Señora Croaker is say to me, 'Gat me a blanket, Refugio, I am going weeth the es-stage. And some washers and paint.' She's poot the washers and paint in back, and she's get inside." He asked gently: "Something is wrong, *patrón*?"

Grif turned and ran to the stable.

26

THE RAIN BEGAN, a tattered gray blanket flapping in their faces as they rode east from the pueblo through ragged acres of prickly pear, winding down the aisles between giant, spread-armed saguaros, and down into a wide, mist-filled valley. Added to Benteen's eight were the only four Regulars Holbrook had been able to find: Sylvester Mowry—the lean, bearded philosopher—Bay-Rum Brown and a couple of others. They rode in slickers with their sombreros tilted to let the rain spill from the curled brims.

Grif had to cut down the pace he had set. The horses would not last at the clip, nor would there be fresh remounts at the swing stations. There would be six muddy, blown coach horses left by a stage clattering on with an untracked team. He jogged down the road, his eyes turbid with worry and self-reproach. There was an axiom that a good stage team could outrun a good saddle horse. And these saddle horses would carry their riders all the way, ten miles or a hundred. They must be treated as traveling horses, not as quarter horses.

He had been so clever in his cruelty, letting her pick the man to ride to death! It served him fairly to be tortured this way. But why must Katie be pulled into it? He glanced at Broderick, wondering what the kid would be thinking of him. Broderick's face had changed. Shiny with rain, it was gray and set. Fearful. That was the word. Him, fearful of anything! The human armadillo beginning to soften.

At the first station they found they had lost a half hour. Jim Cheek had been letting the team run, filled with the importance of his job. They rode on through the endless turnings of the road, avoiding a nest of rocks here, swinging past a towering green devil's candelabra there, while the day lost its newness and afternoon tarnished an already dull sky. They had to rest the horses more often. It grew colder, steam blowing from the nostrils of the ponies and the leather beginning to stink. A low mole of hills thrust up, its peaks lost in clouds. These were the Empires. The tracks of the stage were obscured at times by standing water, or by sand that had lost the imprint of the tires.

They had to think about a night stop soon, or resolve to inch along scanning the road by lantern light for a yellow iron washer. Grif refused to think about it until it was upon him. Katie was somewhere ahead, perhaps in their hands by now. For this last hour of the day he pushed the horses harder. He pulled a wet tortilla from his pocket and chewed on it, rain dripping from nose and chin.

He glanced again at Johnny. The boy looked like a ghost. He was beginning to make pointless remarks about how long did Grif think it would be now; and by God when they caught them what they wouldn't do to those bushwhackers! He felt sorry for Johnny, but at the same time he wondered what had happened to himself. He was sick and scared, but the way you would be over a kidnapped child, rather than a lost sweetheart. It was as if a weary, overworked runner had dropped out of a race. He was sorry and shamed over his failure, but in a self-pitying way rather than in the wild desperation of the deserted lover.

Benteen reined over to Grif. "This hoss of mine's about played out. When are we going to stop?"

There was not over an hour's daylight left. Grif drew in a long breath. "Soon," he said. "We're outrun."

Benteen was not looking at him. He was staring ahead, where dim tracks logged with water crisscrossed the road just beyond a rise. "What's that?"

They dismounted. "Something's happened here!" Benteen exclaimed. "Look at those horse tracks! And the stage was turned, and—look here!"

He held up a flat iron ring smeared with mud and yellow paint.

Grif stood peering southward into the slanting fine rain.

"I'd pay a thousand dollars an hour for sunlight!" he groaned. Out there a short distance was the tangled cactus-and-stone warren called the Whetstone Range, a ridge where two valleys undulated together and the crest of the wave had been torn away to leave hollows and jagged peaks where Indians and jackrabbits loved to crawl.

It might be the spot! Or the trail might swing on to the Mexican border... and after that it would be over. Oh, he and Johnny could poke along on it, but a force of any size, even a willing force, would eventually be spotted by Rurales hungry for gringo hides.

He closed his eyes an instant and in an oblique sort of prayer tried to wish into being a *rincón* in the Whetstones where a dozen Concord stages were getting ready to roll. He remounted. "We can make it by dark. A good place to camp even if we don't find anything."

The wheel paint had been a stroke of genius. Those painted washers glistened in the mud with undimmed luster. The trail was already old, whipping through the brush, lashing across shallow *barrancas*, slamming up over bony hogbacks. At these points, an hour and a half before, a stage with a frightened girl in it had rushed along with a grim escort.

They paused at a lonely spot called Nogales Spring. The trail did a column-left toward the mountains. Grif's heart lifted. "We're a-comin', Katie! Hang on, girl!"

Broderick pushed in beside him. "What do you think? In those hills yonder, maybe?"

"Maybe."

The rain blew back into the sky. Dull reds and black stained the west, as though a child's watercolors had been spilled. But suddenly the light died, sponged away by the clouds, and they reined in almost on order, lost in a wet, wind-lashed mesquite forest under the dripping eaves of the mountains. Grif gave the order he had dreaded.

"Best light the lantern, Syl."

Sylvester Mowry, with a couple of men to make a windbreak, got the storm lantern burning. Its lens was a blurred yellow eye that apologized for not being brighter. Mowry rode for a while in the lead, dipping low here and there to swing the lantern about, and every now and then he gave a grunt and Grif saw a washer in the trail. The route was a natural one that avoided the larger boulders scattered about the base of the hills. The tracks were plainer on this high ground, but the washers gave verification when they wanted it most.

The horses labored up a steep hillside toward a ridge half seen in the failing daylight, a dark horizon against a darker sky, saw-toothed with yucca and snags of boulders. They topped it and looked down into a shallow valley no deeper than a cupped hand, hidden until this instant, the bottom lost in night. A hundred yards farther they rode, and Grif straightened as he saw a handful of washers between the ruts; and simultaneously he discovered that it was not one trail they were following now, but a multitude of them, all slanting in here.

He had a feeling of alarm. "Best snuff out that lantern, Syl. I'm thinking—"

The lantern went out because it had been shot out. As the crack of the rifle reached them, others opened up and the tight little circle of riders burst open like a melon.

The guns were flashing to their right. There were at least four. Broderick grunted and dropped his split reins, clutching the horn and beginning to slip out of the saddle. Grif spurred in beside him and caught him with an arm about the waist. He dumped him across his own pony's neck. There was a frantic sort of firing from the Regulars. Some had been unhorsed and some seemed on the point of fleeing. It was the instant when stands were made, or routs, and Holbrook bawled with the imperative fury of a cavalry colonel.

"Down the slope, now! Follow me but don't bunch!"

He rode straight for the middle of the valley floor, his pony trying to pitch because of the frightening thing across its neck that smelled of blood and fear. He looked back. Mowry had spurred to the rear, chasing someone who was trying to put a scared mount back up the slope. He saw him cuff him on the ear and heard his angry shout.

"Doc! Snap out of it! Stay with us, you fool."

Benteen came back, holding the reins and horn with both hands, a terrified Quixote on a boogered Rosinante. He rode into the mass of them, jouncing on the saddle like a man who had never ridden before, gray and stiff and ashamed.

Grif had in mind a vague cairn of rocks just ahead as a

fortification for a stand. Before they made it, other guns, a regular firing line of them, opened up from the middle of the valley. He sprawled out of the saddle, carrying Broderick with him. Then he ran, with Johnny across his shoulder, for the rocks. Bullets hammered and cried along the ground. It was dark, and the marksmanship was poor. They piled into the scatter of boulders and dug in.

In the brief interval before total darkness descended, he made a map in his mind of what they were up against.

The valley was a tilted, rock-and-brush-choked oval locked in by a high and stony ridge. The ridge formed a half-moon with the horns pointing west. The low but rugged hogback they had crossed joined the horns. The coaches were a huddle of dark boxes near the north end of the valley. Among them were the guns that had stopped their rush, probably a dozen or more. The others still lurked under a slant of granite near the entrance to the valley. Now and then Holbrook's men poured a couple of shots at them just to keep their nerves jumping. The others had gone silent.

Grif made Johnny as comfortable as he could. The rocks broke the wind and Grif's slicker made a blanket over him. The bullet was in his right arm, near the shoulder. Benteen came crawling over at Grif's call. He glanced at Johnny, still in the delusive half-sleep of shock that made a man think he was doing pretty well, though he had begun to stir under the slicker. Benteen only glanced at him, and then confronted Grif with hostile challenge.

"There's a yarn to carry to California with you! The fightin' sawbones with the coward's heart."

Holbrook was puzzled. He had seen many a man flinch before he got his battle legs under him. "What of it? The others might of run too, if they'd been close enough to the ridge. You've got no corner on not likin' to be shot at. See what you can do for Johnny."

But the doctor struck his chest, working himself into one of his frenzies. "But it was Benteen that got there first! Women, children, and Benteen first. You thought I was a rotten doctor because I drank, eh? Whereas I happen to be a drunk because I'm a rotten doctor. I'm telling you you can't make a decent banker or doctor, thief or saloon swamper, without a certain amount of guts."

"You didn't hem and haw about lopping off Sam Granjon's leg."

"Ah! But I was drunk. Drunk is really the only way to operate, except that you lose so many patients by sewing washbasins up in their bellies. Tennessee got uncomfortable after I lost a merchant's wife. An ordinary, uncomplicated delivery; except that I complicated it by passing out on the job."

"Then suppose you take a look at Johnny before you pass out on this one."

A bullet exploded against a tall chimney of rock above them. Benteen started and began to tremble. "That boy," he said, "deserves a better break than to be worked on by Noah Benteen."

"Got news for you," Grif said. He pulled the stopper of the canteen in the bosom of his Dragoon model Colt. He watched Benteen frown over it and then go after the whiskey like a hungry infant taking the breast. He lowered the gun and Grif recovered it, while Benteen let his head rest back against the rock and sighed.

"Now," the doctor presently breathed, "we'll see about Johnny."

He probed a while with a pocketknife. Johnny writhed, the pain getting at him now, but it was a point of pride with him not to make a sound. "This ain't good. Bone's broken. I got the ball, but the thing's going to fester if it ain't properly cleaned out."

Broderick snarled: "Clean it out, then!"

"That'd be a little hard on both of us, without enough whiskey to more'n take the feather-edge off our nerves. Mean a canch of diggin' and then I'd want to cauterize with the blade of this knife. Red-hot, of course. Well, sir, I don't know."

"I'd kind of like to take that arm back with me," Broderick remarked.

Out in the night and the mist there was a small cry, and then a man's laughter. Broderick heard it and tried to sit up, but Grif's hand on his chest pinned him down.

"That was Katie!" Broderick gasped. "God, Grif, that was her! That damned Heydenfeldt! The way he feels about her, and now he's got her—"

"Montgomery's running that shebang. He may be a lobo,

but he won't stand for that kind of business."

"Then why'd she scream?"

Holbrook stood peering through a slot in the rocks.
". . . Propaganda."

Benteen sat with his hands hanging between his
outspread legs, brooding. Mowry and the others were on
picket duty among the rocks. It was growing cold. Grif
speculated on their chances. This was a fair enough hole to
make a stand in, and he liked their chances well enough,
provided these boys could shoot. God knew Benteen had
drilled them at it enough. He did not fear a rush particularly,
estimating that they must have at least half as many men as
Montgomery, so that a rush would be too costly. But he
thought about those wild, woman-starved men who had
probably been living among the squirrels for six months, and
the idea would not leave his mind.

Suddenly Benteen said, "Gimme that canteen again. And
try to light a little fire of paper or something where they
won't see it."

Broderick stared up at them. "I bet," he said, "I'd be good
for a rush, if you'd get me started. We could be within fifty
feet of them before they knew we were coming."

"She'll be all right, kid. Try to rest."

Johnny turned his face to the rock.

Benteen drank most of the whiskey in the canteen, and
after twenty minutes he said whimsically: "If you'll prepare
the patient, nurse, I believe I am ready to perform surgery."

Holbrook managed to achieve a handful of fire with
paper, gunpowder, and some dry oak leaves and twigs
wedged in under the rocks. It made hardly a glow, it seemed,
but presently the balls began to sing over their heads. For a
moment they held their breath; then it became obvious that
the men up at the pass were shooting at no more than their
shadows.

They laid open Johnny's shirt and Holbrook sat by him,
trying to look more like a companion than a strongarm.
Benteen's hand shook violently until within an inch of the
wound. Then it steadied and he went to probing. Broderick
stood it for a while, then a low cry escaped him. Holbrook
pinched a bullet from the flask and slipped it through his
lips. "Chaw on this."

"She ain't broken, after all," Benteen muttered, "but kind

of chewed up a little. Heat this thing."

Grif toasted the knife blade over the flame. Benteen applied it red-hot. Broderick gave a shout of agony and both of them had to hold him down. Four times they went through this, but the last two cauterizations were on an unconscious man.

Benteen finished, dressed the wound with a relatively clean handkerchief, and said cheerfully, "Soberest cutting I've done in years. Let's have another pull at that tonsil varnish, pardner."

27

DURING THE NIGHT the skies cleared. Dawn broke clear and cold. Grif had awaited this hour. He was ready when the first of the outlaws against the cliff showed himself in an endeavor to get a line on the men within the rocks. He let a ball from his saddle gun wing across the broken terrain. Before the hills ceased playing with the echoes, a slickered, Stetsoned figure arose weirdly from behind a screwbean shrub and fell headlong across it.

Now the outlaws across the valley opened up, every man at once, the fire a shattering hail among the rocks. Grif laughed; surprised, fright-intimidated faces turned down from the rocks above him. "Powder's cheap," he said. "Anybody can talk loud, but how many can make it stick? When they get done, take your shots. Then find a new spot before the next one."

The salvo draggled to an end. Among the rocks, gun barrels inched through embrasures and the shots came stutteringly. Someone yelled. "One down—no, two—by God!"

After that there was an exultant quiet, which broke wide apart when a girl's scream echoed through the valley.

Johnny had come haggardly through the night, the raw hole in his shoulder deviling him. He rolled from under the slicker as the cry came, fighting to stand as Grif jumped from a ledge and piled onto him. "No, you don't!"

Broderick breathed sobbingly. "You're not going to set here while they—"

"I'm not going to commit suicide over it. Lay down."

Johnny resisted and then broke, sitting down heavily and covering his face with his hands. "What are we going to do, Grif? They've got us like a fly in a bottle. I don't give a damn for us, but I'd trade those stages for her in a minute."

He looked up. There were tears of pain and desperation in his eyes, and at that moment Grif felt the kinship with him that he had resisted so long. He was witnessing the disintegration of a boy's impossible ideals. Hardness and courage made one sort of man, but it was the sort that made trouble for peace officers. Mix in some sensitivity, and you had a man with the imagination it took to make a decent citizen.

He said gently, "We'd all make such a trade, kid. The Senator thinks so too, and sometime today he's going to try to make a deal. You see, this isn't too good a spot for him either. He doesn't know but what we've got reinforcements coming. And he can't get those wagons out of here until he wipes out the last of us. No, sir. He's going to make us an offer before sundown."

Broderick's eyes glistened. "You think so?"

"Well, I almost wish he wouldn't. Because if Pete Deuce has any brains at all he'll follow us. The tracks we left haven't been muddied out by the little rain we've had since we got here. And I reckon we're going to keep them busy enough that nothing's going to happen to Katie."

Johnny lay back, relieved by the lie Grif had made for him. There was little chance that Deuce would come out, because he would have to build his posse out of a heterogeneous mix of slave men and abolitionists. And there was no telling what a gang like Maroon's and Heydenfeldt's would do by way of retaliation for dead companions.

For a couple of hours he lay in a narrow, upright slot between two boulders, watching the outlaw camp. Nothing showed but thirteen stages in a curving line, and the sleek stage animals in a rope corral against the far cliff. A slim pencil of smoke arose. Someone was going to have coffee, maybe. He took long and studied aim, like a skilled billiard player. It would be a bank shot. His paw squeezed down on stock and trigger in a single patient contraction. The shot jolted him. A man yelled and came into sight briefly. He lunged back to safety and somebody shouted: "Put that danged fire out!"

The smoke perished.

An hour passed that was like the bickering over a conference table—snap shots and barrages; threats and counter-threats—but they were coming to the point where a compromise could be suggested with some grace. It was about noon when Montgomery's rain-barrel baritone rolled between them.

"Holbrook!"

"I hear you!" Grif winked at Johnny.

"We can pick you off a man at a time, if it takes a month. We've got food and plenty of powder."

"Fine! We've got enough tortillas and mesquite beans for a week."

"Will you listen to a compromise?"

"I won't shout my lungs out over it!"

"All right. Come alone to that big mesquite yonder."

Grif waved a handkerchief in agreement. He signaled Mowry and Benteen. "Boys, I'm not going to reach any agreement with that Georgia peachstone, but this is going to be a foot in the door. That mesquite isn't too far from that wallow in the ground. I'm coming back that far and drop. When you see me do it, open up on them, and run like hell for rocks closer to the coaches. You'll have to split up, but so much the better."

Mowry shook his head. "Man, the ones up above will kick the daylights out of us."

"No. Doc, here, is going to pull their teeth for us."

Benteen started. "*I* am!"

"You're the man for the job. There's only three of them. I'm leaving you two boys to help out. All the time we're advancing, you'll be doing the same, running and firing, ducking, and firing again. They're nailed down. They can't move any way but sideways, and there's no point in that; they've got the best spot now that they'll ever have."

Benteen's defeated eyes were accusative. "Are you saying this to shame me into admitting I'm yellow?"

"No. I'm saying it because a man trying to prove something is more apt to keep his eye on the target."

Benteen snarled: "Don't be an ass! If I break down, the whole thing fails."

"That's right, pardner. So you're not going to break down. Keep moving and don't fire till you get a shot."

Benteen was still pleading as Grif, carbine slung back across his shoulder by the barrel, walked into the clear. He stood there until he saw Montgomery's stout form leave the ring of boulders where the coaches were penned. They walked toward a ragged mesquite tree in a stretch of clear wet ground. Montgomery reached it first and waited. Grif stopped ten feet from him. The Senator's jowls pulled sourly, his eyes bloodshot and spiteful.

"We've got a mess on our hands," he said.

"That's nothing new for me. I've had a mess on mine ever since I left Texas. I don't catch on very fast, do I?"

"I did my best to persuade you you were walking into something you wouldn't like. Now we both pay for yo' stubbornness." It seemed to be in his mind that he was being put upon in a very unfair manner.

"Now we're both into something we don't like. What are we going to do about it?"

"One way or another, I know what I'm going to do about it. Go to New Orleans. It will either be by force or because we reached an agreement."

"What's the agreement?"

"You'd like to have the girl and the safe back, wouldn't you?"

"The girl. There's nothing in the safe."

Montgomery's face received this new treachery with acerbity. "However," he snapped, "it doesn't weaken my bargainin' position any. The men seem to think Kate would make good company on the trip. Particularly Heydenfeldt. I'm almost sorry I ever took him into the organization. That man's got a streak of cruelty like a Yaqui Indian."

A stir of movement, a flutter of color, caught Grif's attention. Someone was moving on the ridge behind the horse corral, walking, with little attempt at camouflage, into a position from which she could look down on the valley. He had a kind of sickness of relief. A wagon jolted along slowly behind her, a girl in bonnet, shawl, and dark skirt driving it. Annie Benson stood shading her eyes against the sun.

Grif said, "We get the girl for what?"

"A day's headstart. She'll be in the last coach to pull out. We'll leave her a mile from the foothills."

And once we get into the clear, his thinking seemed to go, you'll never stop us. We outnumber you, even though we'll be slower because there'll be no more changes of teams.

"You know what Butterfield sent me out here for, don't you?"

Annie Benson had turned quickly and taken the bridle of the horse pulling the wagon. She turned it so that the tailgate of the light spring wagon faced the outlaw camp. She dropped the gate. The sun struck a spark from the tarnished brass six-pounder in the back of the wagon, the Territorials' own parade piece. The women were hurrying now, a ramrod working and a keg being opened.

There was a shot from the trio guarding the pass; a shot and some distant yelling. "They've got a cannon!"

"Cannon!" Montgomery exclaimed. "Have you got a cannon in there?"

Grif winked. "We might have."

Montgomery appeared to see through the ruse. He cupped his hands. "Cut out yo' tarnal firin' and rumorin'!" He moved his shoulders restively. "See here. You aren't going to have those coaches, not if God Himself sent you to recover them. They've taken me a year to collect. And they've cost the lives of some good men."

"And some bad ones. No, I don't like your deal." *My Lord, woman, you can't fire a cannon from the bed of a wagon! You'll set it right on the hoss's back!*

"Why, let's see— if you'll tell those monkeys up there to put a cork in it, maybe I can think of something."

Montgomery heard the second shot and cupped his hand to his ear. "They still shoutin' about a cannon," he frowned. He stood in plump, pink perplexity, his small St. Bernard eyes questing about.

"Well, I'll tell you. You leave Kate and six of the coaches, and we'll call it a square shake."

"You know I can't do that."

"Why, that gives me only six and you seven. You're getting—let's see ... thirteen into a hundred, eight times; eight t'ms six, forty-eight ... you're getting fifty-two percent to my forty-eight."

"If you want my opinion," Blaise Montgomery said, shifting the heavy Sharps he carried, "you're a damned fool. There'll be no deal that involves my leaving the stages."

"All right. No deal." Grif turned and started away. He looked back.

After a momentary stare of puzzled anger, Montgomery pivoted and started back to the camp. It was at this point that he saw the cannon on the heights, the women standing aside with their hands over their ears. He shouted a bawl of wild alarm and began to run.

Grif sprawled into the shallow pocket he had picked out. He thought, I hope to heaven Kate's behind a rock!

First he heard the whistling of small objects in the air, then the howling of stricken men and finally the heavy boom of the fieldpiece. He rose and started on a run for the camp. Behind him, Mowry brought the men down from the rocks and across the flats at a dog trot. Beyond, a small, pot-bellied figure led two men up the long slope to the pass.

Annie was dumping another scoop of powder into the muzzle of the cannon. It had broken through the front of the wagon and tumbled to the ground, but the combined efforts of the women had swung the indestructible chunk of metal into position. The horse was dragging a ruined wagon over the hill. Grif kept running until he saw men crawling back to their positions in the brush and rocks. He dropped behind a low stone barrier and squinted for a shot. He put a ball into the brisket of an excited man who knelt on the bare ground.

There was a peppering of fire behind him, some balls singing past him and resounding echoes among the rocks. Annie was ramming the wadding home while the other girl fussed with another charge of assorted hardware. Grif decided to stay where he was for this one. Someone in a plaid shirt who looked like Jim Maroon got one too close to him. He fired back and heard the firing pin fall on a dead chamber. He dropped the gun and went for his half-breed Colt.

The women had their hands over their ears again. He hugged the earth. Grape began to tear the ground about him. Among the outlaws, it seemed to be hell. A man stumbled into sight, holding a wrist without a hand, from which blood dripped hotly. A Regular with no chivalry shot him. Other men were bawling pointless orders at each other. The men with Mowry reached Grif as he came up and started walking toward the stagecoaches. "Spread out!" he yelled. "Take them from both sides!" He stayed in the center himself, where the action would be.

Montgomery's voice was the only dignified thing about the rout. It was shouting an angry, stiff-backed order. In a moment Grif saw him coming through the rocks with half a dozen Territorials behind him. He knew a spot when he saw one, and he was in one now. He dropped to one knee and waited. He had not been so wise in sending the others to the flanks. The whole, mangled wolf-pack of them had ganged to come out in a wedge.

The Senator had a look of madness and glory on him. His coat-tails flapped, his stock had come undone and the thin white hair fluttered. He held a revolver in each hand. As he came into range, he shouted:

"Jeff Davis! Beauregard! And to hell with Yankee dogs!"

He raised both guns and fired them simultaneously. Holbrook had the thought that he was not even trying to hit anything. The balls plowed furrows in the ground at either side of him. It was too close to miss, but he held the shot an instant while the Georgian came closer at his waddling stride. He admired a man who would risk everything for an ideal, admired and yet pitied him, and at last he was convinced that whatever crimes Blaise Montgomery had committed were in the name of a misguided patriotism.

In back of him came Maroon, Gus Heydenfeldt, and three others. There was nothing of the zealot about these men. Heydenfeldt had a bloody gash on the side of his head and he held his carbine like a man who means to empty it and then swing it like a club. Jim Maroon came more reluctantly, unhurt but white and shaken. Suddenly his revolver began to slam; it jolted his arm to the shoulder and the shots went wild.

Grif let the hammer fall. Senator Montgomery stopped. He went back a step and crossed his arms over his belly.

Suddenly Maroon began to run. He flung aside his empty gun and transferred a Colt from his left hand. Gus Heydenfeldt ran two steps and fell flat, going down like a good infantryman, the butt of his gun taking the shock, then slipping up to snuggle against his shoulder. He was the one Grif feared most, but Maroon was almost on him and firing as he came. Scared witless; scared into a fit of heroics.

The Dragoon barked like a bulldog. The shot went into Jim Maroon's body high, where it would stop him cold. He stumbled and his left hand pawed at his throat.

Heydenfeldt fired a shot that slapped a handful of grit in Holbrook's face. He was blinded. When he could see again, he discovered that the others had followed Gus Heydenfeldt's lead and gone down. He had a firming thought without fear: you're going to get it this time, old feller.

Then he saw Mowry coming back with his bunch, filtering through the rocks and brush. They had been into the bastion and apparently found nothing to occupy them. There was some firing from the other side, but Mowry was coming on the run and stopping now to fire into the men on the ground. Heydenfeldt twisted to see them. He shifted the carbine to cover the lanky, bearded man in the lead. Grif's eyes squinted behind the sight, the side of Heydenfeldt's head resting on the framed sight. As the gun kicked, a blur of smoke puffed before it. Heydenfeldt was obscured for a moment; then, his vision clearing, Holbrook saw him lying on his back with his legs drawn up, writhing slowly.

It was sufficient to unman the others. They dropped their weapons and scrambled up, hands high, the focus of the fight lost, with the Senator dead and Maroon and Heydenfeldt both out of it. Grif lay there, burned out. Up on the cliff he saw Annie Benson waving.

After a while, Benteen came down. Doc had a handkerchief wrapped about his head. He looked grim and gray, but there was an adolescent swagger about him. "Just a scratch," he said. "Had to fix up one of the boys after we flushed our grouse. The other boy's holding the two we didn't have to knock over."

"You did all right, eh?"

Benteen spat. "Yes, and no thanks to you. I might have been killed or, worse still, wounded, and nobody to take care of me."

"But you didn't break down, did you?"

"What's the difference between breaking down and shaking till your guts turn to water?"

"Quite a bit. They give medals to the ones that don't break down. You may even be of some worth to those julep merchants down there. Though, feeling the way I do, I hope you won't."

Benteen gave a loud and derisive snort and went to look over the downed men. A queer little hombre, thought Grif, but not hard to understand once you had torn away the bandages and looked at the wound he was trying to hide. Thinking he had a corner on cowardice. And yet, having at last acquired something to think on with a little pride, he might find less satisfaction in his desperate, drunken soul-searchings.

They found Katie imprisoned in one of the stagecoaches. She became hysterical when she realized it was all over, and Annie had to take her in hand for a few minutes. Annie made herself busy with something else while Katie went up to Grif. Excitement had washed all the color from her face, but she tried to smile as she took his hands.

"I just knew you'd find me. I wasn't worried once, except when Heydenfeldt tried to get in the stagecoach with me. I guess it was the Senator, more than my hitting him, that kept him away. But it's over. Grif, I want to tell you what you wouldn't let me tell you the other day."

He shook his head. "I just took off those yellow boots thirty-six hours ago, and I'll be horsewhipped before I'll pull them on again, even for you. It was nice while it lasted. But I guess we know, now, that admiring is a pretty yonder piece from loving. Well, you know me: a girl in every swing station. Don't worry about old Grif."

She felt the bitterness in his voice and tried to speak again, but he looked toward the rocks where they had spent the night. "I guess you didn't know Johnny got hit."

"Johnny! Oh, Grif! You don't mean—"

"No, but he's a pretty unhappy boy. Better go see how he's making out."

She pulled her skirts up and started running for the rocks, calling, "Johnny! Johnny!"

Glumly, Grif saw to getting things ready. He figured this was as good a rendezvous as any for the coaches and stock that would be streaming in any day now. Here he could assemble his drivers and supplies; through that gap they would roll on the first mile of a trip that would take them across Lee's Ferry and on up to Salt Lake City. Mowry agreed to stay with the coaches until Grif returned with his own force.

Annie came picking her way across the rough ground. "Going to hitch up a stage and drive us back?" she asked.

"You bet! That was a pretty fine thing you did, Annie.

But don't ever try to fire a cannon off a spring wagon again."

He had a team backed onto the pole, and waited to help Annie into the coach. She shook her head. "I'll ride up with you."

He shrugged and gave her a hand. He put the other girls into the Concord and climbed to the box. Someone handed up the lines. He sorted them awkwardly. He was strictly a relief driver, though it seemed the least he could do was to escort her back to Tucson personally. He kicked off the brake and the coach lunged forward. As they passed the cairn of rocks where Johnny and Katie were, a wave of self-pity went over him. He sighed and drew a snuffling breath.

"Seems like old Grif gets the south end of the chicken again. Johnny gets Katie, Katie gets Johnny. Butterfield gets his stages, and I get a kick in the britches. Everybody's doing all right but Grif."

Annie turned on him. "See here! I'm getting mighty tired of all this. You're not heartbroken. You're just suffering from a slightly dislocated pride. You've been nosed out by a younger man. That's all."

He clucked the leaders up over the ridge and they swayed down the foothills toward the desert, gray and tan and purple in the spring sun. It occurred to him that there was something almost pleasant in being scolded by Annie. She rolled the most palatable pills in the world.

She moved a little closer. "It's hard to get it straight, at first, that life is something you can't slow down or speed up, like a team of horses. There's a bridge between youth and middle age, but you can only cross it once. You can look back, but it will only hurt you. That's what you've tried to do, Grif. And you needn't because you've got something no young man has—strength! Real, rock-bottom strength."

He let his foot rock on the brake, and gave the off wheeler a tap of the whip. "Shoot!"

"You know," she said brightly, "I'm going to sell the saloon! It doesn't seem like a business for a lady, and I'd rather be a lady than anything in the world. So if you've got room, I might just go along with you to California. If I wouldn't be in the way."

"Shore not. Got room for the girls too, if you want to

bring them," he said gallantly.

"The girls can take care of themselves. They always have before."

A wind rustled through the sage, an abundant wind filled to bursting with the fragrance of early spring. A wind to make a not-old man feel buoyantly young and a not-young woman bloom like a girl. He reached down and patted her hand.

"Grif," she said.

He continued to hold her hand, and, shaking up the lines, let the horses run.